A
CIRCLE
OF
WIVES

Fiction by Alice LaPlante
Turn of Mind

A CIRCLE OF WIVES

Alice LaPlante

Atlantic Monthly Press
New York

Printed in the United States of America
Published simultaneously in Canada

ISBN: 978-0-8021-2234-6
eBook ISBN: 978-0-8021-9274-5

Atlantic Monthly Press
an imprint of Grove/Atlantic, Inc.
154 West 14th Street
New York, NY 10011

Distributed by Publishers Group West

www.groveatlantic.com

To David, with much love

Alas! the love of women! it is known
to be a lovely and a fearful thing.

—*Don Juan,* Lord Byron

1

Samantha

I AM NOTHING IF NOT irresolute. Excuse the double negative. What I mean to say is that there is little I won't waver over. You know how squirrels flirt with death by the roadside, and how some actually lose their heads and rush into traffic to their doom? I had to give up riding my bike around campus as an undergraduate because of those damn squirrels. They'd make a dash for my tires, and if I would just hold firm and keep going, chances were good they'd scamper back to safety. But if they'd freak, I'd freak, and the result was too many crashes, too many injuries. I walked everywhere my junior and senior years. So. A waverer I am.

Peter and I are at Cook's Seafood Store on El Camino. We're warmly greeted as we walk in. I love this place because the men behind the counter—all men, a variety of ages between twenty and seventy—look so happy to be there. I believe the word to describe them is *fishmongers*. Such a lovely word. And apparently a lovely place to work, as most of them have been there for decades. I like the way they closely attend to customers describing their dinner plans, how they take the time to think before suggesting the exact number of shrimp for a party

I

of four, the precise weight of ahi tuna for six. No, they can't recommend the mackerel; it's a bit spongy today. Then, after placing the slabs of raw fish or the handfuls of shellfish on the scale, they wrap the purchases in crisp white paper as carefully as if they were the most special of birthday gifts. The taking of money appears a casual afterthought; the real business of the place is in the human interactions. If I were lonely, here is where I would come for solace.

The store is crowded, but we're patient. They know what we want, and sure enough, there's a wink and a broad smile from Eddie today, and out comes a beautiful specimen of smelt, Hypomesus transpacificus, that Peter has been seeking for quite some time. The fact that I use the words *beautiful* and *smelt* together in a sentence shows what living with Peter has done to me. As usual, Peter jingles the coins in his pocket and as usual Eddie waves him off. Peter is a scientist, an anthropologist, or, to be strictly honest, an academic wannabe. His doctoral dissertation involves researching the diets of the indigenous peoples of the San Francisco Bay area. He spent all last summer across the bay at the Emeryville Shellmound, wallowing thigh deep in what they now know is a toxic swamp. He will take this tiny smelt home and dehydrate it, carefully preserving the skeleton, and use it as a model to draw in his workbook. I'm wild about his meticulous sketches of these dried carcasses. For pleasure I often go leafing through the pages of his dissertation notes, and for my birthday I requested to have two of my favorites copied and framed. He thought I was kidding. But no. The delicate renderings of the fragile structures truly delight me. God is in those bones.

So here's where we are: Together almost ten years after we met in freshman rhetoric and I helped him understand the difference between *its* and *it's* and *which* and *that*. We became instantly inseparable, although I hesitated to call myself *committed*. It's not a word I would use, ever, to describe myself. Now, a decade later, Peter is still in school, and I'm still wavering. I wavered my way from an undergraduate degree in history into a quickly terminated semester of law school, then into a master's program in education and then less than a full term teaching eighth-grade social studies in nearby Portola Valley, recently rated the second richest town in America by *Time* magazine.

And here's something else you should know about me. In addition to being irresolute, I'm also a quitter. I'm not ashamed. I find that it often takes more courage to stop doing something you despise than to continue blindly along the wrong path. You usually save yourself, and others, a lot of grief by acknowledging your failure and moving on. But walking out on those kids—entitled spawn of venture capitalists and software magnates that they were—in the middle of the day, in the middle of the term was wrong. Plain wrong. The thing was, I couldn't have *not* done it. Another double negative. But seriously. If I'd had to spend another minute in that beautifully appointed classroom overlooking the rolling hills of the San Francisco Peninsula's richest real estate, I would have slit my wrists. Peter, reasonably enough, asked me whether I'd feel more . . . useful . . . teaching inner city kids. But the point wasn't that I felt *useless*. I'm not sure what the point was, except I got the same kind of choked-up-difficult-to-breathe feeling that had been the breaking point in Sam Adams's (yours truly) legal career misadventure. No beer jokes, please, I've heard them all.

I stumbled into my current situation, like I stumble into everything. About four years ago, Peter and I were living on Curtner in a dismal two-bedroom apartment. I'd just quit teaching. Peter was finishing up his master's. Palo Alto doesn't have many streets that aren't safe, but Curtner is one of them. Do a search of the California Sexual Predator's online database, and all the little red dots congregate around Curtner—about the only area in town where a sexual predator wouldn't be kicked out five minutes after he moved in. I'll say this about Curtner: People were tolerant. Well, I was back to using my bike after a four-year hiatus—depended on it, in fact, to get around as my car had died and I didn't have the money to fix it—and so was mad as hell when someone sawed through the heavy chain I'd specially purchased and made off with my ride. I loved that bike, had viewed it as my vehicle of liberation. An antidote to my stint as a teacher of the privileged.

3

My fit of rage over the theft propelled me onto a bus downtown and into police headquarters. I was given a form by a bored clerk and began filling it out despite the fact that my bike was probably worth less than two hundred dollars and therefore the report wouldn't be considered worth anyone's time. Then I saw the notice, tacked on the bulletin board. The police department was hiring. All that was required was an undergraduate degree and a clean record.

As it turned out, they mainly needed bodies to patrol the Stanford campus and try to prevent the kids from doing anything too dangerous. I tend to interview well, so that part was easy. They also gave me an aptitude test, and I passed with flying colors. Apparently my whole life I've been aching to lay down the law—not in the courtroom, but in the streets. It figures. I tend to be a little prissy about rules.

I know about as much as anyone what kind of bad things good kids can get up to, and I have a lot of tolerance for the undergraduate age group. This made me fairly popular on campus, and I gained a reputation as a trustworthy person among all parties. Surprisingly, the work suited me. I liked the camaraderie at the station house. I wasn't scared of drunk freshmen, even if they were bigger than me. I didn't mind getting yelled at or wept on. I had more trouble coping with the suicide-minded kids and the violent crimes—we generally had one or two sexual assaults on campus per quarter. But I found I had a cool head and sufficient authority to handle even these difficult cases, and so the first year passed rather quickly and satisfactorily. After that, three more years whooshed by. Then, just when I was beginning to think I had gotten into a rut, a detective position opened up. It offered a bigger paycheck, which sounded pretty good to me. But it was also a chance to get out of the itchy uniform into some comfortable clothes and use my brain. I'd begun to stagnate, to stink, even, with what was getting dangerously close to boredom. Again interviews. Again the aptitude test. A bunch of tedious training. And I got the promotion. Detective Samantha Adams. But everyone calls me Sam.

So it's about 1 PM on a sunny May day. We've just gotten home from Cook's—home being the smallest rental house in Palo Alto—and kick off our shoes. Peter is about to make a pot of his world-famous veggie chili when I get a call.

I put my shoes back on.

"What's up?" Peter comes out of the kitchen. He looks sad. Our schedules don't always sync, and Saturdays are supposed to be sacred.

"Someone croaked over at the Westin," I say. I'm still in a bit of shock.

Peter groans. "Can't it wait?"

"No. This is serious. I need to meet Jake and the county's CSI team there." Jake is the Santa Clara County medical examiner. "Mollie says it looks suspicious."

"So?" Peter asks.

"So, what I'm saying is that this might be an actual *murder*. In Palo Alto."

I couldn't have picked a more tranquil town to play cops and robbers. Palo Alto is an upscale university town about thirty-five miles south of San Francisco. Peter likes to tease me by reading out loud at the breakfast table the "Weekly Crime Watch" section of the *Daily News*. East Palo Alto and Redwood City get their share of drug busts and even shootings, but here we mostly issue tickets for barking dogs— a Palo Alto canine has fallen afoul of the law if it barks for more than ten minutes—and pick up intoxicated homeless people, to whom we give a meal and a place to dry out before releasing them back onto the streets.

I pull my new Toyota—recently financed by my promotion money—into the Westin's circular drive off El Camino, and park it in a no parking zone. When a doorman gestures to hurry me along I show him my badge and he, suddenly gracious, opens the door for me. I'm still not quite used to this—the deference shown to me as an officer of the law. Although sometimes, of course, I get the opposite reaction:

impudence or scorn, especially given my small stature and the fact that I'm a very young-looking twenty-eight years old. At least, when wearing the uniform, people believed I was an officer. In street clothes, even when I show my badge, some people openly express their doubts about my authority. I've had both men and women reach out and pat my head when I'm in the middle of questioning or even issuing a warning. Mortifying.

The Westin has been open less than a year, and although situated right off campus, I've never had cause to visit it before. They'd hardly find many reasons to call in the police. Mostly the hotel is frequented by well-heeled Silicon Valley types. The lobby is full of them when I arrive, milling around with cups of Starbucks and carrying binders that say EQUIS RESEARCH in bright red block letters. A placard proclaims *High Tech Investments: A New Paradigm for Risk Assessments*. Just another chance for the haves to help themselves to more.

I look for stairs, but none are obvious so I do something I hate, which is to take an elevator to the second floor. Once I exit the elevator car, signs indicate that room 224 is to my right. Deep plush piled carpet. Elegant gold-leafed tables holding elaborate bouquets of flowers, implausibly fresh and blooming—so implausibly that I surreptitiously pinch off a bright red blossom. I bring the flower to my nose. Real. Incredibly sweet, almost nauseating. Then I turn the corner and bump into a crowd gathered in front of room 224. I drop the flower and kick it to the side, hoping no one notices. The two cops guarding the door, Mollie and Henry, wave me through. I recognize Jake, a slight, balding man in his forties, kneeling on the floor over the body of a heavyset man dressed in jeans and a blue T-shirt, newish-looking sneakers on his feet. The body is on its side. A violent red contusion mars the forehead, and blood is spattered across the man's cotton top. Behind Jake, a woman armed with a large camera and with an official badge hanging around her neck is photographing the area around the body. Two men, also with badges, are carefully filing away plastic evidence bags. I assume that they, like Jake, are from Santa Clara County.

They've got a CSI Crime Lab there. We don't even have a photographer on our staff. At crime or accident scenes we use our phones to take photos.

One of the cops guarding the room is Mollie, a new hire—the officer who called me. The other is her more seasoned partner Henry. Mollie seems a bit ill, but is doing a valiant job keeping what appears to be the hotel manager—he's wearing a suit and a name tag—and a couple of women, also wearing name tags, from getting inside the room. They are pressed up as close as they can get, though, trying to get a clear view of Jake and the body. A Latina woman in a housekeeper's uniform is standing off by herself. I push past them.

"It looks like he hit his head on the corner of the dresser when he went down," says Jake, throwing me a pair of rubber gloves. We've worked together just once before. Last month, in fact. A homeless man had stepped in front of a car on University Avenue, the only other death I've had to deal with since I'd made detective. Open-and-shut case.

"What caused him to fall?"

"That's the question," Jake says. "I'm thinking heart attack. This fella doesn't seem like he hit the gym very often. Although he may have died from striking the dresser here. There's a lot of blood, but head wounds tend to be bloody."

"Any ID?"

Henry hands me a wallet. Even I can recognize that it's damn fine leather, there's a buttery sheen to it that my fake leather purse could never aspire to. I begin pulling out cards. "John Taylor," I read off a Visa then find a driver's license in the same name. The always-unflattering DMV photo made this John Taylor look tired and somewhat older than his sixty-two years. A reddish, corpulent face. Nice head of hair, though, for his age. I find a Stanford University Medical Center ID.

"He's a quack," I say. "John Taylor, of Stanford Hospitals and Clinics. A fat doctor. Go figure."

"What makes you think he was a doctor? Lots of people work over at the hospital, he could be a nurse, a technician, an orderly . . ."

"Yeah, but how many of them can afford a room at the Westin? Besides, it states it right here on his ID: *Dr.* John Taylor."

Jake is frowning.

"What is it?" I ask. I've been careful not to stare directly at the body. I'm not particularly squeamish about blood, but I haven't been in the presence of too many dead people.

"I'm seeing other signs of trauma. Unless this guy was in a bar fight recently, he's got some 'splaining to do. See?"

Jake shows me an ugly raised bruise on the upper right arm.

"Seems like someone pummeled him."

"And here." On the left shoulder, another bruise.

The manager tries to step forward at this point, but is pushed back by Mollie.

"Officer," he says to me.

"Detective."

"Detective, I should tell you that this man checked in under another name. As Jonathan Tinley."

One of the women with him speaks. "I was the one who registered him. He paid cash, so I didn't ask for ID."

"You didn't do anything wrong," I tell her, then add, remembering my training, "and neither did he. There's nothing wrong with staying at a hotel anonymously. Wanting privacy isn't a crime." When Peter and I go on our low-budget vacations, he delights in giving ludicrous names when we check into the Motel 6. Mr. and Mrs. Tiny Thumb. Rapunzel and Vice Chancellor Charming. He's still a boy, really, that Peter.

"Depends on what he wanted the privacy for," says Jake, still kneeling on the floor over the body. "And cash in a place like this?"

"How much do the rooms cost?" I ask.

"The rates fluctuate depending on demand, but mostly four hundred dollars plus a night," says the manager. "We rarely have cash customers, so Emma actually remarked upon it to me when she ended her shift. Apparently, he pulled out four one-hundred-dollar bills."

"How long was his stay with you?"

"Just last night."

"Who found him?"

"Rosa," says the manager, and points to the woman in uniform. "One of the maids. Our checkout time is 11 AM. She knocked on the door at noon, and when she didn't get an answer, let herself in."

Jake makes a noise. I turn to him.

"Here's something else. On the upper back." He stretches the neck of the T-shirt to expose the man's shoulder.

I lean over and squint where he is pointing. I can't see anything. Jesus, this man has one hairy body. On the whole, I like furry men. But this is almost grotesque. Underneath the hair the skin is mottled red and white.

"It's small, but it's there," says Jake. "A slight puncture. Like a hypodermic needle would make. Can't you tell? The small hole with the raised flesh around it?"

I squint again, but shrug. "If you say so."

"I do say so. And I'm going to need to do a more complete examination at the lab. We definitely need an autopsy on this one."

"What does that mean?" calls the manager from outside the room. He has that look people get when they're trying to appear concerned but they're really eager for dirt of some kind. We both ignore him.

"Have we got a wrongful death here, Jake?" I ask.

The manager can't contain his excitement, and lets out an *ohhh*. The news will be all over the hotel the minute we leave the premises.

"No, not definitely." Jake rubs his thinning hair with a gloved hand. "Just that I'm not signing off on this right away." He picks up his cell phone and begins dialing.

I feel at a loss. I walk over to Mollie, my fellow newbie. "I guess our first step is to notify next of kin." Jake nods at me as he waits for his call to be picked up on the other end of the line. "Whoever it is—I assume a wife," I gesture at the wedding ring on the man's left hand. "They'll have to do a positive ID of the body as well."

Mollie isn't happy.

"Yes, I'm afraid that's you, dude," I say. "And you," I point at Henry. "Go to his house in Palo Alto. Hopefully someone will be home."

Mollie leaves with Henry, and I close the door to the room before turning to Jake, who still has the phone pressed to his ear. The photographer continues to take photos of the room, even the parts that look innocuous to me, like the professionally made bed.

"I dunno," Jake says, covering the mouthpiece. "I have a feeling about this one."

So do I.

I think longingly of Peter waiting at home with a fresh pot of veggie chili, pull my notebook and pen out of my backpack and say, "Okay. Let's get to work."

2

San Francisco Chronicle

Prominent Stanford Doctor
Found Dead in Palo Alto Westin

May 12, 2013

PALO ALTO, CA—Dr. John Taylor, a prominent plastic surgeon and head of the Taylor Institute of Plastic Surgery, was found dead of a presumed heart attack in the Palo Alto Westin on El Camino Real on Saturday, May 11, 2013.

Colleagues expressed shock on hearing of the demise of Dr. Taylor, who specialized in helping children with facial deformities due to trauma or birth defects. "John Taylor will be sorely missed, both in his personal life, and for the advances he has made in reconstructive surgery," said Dr. Mark Epstein, a partner at the Taylor Institute.

Dr. Taylor is survived by his wife of thirty-five years, Deborah Taylor (55) of Palo Alto, and three children: Charles (32), Evan (31), and Cynthia (27).

Preliminary reports have determined Taylor died of a heart attack, sources say.

3

MJ

I'VE ALWAYS HATED THE TEDIOUSNESS of Mass. The empty words, spoken with such grandiose reverence. Try to figure out their meaning, though, and you come up empty. Slippery words spoken by slippery folks. I've had little affection for priests since our parish rector violated a good proportion of the altar boys entrusted to his care, including my little brother Thomas, now a sad and troubled man. The annual altar boys' picnic back in the 1980s was a bacchanalian orgy that effectively polluted a generation of young men in Gatlinburg, Tennessee. *Glorious Gateway to the Great Smoky Mountains*, my ass. *That dog won't hunt*, as I used to say. Talk about a wasteland of the spirit—Gatlinburg was it.

I'm standing in church now, trying to find a place to sit. For John. John's funeral Mass. I haven't been in a church for many years, much less a Catholic one. All the back row pews are taken. I certainly remember that phenomenon, Catholics wanting to put as much distance as possible between themselves and their dubious priests. I'm forced to keep moving up the aisle to find a space to squeeze into.

I'm in a strange state. I've spent the two days since I read about John's death in the newspaper wandering around the house in a kind of trance, fits of crying interspersed with those of absolute fury, and bottomless panic. I'd managed to call some friends, listened to their disbelief and outrage, but nothing really penetrated the numbness underlying all the emotional outbursts. I told my two sons, who despite being adults couldn't refrain from rather hurtful told-you-sos. And my brother Thomas accepted the news with silence. John's death effectively quenched a few of Thomas's grand financial schemes. But everyone is pushing me to move past the shock, and the hurt, and to be practical. To *take action.*

In particular, my friends are urging me to get a lawyer. Last night I went so far as to start reading Yelp reviews of local divorce attorneys. Surely that type of lawyer would have experience with property rights. I don't know where else to turn. I doubt anyone would have any legal advice for my particular situation.

For what do you do when your husband not only turns up dead, but already married?

According to the *Mercury News,* he was wedded for thirty-five years to a Deborah. *His beloved wife.* So where does that leave me?

We had (I thought) been married for five happy years. Our house is in my name, and in John's will—stored safely in our safe-deposit box—it is clearly left to me. But what if there is another will? What's my legal standing? This Deborah predates me in John's life by at least twenty-eight years. And California is a joint property state. Do I need to tell the bank holding the mortgage about John's death? Will John's *real wife* have any grounds for claiming the house? After all, John contributed a substantial down payment, and we've built up quite a lot of equity in it. Even if she doesn't, can I manage the mortgage on an accountant's salary? As my daddy'd say, *I'm in a seat so hot it's making my teeth sweat.*

If all this sounds cold and calculating in the face of the death of the man I'd called my husband for five years, forgive me.

Walking up the aisle of the church, I am getting uncomfortably close to the front, where John's real wife is certain to be. His *real wife.*

I can't help it, that's how I already think about the situation. Her, real. Me, false. My life as a fraud.

My shrink tells me this is my fault, that I keep seeking out life situations where I am bound to be an outsider, creating scenarios where I hover on the periphery. I had actually thought, in my marriage, that I had overcome this unhealthy tendency. I was finally *inside,* I finally had found a place where I belonged, had created an intimate circle that for the first time excluded others, rather than being excluded myself. What a joke. Now I'm not even sure I own the bed I sleep in.

When I do find a seat, it's alarmingly near the people who are clearly relatives and dear friends. I sit down and watch a tall, commanding woman whom I assume is the Deborah from the newspaper article. She is quietly greeting guests, accepting their condolences with such assurance! Such poise! She is obviously a force to be reckoned with. Even if she weren't the widow, she would have been the focus of our attention.

I'd nursed a faint hope that perhaps a mistake had been made. Perhaps John had once been married to this woman, but long divorced, and she was attempting some sort of con upon his death. But when I observe her straight square shoulders, her perfect silver hair—almost shellacked, it is so shiny and perfect, every strand in place—her placid coolness, and her clothes that just scream money and privilege, I despair. This is not a woman who would allow herself to be left behind, certainly not the type who would need to pull any such shenanigans. She is a keeper, of husbands, of power. You can tell from the way she greets each of the priests (four of them!) personally, and from all the men and women eager to approach her, shake her hand, or give her quick hugs (they are all quick, none lingering or overly intimate). Mostly the former. She's like *that,* then. Someone who largely inspires handshakes even from other women.

She stands in front of the coffin, elegant and self-possessed in a way I can never hope to be. I look down at my yellow skirt, the most expensive and colorful item in my wardrobe—John loved it—and cringe.

I stand out in the sea of black like a canary in a cave. I *feel* like a trapped canary, about to asphyxiate from the lack of oxygen. *She* would never be inappropriately dressed. Rather, how she dressed would determine what was appropriate in others. I think of the parking lot full of late model Mercedes and Lexus and BMW cars, and despair even more. She could squash me like a bug.

Yet do I envy her? Not particularly. I prefer the sloppy embraces of my ragtag friends to the brisk handshakes she is getting from even those people who seem to know her well. And I don't believe that John preferred her to me. I have that smidgen of confidence. After all, he married me *after* he married her. So I trumped her, in some oddly satisfying way.

I have to admit, she did organize everything splendidly in just three days. The prominent obituaries published in the *Mercury News,* the *Chronicle,* the *Daily News.* The huge displays of flowers carpeting the front of the church and overflowing down both side aisles of the packed church. And musicians—in addition to the organist, a cellist, a flute player, a singer with a heartbreakingly lovely contralto voice. It is all done in the most exquisite taste.

I think of what a sorry showing I would have made if the funeral arrangements had been left to me. We—John and I—didn't even belong to a church. What do you do in such cases? Rent one? I would have invited our little group of friends (*my* friends, I realize now, John had never introduced me to any of his) over for sandwiches and tea in our garden. Our garden! John had loved it so much! He would have objected to all the cut flowers here, sliced down in their prime. He loved growing things, things rooted in the earth. He was a natural healer.

He was often up at 5 AM to water the garden in the pale dawn light; then he was off to the hospital, where he would grab a shower and breakfast before making his rounds. But no, I have to stop when I find myself thinking like this. So he had told me. *So he had told me.* And now I understand that nothing he'd said can be trusted. With this thought, I collapse against the hard back of the pew even as the rest of the congregation stands up. The priests are at the altar and the service is beginning. I somehow haul myself up to my feet. How reassuring this hard, cool surface beneath me is. Nothing else is safe, nothing solid anymore.

As I compose myself I catch the woman I've guessed is Deborah looking over her shoulder at me. I try to read her expression. Hostile, I decide. *Who are you? Interloper. Gate-crasher. Imposter.* I turn my head to evade her glance, only to find myself staring at the casket, which I have been avoiding. Hard to believe John's body is in there, inert and rigid. He'd come into our bedroom to kiss me goodbye Thursday morning as usual, smelling of damp and earth. His hands were cool as he placed them on my shoulders and gently shook me. He didn't like to wake me up at such an early hour, but I always insisted. I needed to feel his lips against mine before losing him for the day, the pressure of his shoulder on my chest as he leaned in. I needed him to be *real*, that's how blessed I'd felt every day of our six years together.

Being practical? Who am I fooling? I am suffocating under the weight of grief and rage.

We had agreed, in our wills, on cremation. Clearly he had another arrangement with Deborah. Either that, or she determined to override his wishes. His body is going into the earth intact. I'm unsure how I feel about that. I'd found the idea of cremation to be reassuringly *final* and safe. *If I can't have him, no one can.* Crazy thoughts—being jealous of even the earth for embracing him so wholly when I can't.

He never knew how jealous I was, how I carefully watched him when we were out in public for any sign that he was looking at, perhaps evaluating, other women. But he never gave me a moment's worry. Funny, isn't it?

The Mass begins. First we are kneeling, then we are standing, then everyone is sitting again; I had forgotten all this popping up and down. I am squashed between a young man dressed elegantly in a gray suit and a wizened elderly woman who seems to be someone of importance, given that earlier people had paid her court. Some sort of relative?

It strikes me she could even be John's mother. He'd told me both his parents were dead, but I realize I am on quicksand here, too, that I can't trust any of John's so-called facts.

The young man (well, younger than me) on my right is wearing a suit that I take for silk since it's so soft when I accidentally brush my arm against him. A wisp of a mustache. People have been addressing him as either Mark or Dr. Epstein, whereas the elderly woman is called just Georgette, despite her age. I put her in her late eighties, perhaps even older. Around us are other well-dressed guests, all properly solemn. Before the Mass they had been quietly and cordially talking to one another. Not to me, but over and around me. The outsider. What else?

And the children! They're in the front pew, to the left. There is so much of John in the girl it nearly breaks my heart. She is clearly in pain, crying silently. One of her brothers has Deborah's sharp, chiseled features but—as we stand once again—not her height. He is easily six inches shorter than the other brother, and a couple of inches shorter than his sister. He too has a lost look on his face, and my heart goes out to him, the runt of such a tall, handsome family. He has to reach up to put his arm around his sister's shoulders. The other boy stands apart. He is tall, more than six feet, and resembles neither Deborah nor John. He doesn't look particularly sad, but angry.

What are the stages of grief—don't I have to go through denial, anger, and bargaining before acceptance? If so, I'm certainly angry enough, and the full force of John's death hasn't yet hit me. My emotions, as intense as they feel, are just shadows of what they will be when I'm able to fully absorb this.

But I find I can be openly calculating in the face of my own imminent breakdown (I can't think of any other word to describe what is happening to me). I'm almost clinically observing myself while plotting to somehow seize advantage over this situation with the formidable Deborah. Because I very much feel that the two of us are in a *situation*. I take solace in repeating to myself that I'm the only one who understands that. Deborah knows nothing about me. Perhaps for once, I think, my outsider status will serve me well.

At this precise moment, while I'm thinking these vaguely reassuring thoughts, it happens. The Mass ends, the presiding priest bids us to go in peace, and the organist starts the recessional. I see (as if in slow motion), Deborah detaching herself from her children, and edging out of the front pew. As the priests line up behind the casket, she quietly slips across the aisle. She eases over to my row. She seems to be looking at me. My hands begin to sweat. I tell myself that she has something of urgency to share with Georgette, or that Dr. Epstein is needed for some reason, and I stare straight ahead, mouthing the words to the recessional, dimly remembered from childhood. *Praise God from whom all blessings flow.* As if from a long way off I hear my name. "Hello, MJ." I am frozen. *Praise Him all creatures here below.* "I'm so glad you could come." It is Deborah. She pauses, but I still refuse to look at her. *Praise Him above ye heavenly host.* People around us are beginning to take notice, are no doubt wondering at my rudeness. *Praise Father, Son, and Holy Ghost.* I don't think I imagine the emphasis on my name when she says it again. I hear *I know who you are* as clearly as if it has been said out loud. "*MJ.* You'll attend the reception at the house afterward." It isn't a question. Then she turns to follow the priests and the flower-laden casket down the aisle, her children treading dutifully behind. The daughter turns her tearstained face toward me as she passes. I can't meet her eyes. God knows what she, and others, are thinking.

4

Helen

I GOT UP AT 4 AM to catch the first flight from LA to San Francisco. Now it's 9:30, and I've finally arrived at the Stanford University campus. I've been here before, of course, but under infinitely more pleasant circumstances. It's not every day that you attend the funeral of your husband as organized by his other wife. Or, rather, the funeral of the man you've been calling husband for six months. Who *was* John Taylor? I no longer have a clue.

John's obituary hadn't mentioned a wake, or "viewing," just a time and date for the funeral service: 10 AM, Tuesday, May 14, 2013, Stanford Memorial Church. As you would expect for a successful professional, a prominent member of his community, the turnout is impressive. A large throng is milling around the church entrance, and the atmosphere is almost festive, people shaking hands and hugging and chatting. If not for the preponderance of black you might mistake the gathering for a wedding or christening.

It has been three days of shocks. Multiple shocks, one after the other. That first bewildering call from my friend Annie who works at the university, followed by her email containing the link to the news article in the campus paper. And of course, denial kicked in immediately after I read it. No. No. Not my John. Not *my* Dr. John Taylor. But the facts—I couldn't ignore the facts. A prominent plastic surgeon at Stanford. A thriving private practice that did pro bono work for children with birth defects. Proof. Whatever John had lied to me about, it wasn't his professional achievements. John was dead. First I had to absorb that. And then, this Deborah. This other wife. One who apparently superseded me. And the children. The children.

I had thought of calling this *wife*. I should be honest, I more than thought of it. I tried to find her number, an email address, anything. All unlisted. The only things that my Googling turned up were some clubs and associations she belonged to: The South Penninsula Garden Club, where she was the longtime secretary. *Mrs. John Taylor Hosts a Tea Party in Beaufort Park.* The Women's Guild of Santa Clara County, where she had been elected president twice. A number of medical charities. Some out-of-focus photos of a woman with gray hair, stiff shoulders. A general air of rigidity. No other data available. No photos of the two of them together. John was either very cagey, or she was a very private albeit civic-minded person.

I even called Stanford Memorial Church, where the service was going to be held. They refused to give me any information, referred me to the funeral home managing the arrangements. But the funeral home also declined to release her data. God knows what I would have said if I had actually gotten this Deborah on the phone. I was distraught, not a word I use lightly. Not a state I'm used to being in.

That's when I bought my ticket to San Francisco.

I push through the throng in the vestibule and enter the church. Inside, people are quieter, have put on their serious faces. The casket is already there, on a platform at the front. I am a little puzzled by this, I thought the traditional way was to carry it in at the start of the service. It isn't open, thank God. That would have devastated me. No. Despite the size of the church, the seats are filling up. I wonder if I should feel proud of this, that my John commanded such devotion. I feel nothing. I have yet to feel anything at all.

I dressed carefully this morning, spending more time than I usually would. Given my personal taste in clothing, I'd had no trouble finding something black to pack in my overnight bag. I surveyed myself in the mirror of my room. I happen to be staying at the hotel John died in, according to the newspaper article, which also happens to be closest to the church on campus. I keep my hair neat, a dull brown shoulder-length bob that I pull back into a ponytail when I'm working. A little gray has started to creep in, not surprisingly, at age thirty-six. Let it. I'm not ashamed to be the age I am, to have earned the gray at my temples, the slight crows' feet at the corners of my eyes. I don't yet have to wear glasses. I wear no jewelry other than my wedding ring, and I had even protested against that when we got married. But John had insisted. And since he made few demands, I agreed. It was a small thing, but it mattered to him. *Had* mattered. It still feels so foreign, six months later, the cold metal against my finger.

I slide into a pew close enough to the front of the church to be part of the assembling congregation, but far enough back that I can observe the proceedings without being noticed. I first note the flowers. They are certainly exceptional—gorgeous arrangements wrapped around the altar and overflowing on either side of the casket. So very many tributes. Hundreds of them. A profusion of bright colors in that somber place—deep reds and blues and yellows splashed against the dark wooden pews. And the smell, overwhelming. The flowers' cloyingly sweet perfume making breathing difficult. People are holding Kleenexes to their noses, popping pills. You can barely see the wood of the coffin, awash as it is in this sea of flowers.

I am most interested in the group congregating in front of the coffin, on the steps leading up to the altar. Clearly they're the family and closest friends of the deceased. Of John, I remind myself. Right away I spot this wife, Deborah, from the photos. A tall, silver-haired woman impeccably dressed in a tailored black suit. She appears completely composed as she greets people. From where I'm sitting I can see she has makeup on, something I had thought of, but dismissed upon considering there was the possibility I could shed tears. Not that I'm a weeper by nature. But even the slight chance that I would suffer the indignity of a mascara-smeared face made me show up here with a naked visage. John's children are less self-possessed than their mother. They stand apart from her, three young adults, smiling politely when approached, submitting with dignity to handshakes and hugs and quiet whispered words. The girl and the younger boy are both openly crying. The older boy—man—is trying to appear unmoved by what is happening, but failing altogether. His misery written on his face. They look like nice kids. Then a bell chimes and everyone takes their seats.

It is a Catholic service. I know from attending too many funerals for children I couldn't save that having four priests processing up the aisle to stand at the altar is significant. Catholics take these things seriously. A four-priest Mass, like a four-alarm fire. A person of importance is being prayed into the afterlife. The John Taylor I knew would not have cared, but you can tell by watching this Deborah that such things matter enormously to her. She kneels, and stands and crosses herself, always a few seconds before everyone else. I find her the safest role model for what to do next. She never falters. If a tear cracks the smooth mask, I miss it. Although I do see her surreptitiously yank the robe of one of the altar boys to hide his torn jeans and sneakers as he and the priests walk back down the aisle.

I hesitate about whether to go to the cemetery. I'd hoped to briefly corner Deborah at the church, if I could get even half a minute, enough to get a phone number, an email address, something to follow up discreetly later. Given the size of the crowd, I now doubt whether I'll have any further opportunity at the graveside. Nevertheless, I go. My other options are to hire a lawyer to contact Deborah more formally or bring in the police to charge a dead man for committing bigamy. Neither attracts me. I'm not even sure what I want. If only it were possible to forget the whole thing ever happened. Erase the last year of my life, obliterate the twelve months since I met John Taylor. I still feel married. I don't even feel widowed—not yet. I know from my experience with grief counselors how that comes later.

Although the line of cars trailing behind the hearse is long, when we reach the cemetery it becomes clear that most of the funeral attendees hadn't bothered, we are down to about one hundred people at most. The weather is gorgeous, one of those Northern California days with a deep blue sky of the type we rarely see in LA. A perfect mild temperature that allows people to go without a sweater or jacket. The cemetery is on a high hill overlooking the ocean. You can see a fog bank hovering offshore, but otherwise every object in the landscape for miles in every direction is visible. Below us a small seaside town, its back to the ocean. Farther north up the coast, is what looks like a military installation on a hill, complete with huge satellite dishes and control towers. Far to the south, where the coastline curves in a half-moon, another, larger town with a preponderance of white buildings that glow in the sunshine. John would have been happy on a day like this, in a place like this. Although he hated extreme weather, both hot and cold, he loved the sun. He'd open the patio doors of my condo in the early morning, before the day heated up, would drag one of my upholstered armchairs out onto the balcony and bask in the sunshine, have his coffee there. He hated my patio furniture, found it too unyielding, too uncomfortable. I'd been planning to replace it so he didn't have to rearrange everything just to enjoy his coffee. He'll never do that again, and the thought gets me right in the gut. I actually give out a little gasp of pain, so visceral is it. The man next to me leans closer. "Are you all right?" he asks. "Yes," I manage to say, but I'm not. No.

The cemetery employees don't lower the casket into the earth, but leave it sitting aboveground on a sort of metal apparatus. We are down to one priest, and he speaks only a few brief words. Amidst a few scattered *amens* people lay individual flowers on top of the casket, and that is it. No drama. Deborah reaches over and pats the coffin. A quick, almost impersonal touch, as if it were a piece of furniture, or a neighbor's dog. Then the priest announces the reception, invites everyone to join Deborah at her house. And I hear Deborah's voice for the first time. Deep and compelling. She cups her hands around her mouth so everyone can hear, but if you hadn't actually seen her lips moving, you could have thought a man was speaking. "Everyone is welcome," she calls out. I take one of the leaflets being distributed with the address and directions, get back in my rented car, and drive to the house of John's real wife.

5

Helen

AS A PEDIATRIC ONCOLOGIST, I know grief. I've witnessed it in its rawest form, for nothing good ever comes from the death of a child. There are no mitigating circumstances. There are no words that comfort. "She's no longer in pain" comes close, perhaps. But little else. I have been through this with parents dozens of times. You might consider that I would be inured to it.

But no. Sitting in my hot rental car in front of my husband's house on a leafy Palo Alto street, I suddenly know the intimate meaning of the word. *Grief.* Bereavement. Bereft. *So this is it,* I think. The moment before, I had been considering a new case, a patient, six-year-old Cecilia, who has been suffering from what seems like a prolonged bout of flu. I had probed further. Bleeding from the gums. That is bad. Frequent nosebleeds. That is worse. The lab report has just come through by email. Not good results. Actually, terrible results. The problem with these mobile devices is bad news coming all the time. *Should I inform the family of the lab results?* my colleague wrote in the email. Ten minutes later, only after I have repeated the words *family* and *lab* and *results* until they are meaningless do I realize how

27

large is the hole that has been blown in my heart by John's death, his infidelity.

I roll down the window and try to fan some air into the hot car. I don't want to approach the house yet. I have somehow beaten the crowd here and rather than knock on the door too early, I settle in to wait. The house surprises me. It's a majestic colonial with white columns in front and a circular driveway edged with verdant bushes. A manor house from the Deep South. Tara. John had lived here, had been here when he wasn't with me—not in some funky Victorian on Potrero Hill in San Francisco, as he had led me to believe. He must have been indulging in a fantasy when he talked about his San Francisco home. How the original ana-glypta wall decorations were still intact, that the tall wooden windows wouldn't open, that his office was lined with quarter-hewn oak. He'd been so convincing in his stories of the ancient plumbing, of the termite infestation. I'm stunned by the elaborateness of his fabrications. Such lies require forethought. He'd spoken of nights staying up until 3 AM doing dictations, pausing intermittently to admire the lights of the city below. He even described the pad thai of his favorite late-night delivery restau-rant, his neighborhood café with Wi-Fi where he went over case notes, and how the noise from southbound 101 troubled him on evenings when the wind blew due south. He'd drawn me a picture of a life brim-ming with innocent busyness. We'd be sitting on the sofa, talking lazily about ourselves, still in that stage of discovery, and these things gradually came out. And all a fantasy. No. That is too kind. A con.

His reality was quite different. The house in front of me is pristine, perfect. No plumbing problems or termite infestations would be toler-ated here. The hedges trimmed with military precision. Even the flow-ers are orderly, organized into discrete clusters in beds lined with evenly matched rocks, nothing growing free of constraint. The rosemary has been cut into boxy squares, the lavender shaped into neat hillocks. So this was John's real life.

Oddly enough, my sense of being injured, of being betrayed, doesn't take away from my grief. I still ache for him, for the John I had known. *We could have worked it out,* I tell him, now. *You didn't have to go and die over it.* At the funeral, amidst the interminable readings and sermons and eulogies some dim-witted medical technician from John's practice mixed her metaphors in an eager attempt to pay him homage. *His heart was as warm as Texas.* But Texas isn't warm, it's damn hot, I'd found myself silently arguing with her. Besides, that comparison was supposed to be about size. *A heart as big as Texas,* was the cliché she'd been searching for.

We did have a love that big. And I'd been proud of the drama-free life John and I were leading. So different from my early years. Little did I know what drama I was actually involved in. I thought our quiet conversation signaled contentment, two pleasantly exhausted professionals communicating in ways deeper than words. And then to bed. And then to bed. I'm going to miss that. For John adored my body. That's his word, not mine. *Adored.* I've always found the sight of my slight, bony frame distasteful. But he'd clasp his hands around my waist and marvel that his fingers could almost touch. He'd lift my arms up to admire their leanness. I had begun to think of myself differently. As attractive. The fact is, I simply don't much care for eating. I think of it as consuming the necessary units of nutrition. My vegetable matter, my proteins, my fluids. I'm indifferent to the forms my units take. I wouldn't say I'm fastidious—if anything, the opposite. Everything is bland, nothing sticks out as particularly appetizing. A mild form of ageusia. Hypogeusia, to be accurate. An inability to taste. Not enough to put me at risk, healthwise, but it doesn't lend itself to overeating. I tend to pick my foods by colors. Deep greens, deep yellows, deep reds.

I am equally indifferent to alcohol. Yet John and I sat down each evening we were together with our wine. I think it was the image of the chardonnay in the glass that attracted me, the rich golden color, the cool feel of the glass containing the chilled liquid on my fingers. What sense I lack in my taste buds is most definitely compensated for by my epidermis. John had only to brush his fingers against my shoulder for me to shiver with desire.

I notice that cars are parking behind me, people are starting to walk up the pavement to the house. Deborah is in the doorway, beckoning people in.

I glance at the *Chronicle* obituary I brought with me. It is lying on the passenger seat. The photo of John when young, playing the piano. An unconventional one to choose for a death notice. John had been devilishly handsome—that youth, that mischievousness. No, the John I'd known was a tired man, a man beaten down by too much responsibility. Someone who had lost touch with joy. Yet he brought me joy. And I had believed that I introduced some pleasure to his life.

At this, the grief hits again. Strange how transient it is. Usually my emotions are stable, with predictable transitions from one state to another. But not this. The throbbing in the chest, why does it *feel* like the pain is centered there? Even the smallest children, who can't know anything of the location of the heart, point to their chests when they're in emotional distress. One could argue it has to do with our lungs, that the physiological pressure on them during times of extreme stress makes us associate our chests with emotion. After all, there's no real connection between the heart and the mind. The heart is just a motor for channeling blood to the body's extremities. Yet it does hurt there. One could hold both hands to one's left breast to try to contain the pain.

If John had genuinely been my husband, I could announce his death to close friends and associates we had revealed our marriage to. I could grieve publicly. But I can't slink back into my condo, husbandless, leaving people to wonder *what the hell happened?* For perhaps the first time in my adult life I find myself wondering what others might think. No. If nothing else, I'll need to untangle the legalities. I suspect that will involve going to court to get my marriage annulled. So be it. If I can't claim widowhood at least I'll be single again. Not that I'll ever remarry. I had been right to think it inhospitable territory for the likes of me.

I slowly get out of the car, smooth my dress down, and walk up the perfectly fitted gray flagstones to the imposing white house. No, I wouldn't have placed John here, not with his missing buttons and his protruding stomach. He couldn't get through a meal without staining his shirt. Yet I've seen his surgical handiwork, seen the children whose faces he'd fixed. He was a true artist, a perfectionist. He'd get calls at his office from women—and, increasingly, men, too—begging him to consider using his skill for cosmetic face-lifts, nose jobs, and cheekbone sculpting for vanity's sake only. He refused, although his partners took such cases. Or maybe that was another smoke screen, another fantasy of the honorable life he wanted to live. It occurs to me that one can't support a wife in a style like this in Palo Alto without raking in some pretty big bucks.

I slip quietly into the house. Quite the crowd. Easily two hundred people milling around, talking, even laughing—the solemnity of the church and cemetery shattered. Deborah had the sense to have the reception catered; young people in white shirts and black trousers are carrying trays with glasses of red and white wine and mineral water. Again, I'm struck by how composed Deborah is, by her apparent lack of sentiment. Only once does she betray any emotion, and that is when an unfortunate guest, a portly middle-aged woman, bumps into another guest and spills a glass of red wine on an Oriental carpet. Everyone freezes for a moment. Conversation ceases. They look at Deborah. She is in the center of a little group, and she also stops talking, her hand goes to her heart—that gesture again—her face reflecting the kind of horror and woe I've seen when giving my patients' parents terrible news. Yet this is over a rug. Her reaction might be due to projection—after all, the woman just buried her husband; perhaps this incident triggered pent-up emotions. But Deborah is indeed distraught over the rug itself. When the guilty woman bends and starts scrubbing at the stain with a cocktail napkin, Deborah hisses at her to stop. She grabs the woman's wrist, staying it while calling loudly for a wet towel. One of the waiters races into the kitchen and emerges with a damp tea towel. Even then, Deborah doesn't trust anyone else. She kneels on the floor, places the damp towel on the stain, presses gently, then hands the towel to be rinsed off and brought back. She stays on the floor repeating the blotting cycle for so long that people start talking again, and gradually the noise level of the room is what it was before the incident. Deborah continues for a good twenty minutes, tending to the rug as if to an invalid.

Even though the crowd is still thick, I can't help noticing one person. She stands out. Older than me by perhaps a decade. Midforties. Long, wavy, graying golden hair. An ankle-length, shimmering gold skirt that screams in the sea of black and gray. A long-sleeved, green sweater too heavy for this heat—you can see the sweat visible on her brow and neck. The kind of person who has *take pity on me* written all over her, and as a result creates a virtual black hole in the center of any room. I've never felt uncomfortable being alone. Being an observant wallflower pays off. I sip my mineral water and lime, and speak when someone addresses me, but feel no need to be constantly engaged.

I am so lost in thought that I realize I have inadvertently locked eyes with the woman in the gold skirt. I am dismayed to see her bearing down on me. She might have mistaken me for someone who needs rescuing. Perhaps she hopes I am another social outcast looking to commiserate. She stumbles as she approaches. I assume she's had a bit too much to drink—an accurate assumption, as it turns out.

She opens just as I would have predicted. "I don't really know anyone here," she confesses, obviously expecting me to say something similar. Her voice, despite her nervousness, has a pleasant slow twang to it. *Ain-ee-wun hee-ahh.* Not a California native. I shrug, not wanting to encourage her. Sloppiness. It always repels me.

"So how do you know . . . the people here?" she asks. *Hee-ahh* again. She doesn't wait for an answer. Her eyes and mouth both open wide. I can hear her breathing through her mouth. Distasteful.

Then I feel a hand at my elbow. It is cold and damp. I turn. It's Deborah herself, who has apparently finished administering to the rug. The gold-skirt woman is staring at her, her mouth still open, clearly flummoxed. "So you two found each other," Deborah says, gesturing at me, then at the woman. "Why am I not surprised."

I am at a loss for words. Finally, I inanely stick out my hand. "Helen R—"

"Richter," says Deborah. "Yes, I know. Helen Richter, meet MJ Taylor. I'm assuming you both know who I am."

"Taylor?" I ask the woman in gold. "Are you related to John?"

"Related?" the woman begins to laugh. She's most definitely had too much to drink. "I guess you could say so."

"But not by blood," suggests Deborah. She is smiling.

"No, not like that," the woman says, then falls silent.

There's an awkward pause as Deborah briefly accepts the goodbyes of a couple of guests, then gives us her attention again. "You two have more in common than you realize," Deborah says. She appears as composed as ever. "In fact, we all three share something quite . . . intimate."

"I don't understand," I say, but a drum has started pounding in my chest. I can feel blood rushing in my ears. I realize I haven't eaten anything for nearly forty-eight hours.

"Excuse me," I say, and stumble over to the nearest empty chair. I put my head between my knees. The dizziness passes.

I stay there for a moment, then gradually sit up, hoping to be left alone. But no. Both Deborah Taylor and MJ Taylor are standing next to me. MJ looks genuinely concerned and is holding out a glass of water. Deborah simply observes me.

"I think you're beginning to get it," says Deborah. She smiles. It strikes me that she doesn't have a very nice face.

MJ still looks bewildered, she glances from me to Deborah and back again. "What's going on?" she asks. *Goin aw-an.* Definitely southern roots.

"What's going on is the inaugural meeting of John Taylor's spouses," says Deborah. "Would we qualify as a coven? A harem? What is the term for a group of wives?"

"Circle," I say. "We are a circle of wives." Then I close my eyes and this time don't fight the dizziness.

6

MJ

I SOMEHOW GET HOME AFTER that disastrous reception. How I did it without ending up with a DUI I don't know. I'm not a drinker. It only takes a couple glasses of wine on an empty stomach to put me way under, and the wine coupled with the stress, and then the shock unhinged me completely. Three wives! And of course it had been me who jogged that woman's elbow so she spilled her red wine all over Deborah's apparently very valuable carpet. Well, despite knowing everything else, she didn't seem to know *that*. Be grateful for small victories, I tell you. Or "Yee-*haw*" as my mother would say sarcastically when underwhelmed by an event.

How do I feel? Humiliated. I've clearly been outsmarted and outgunned at every point. Those fantasies I'd had of starting a quiet conversation with Deborah in which I calmly informed *her* of the situation now seem borderline hallucinogenic. Not since I dropped acid in my twenties have I felt so displaced from reality as standing in Deborah's living room with her and that other "wife." What was her name, Helga? Heidi? Something that begins with an "H." She managed to hold on to her wits and, more importantly, her dignity. Even at my best I only muddle through life, grateful for the goodwill most people bear toward dumb creatures. At least Deborah doesn't seem inclined to strip me of my assets, meaning, this house. "We'll have that talk later," she said to me before I left. Of course, only to me, as this . . . Henrietta? Haley? . . . clearly isn't as concerned as I am about finances. I can't help wondering what her circumstances are. Thank God I never quit my job. John had told me I could quit anytime, but I just hadn't been able to imagine what I would *do* with myself all day. Come to think of it, John might have had similar worries, probably thought I'd be more likely to pry into matters if I didn't spend eight-plus hours at the office every day. Besides, I don't mind my job. I rather enjoy it. Bookkeeping for a software company in Silicon Valley distracts me—and affords me a certain level of respect. The sanity of numbers, the rationality of ratios, percentages. Accounting has always kept me grounded during rough patches in my life; I can only pray it will this time, too.

Since Deborah was constantly being interrupted by departing guests offering their final condolences, we didn't discuss the details of our situation. Deborah had said, "Of course there's no need for anyone else to know," at which point I felt a certain amount of relief, but even so I'm unclear how it will work out. Will I claim John as dead? Will I take the death certificate to a lawyer to make sure the house is truly, officially, mine? That other *wife,* she'd nodded calmly, took it all in stride. The indignity of not being the final wife! It confirms that I lack something, that I hadn't given John what he wanted, what he *really* needed. Not that Deborah seemed to feel anything of the sort. At least she was left twice. Not that I was actually *left.* (I have to keep reminding myself of that.) He could have done so. He could have asked me for a divorce when he met this third wife, this who*ever*. He could have just abandoned me. That he didn't means something, it's something to hold on to.

In the meantime what will I tell people? I suppose I can say that my husband suddenly died of a heart attack. That's what the newspapers reported anyway. As Deborah said, "no one needs to know." But this is all for another day when I can bear it. I am still a little tipsy and not exactly thinking clearly. I begin to get ready for bed when my house phone begins to ring.

I usually ignore numbers I don't recognize from the caller ID, but this is a local call, which makes me curious, as does the fact that no one who knows me ever calls the landline. Everyone who needs to reach me knows my cell number. But this caller is extremely persistent, really, *aggressive* is a better word: The phone keeps ringing, and I let the call go to voicemail five times before I finally answer. "This is MJ."

The caller turns out to be a reporter from the *Chronicle*. She got an anonymous tip. No, she doesn't know from whom—it was anonymous. *Duh*, she practically says. Then, "Is it true that you were married to Dr. John Taylor? And that he had two other wives?" she asks.

I am floored. Who could have told her? How many people know? Deborah, or perhaps that other wife, although she hadn't seemed the type to give much away. That type can surprise. This . . . Helen—that's right, that's her name—might have looked as though she had everything under wraps, with her elegant black sheath and those cheekbones and collarbone, but I've seen some truly spectacular meltdowns from her kind. My own tightly buttoned-up mother was a master of self-restraint, but when she broke, she broke big.

This reporter, she hits me with the facts. So smoothly! No hint of judgment or shock in her voice. She fools me, she makes it sound like no big deal.

"And you had no idea about your husband's other wives?" she asks, and her voice is so . . . *understanding* . . . that I lose my head. The booze coupled with the confusion. I spew words, many words, before hanging up the phone and collapsing.

7

San Francisco Chronicle

Deceased Stanford Doctor
Had Three Wives

May 15, 2013

PALO ALTO, CA—Dr. John Taylor was a prominent plastic surgeon, an associate clinical professor at Stanford, and director of the Taylor Institute, a thriving private clinic that specialized in facial reconstructions. It wasn't until Taylor passed away last week, at age 62, of a presumed heart attack, that he was discovered to have had three concurrent wives in different households in Palo Alto, Los Gatos, and Los Angeles.

"My world has just fallen apart," said MJ Taylor (née Johnston) of Los Gatos, who hadn't known that her husband was married with three children. In fact, he had never divorced his wife Deborah Taylor (55) of Palo Alto. MJ Taylor (49) had married Dr. John Taylor in a quiet ceremony on the beach in Santa Cruz five years ago. At that point, Dr. John Taylor had been married to Deborah Taylor for nearly thirty years. Then, six months ago, Dr. Taylor married again, this time to fellow physician Helen Richter (36) who lives and works in Los Angeles, where Dr. Taylor was a visiting professor at the UCLA medical school. Dr. Richter kept her own surname after the ceremony. MJ Taylor, a financial analyst at WebSys Corp., in Santa Clara, also claimed to have no knowledge of this later marriage. "Until the funeral reception, I had no idea. Not a clue," she said, adding, "She *does* seem like a nice woman."

Dr. Helen Richter and Deborah Taylor were unavailable for comment.

In the United States, the Model Penal Code (section 230.1) defines bigamy as a misdemeanor. In the state of California, if a married person marries an unmarried person the penalty is a one-year prison term or a ten-thousand-dollar fine. If an unmarried person knowingly marries another person's husband or wife, then the penalty is five thousand dollars or a one-year prison term. Samantha Adams, a detective with the Palo Alto Police Department said the state was unlikely to pursue charges against MJ Taylor or Dr. Richter, as they appeared ignorant of Taylor's original marriage.

8

Samantha

"SO YOU'VE CAUGHT A LIVE ONE." That's my boss, Chief Elliot, although everyone calls her Susan. Officers visiting our station house from other cities are appalled at the informality. But despite the fact that we're on a first-name basis, she doesn't stand for nonsense. A tall woman in her midfifties, she's been running the Palo Alto police department for almost twenty years. She was the one to tap my shoulder and ask if I wanted to take the detective exam, the one who put the idea into my head. I wouldn't exactly call her a mentor, although others in the department hint that I'm a favorite. She's a remote sort of person, not overly warm, and despite the first-name thing, not terribly approachable. Once I bought her a Diet Coke from the machine, having noticed that she swills them down in a constant flow all day. The look I got still sends chills through me. But I've witnessed her in action enough to note that she has vast excesses of patience and, I've always thought, wisdom. She has a nickname that people are careful to use only out of her hearing, *Suicide Suzie,* due to a famous incident where she talked a guy down from jumping off the Sand Hill 280 overpass. The mayor gave her a plaque *for an act of valor* that someone had to rescue from the garbage can after the award ceremony. To Susan's chagrin, it now hangs above the entrance to the station house. I have enormous respect for her. She doesn't seek glory for its own sake, but values a job well done.

Susan sits at her desk, fiddling with a pen, then leans back in her chair. She is large, with massive shoulders and a double chin, the type of woman that unenlightened persons probably wouldn't take seriously, given her size and indifference to fashion. Strangers might mock her for her weight, might see it as evidence of laziness or lack of control. Yet I've never known anyone so disciplined. No matter how early you get to the station, Susan is already there. The station house is a spotless engine of efficiency. She computerized all the records a full decade before other police departments in the state. Of course, a lot of that has to do with Palo Alto money. But also Susan's vision. She's married to the head of Palo Alto's firefighting division, himself no Skinny Minnie. People like to joke that one of the reasons Palo Alto is such a placid community is that the two of them hate having their dinner interrupted.

"I'm mostly talking to myself here," she says. "I'm wondering if this case shouldn't go to a more seasoned officer. Someone used to handling those ghouls in the media. After that *Chronicle* nastiness, the media is calling for an official statement. You'd have to write one today and present it tonight or tomorrow morning. You up for that? Or do you want me to pass it on to Grady." Grady being our only big-city cop, having retired from the Detroit police force before moving west and signing on in Palo Alto as a detective at the ripe old age of fifty. *Easy money*, he calls it. You can see him trying to stifle a smile when anyone complains about having a bad day. I Googled him once, way back. He was put on administrative leave twice in Detroit for having killed while on duty. The words *excessive use of force* were used throughout the various newspaper reports. Scary stuff. I tend to tiptoe around Grady.

Part of me wants to say, *sure, why not, throw it to Grady,* and let this case go. That's the quitter in me. Though I'm also kind of hooked.

"I can handle that," I say. I try to exude the air of someone competent, yet not foolishly overconfident. Mostly this involves standing up to my 5'4" height and brushing my bangs out of my face.

"But we know nothing yet," I say. "Jake sent the body to the pathologist for an autopsy, and he said we won't have the results for days."

"Then tell them that. Keep it short and sweet," Susan says.

"Do I mention the bruising? The needle puncture?"

"Absolutely not," says Susan. "You speculate about nothing. They'll press you to say more. They'll try to get you to say this is murder, whatever. Just stick to the facts, Sam."

The facts, I think, not unhappily, are doozies. Although I'm not unmindful of the fact that a man is dead—a man with responsibilities and a family who is grieving—I'm excited to be doing something other than processing theft reports that will come to nothing or investigating break-ins fumbled by pot-smoking sixteen-year-olds. They're not the cleverest criminal minds. The last one I'd been assigned to, the perp had two of his friends on bicycles acting as lookouts. A couple of kids riding in perpetual circles in front of the target's home naturally aroused the attention of the neighbors. When we arrived, the perp was trying to get away on his bike with a MacBook in his backpack and two iPhones in his pocket, but not before he'd paused to make a phone call from one of his ill-gotten phones. Like I said, not the brightest criminals in the world.

"I'd like you to stay on the case," says Susan, with an air of having made up her mind, "For now, you're our homicide department, Sam. Use Grady or Mollie as backup. I want daily briefings."

"Oh, and Sam," she calls after me, as I'm walking away, "Find out who tipped the newspaper off about the three marriages. Talk about a shocker! It must have been one of the wives. I'd like to know which one thought it would be advantageous for us to know about the bigamy—I mean, multiple marriages."

"The *trigamy*," I quip, and get a smile out of Susan. It makes my day.

9

Excerpt from Transcript

Police interview with MJ Taylor, May 18, 2013

[Preliminary introductions, explanations of processes and procedures]

Samantha Adams: When did you realize your husband had two other . . . relationships?

MJ Taylor: Not until I read the news of his death. And actually, I only found out about his first wife from the paper. The other wife I learned about at the funeral reception. No one accepts that, though. No one can believe I didn't suspect something, anything.

Samantha Adams: Well, didn't you?

MJ Taylor: Not at all.

Samantha Adams: How could that be?

MJ Taylor: I have to tell you, John simply inspired confidence. That large, imposing physique. His soothing authoritative voice. And don't forget I was in love. I felt like a bride even after five years of marriage. I had no idea I was married to a Bluebeard. And unlike Bluebeard's bride, when he told me there were places I couldn't go, questions I couldn't ask, I obeyed. Unlike her, I absolutely obeyed.

Samantha Adams: Do you think others suspected? His secretary? His colleagues?

MJ Taylor: I never called his office; he forbid me to, said it would disrupt his work. I was only allowed to contact him via email, or through his cell phone. I didn't call the hotels he stayed at when he was out of town, I never showed up unannounced at any of his award dinners honoring him, any of the celebrations of his professional success. He wanted to keep his professional and personal lives separate, he told me, and I obeyed.

Samantha Adams: Didn't any of this strike you as strange?

MJ Taylor: Not at the time. Or rather, John *was* strange. It was one of his charms, his eccentricity. He danced naked in the garden after dark. He kept caramel candies in his bedside table, popped them in his mouth during his frequent awakenings in the night, sucked them until he fell back asleep. Like a two-year-old, he suffered from night terrors, needed sweets as pacifiers.

And I was—am—a little strange myself. The hippy accountant. Fish out of water almost everywhere. Except when I'm with my brother, of course. I'm nothing if not a good big sister. But other than that, an oddball. Until John. I was truly known to him. Do you understand what I mean by that? That was John's particular magic. My friends said this, too, you felt he saw you, really *saw* you. Such a man was worth waiting for. Even worth compromising for.

Samantha Adams: Well, how *did* you meet John Taylor? You seem to come from such very different worlds.

MJ Taylor: We met cute, as they say. Six years ago. I had just been laid off in one of those Silicon Valley purges that seem to happen every ten years or so. *Downsizing*. Or, as our CEO said when he made the announcement, *rightsizing*. Meaning me, and about forty thousand other people, were wrong. I went out for drinks with my fellow superfluous humans. Unusual, for me, I'm not a drinker. Neither was John, it was something we had in common. That's what makes our first encounter in a bar so odd. That day I had a beer. And another. And another. One by one my fellow ex-employees left, and eventually I looked around and realized I didn't know anyone. Surrounded by strangers! I'd drunk enough to become cranky, but I signaled the bartender, and ordered a real drink, in a real drinker's glass. That's how I ordered it, "Give me the drink that comes in that glass." And I pointed. When it came, I gagged, it was so strong, so bitter. And I hate olives. I sent it back. I rejected it as inferior, as I had been rejected that morning. *Right-sizing*. Rightdrinking. My voice was too loud, and heads turned. Who expects to see an aging hippy, complete with long flowered skirt and beads, at a watering hole for software project managers and semiconductor sales reps? I was surrounded by young men (all young, young, *young*) in identical uniforms, khaki pants and blue button-down shirts. Very few women, very few of anyone over the age of thirty. The guy sitting next to me at the bar was the exception.

This man—I guessed his age as midfifties—he reached out across the bar to my rejected drink, picked it up, and took a sip. He made a face. "This is clearly unacceptable," he said, and smiled at me (an understanding smile). "Wait. Just you see," he said. "I'll make you the perfect drink." He somehow commanded from the bartender the vodka bottle, a handful of lime wedges, a can of cranberry juice, packets of sugar. How did he manage that? He had that way about him. He was clearly used to being in charge, he didn't even need to raise his voice. If anything, it was the reverse, he was so soft-spoken that you had to lean forward, *you* had to go to *him*. And you did so willingly.

John wasn't dressed particularly well, a worn pair of jeans, and a T-shirt advertising some sort of golfing charity. It turns out he'd been at a boring function at the hotel next door, had slipped away for a break, decided to come into the bar. And he did exactly what he promised. He made me—us, because we shared it—the absolutely perfect drink, semisweet, with a sharp tangy aftertaste. And I was just *gone*.

Samantha Adams: So what did you know, and when did you know it?

MJ Taylor: Are you recording this? It's just that you're not taking any notes.

Samantha Adams: Oh right. I forgot to tell you. Yes, we are videotaping this. See the camera? Is that okay? Or rather do I have your consent to record this interview?

MJ Taylor: Of course, that's okay. I have nothing to hide. Record away . . . What was the question again?

Samantha Adams: When did you find out about the other wives?

MJ Taylor: Oh, yes.

I was completely in the dark until I saw the death announcement in the *Mercury News* on Sunday. I'm one of the few people on the planet who still gets a newspaper delivered in the morning, one of the few who still enjoys turning the physical pages over coffee. I don't usually read the death notices (I'm not that old, not yet) but I tend to flip through the various sections methodically. And a particularly large obit caught my eye. The photo alone was a quarter of a page. Then I saw the name. John Taylor.

I hadn't known before then, how could I? John had called me Thursday morning, said he had to make one of his trips down to UCLA, there was an emergency case. He suggested I might want to visit friends in Oregon, I'd been talking about doing that for a while. But I decided I'd stay home, catch up with the house, work in the garden.

Samantha Adams: Did John often take off like that?

MJ Taylor: Of course, he had his hospital duties. Trips to conferences. His academic appointment down at UCLA. Nothing that struck me as unusual given the professional commitments of a man of his stature. Of course, now I feel like a fool. Bluebeard's wife, finding the bloody chamber only after her vile husband has been apprehended.

Samantha Adams: So you hadn't seen him for three days when you read the obituary?

MJ Taylor: Right. For two days he'd been dead, and I didn't know, hadn't felt it. I should have *known*; I have certain gifts in that direction, I could tell you stories. But no. I *had* thought it odd John didn't call, didn't return my calls to his cell phone since Friday. That was unusual. But not completely unprecedented, either. He was a bit of a free spirit, John. It was one of the things I loved about him.

Samantha Adams: What was your reaction when you read the obituary?

MJ Taylor: My first thought was, what a good-looking man! The handsomeness of the man in the photo caught my eye, not the fact that it was John. A young man sitting at a piano, his fine fingers poised to play what you knew from his smiling face would be a happy song. I remember thinking, *how sad, this attractive man dead,* then I saw the name, went back to the photo, and recognized John.

Samantha Adams: And that was how you found out about Deborah?

MJ Taylor: Yes. *A beloved wife.* Of course, they have to say that, but it still hit me, hard. And three grown children! I thought of John's lack of warmth (hostility even) to my boys, which I attributed to his never having had a child himself. How wrong I was. My life blew up, then, sitting at my kitchen table. Just shattered.

10

Excerpt from Transcript

Police interview conducted
by telephone with Helen Richter,
May 19, 2013

[Preliminary introductions, explanations of processes and procedures]

Samantha Adams: Can you hear me okay? Sometimes our phone connections at the station house aren't so great.

Helen Richter: Yes, I can hear you fine. Can you hear me?

Samantha Adams: Yes. And I'm supposed to inform you that I will be taping this telephone conversation. Is that all right?

Helen Richter: No problem.

Samantha Adams: Okay. I don't want to take up more of your busy day than necessary, so let's just jump into it. I guess my first question is how did John Taylor get away with it? I mean, having three wives? How could you not have suspected something?

Helen Richter: Isn't that *the* question. The question everyone wants answered. *How did he get away with it?* [pause] It's the elephant in the room at work. Some people manage to restrain themselves from asking. Most don't. They seem to forget you're one of the "its" being referred to. Meaning wives. And people have an almost clinical curiosity about the logistics. I suppose I can't blame them. *What did he tell you when he went away for long periods of time? Did he keep separate credit cards, bank accounts for each wife? Did he ever show up wearing something you didn't recognize, or smelling of a strange scent?* You wouldn't believe the things people you barely know will come straight out and ask.

Samantha Adams: So, did he do any of those things? You have to admit, they're the kinds of questions that immediately spring to mind.

Helen Richter: I still don't know the answers myself; he did such a masterful job. Not of coming up with clever responses so much as erecting a kind of force field against them ever getting asked.

Samantha Adams: It must be hard.

Helen Richter: [pause] It is. [pause] You know, if your husband has an affair with another woman, you get a certain amount of sympathy. You see, there's an acceptable social protocol for consoling the wives of middle-aged men who wander. But if your husband has another *wife* . . . well, we don't exactly have a boilerplate for that. And people are lost without their boilerplate. They mostly lose control of their mouths. Ask a lot of stupid questions. And the most stinging of all is, *How could you not have known?*

Samantha Adams: How did you find out?

Helen Richter: By his death. The news article in the *Stanford Daily. Survived by wife Deborah, and three children, Cynthia, Charles, and Evan.* Devoted wife, I should say. Or was that the obituary? In any case, a wife that was not me. Not that I would ever describe myself as *devoted*—that has the connotation of blind, adoring worship. That wasn't what John felt for me. Or what I felt for John. No.

I didn't know he had children, either. That had been one of the conditions for *our* marriage. No children. No discussion. No regrets.

Samantha Adams: Tell me more about your marriage.

Helen Richter: It was very short and very sweet. We had just six months together, barely made it out of the honeymoon stage. Then again, it was a commuter marriage. With me in Los Angeles, him in Palo Alto. I had my job, and he had his. I liked LA, he liked Northern California. And we liked each other. So we agreed, we would have a long-distance relationship. He came down twice a month for three or four days at a time.

Samantha Adams: You never came north, to visit him in Palo Alto?

Helen Richter: No, never. It didn't come up, was never an issue. You have to keep in mind, we were both very busy. When you choose a medical career, you accept a lifestyle most people would find intolerable. The long working hours, mostly on your feet. The fatigue, both physical and emotional. I'm a pediatric oncologist at the UCLA Children's Hospital. I see fifty to sixty children every week, all very sick. No month passes without at least one, usually more, of my young patients dying. At any given time, our department is running four or five drug trials that I need to stay on top of. And when I'm not actually at work, I'm reading the latest journal articles, and trying to catch up with my dictations, my own writing.

Samantha Adams: Didn't you miss him when you weren't together?

Helen Richter: Obviously. On some level. But what you don't seem to get—what no one seems to get—is that I didn't have much room in my life for more than John was willing or able to give me. Until I met him I expected to remain single, and very happily so. He didn't fill a void; there was no emptiness in my life. I even felt uncomfortable at first, shoehorning him in. Yet I wanted it, wanted him. Surprised myself by the urgency of the wanting.

Samantha Adams: Whose idea was it to get married?

Helen Richter: John was the one who demanded marriage. I resisted—especially since no children would be involved. I saw little need to formalize the relationship. He was insistent, even told me that without marriage he didn't feel our . . . liaison . . . could continue. We completed the paperwork and one Friday morning went down to the courthouse and did the deed.

Samantha Adams: Strange. I mean, *why?*

Helen Richter: Yes. He could have had an affair with me; I'd have been no wiser. I'm not the suspicious kind. The marriage certificate was important to him. The day of the ceremony, we went back to my condo and drank wine and sat on the sofa. Just sat, not touching. He asked me, "Do you feel any different?" I had to admit I didn't, although I was certainly very happy, was deeply happy. John said he felt like a great weight had been lifted off his shoulders. "I feel so free," he said. An odd thing to say, once you know the facts. Shouldering yet more responsibility, and complicating his life with more intrigue and lies. *So free.* What was he thinking?

Samantha Adams: After the wedding, what happened?

Helen Richter: Little changed. He moved some clothes and personal effects into my condo. We redid our wills. Otherwise, we carried on as before. We made no announcement. I informed my small circle of friends, and that was that. I don't think most people at the medical center where I taught and where John was an adjunct knew. Although they might have realized we were attached in some way.

But all this is making our relationship sound . . . uncaring. Tepid. It wasn't. I'm not good at talking about such things. I'm a very private person. Insular, even. So this is hard. I will say that what happened after the marriage was official took me by surprise. I hadn't foreseen how much it would matter. I hadn't anticipated the absolute happiness. And what could arguably be called passion. Yes, physical. Yet also more than that. Before, I knew what we had between us was good. I knew we had a reasonable shot at making each other happy. But I hadn't anticipated bliss. I'd never before encountered *ecstasy*.

Samantha Adams: [long pause] Strong words.

Helen Richter: Yes. Still, inadequate for describing how I felt about John Taylor.

11

Excerpt from Transcript

Police interview with Deborah Taylor, May 20, 2013

[Preliminary introductions, explanations of police processes and procedures, notification that the session would be videotaped]

Samantha Adams: So did you know that your husband had taken two other wives?

Deborah Taylor: Of course I knew. How could I not? I made it all possible. Did you think John capable of scheming on this level with any degree of success? Nonsense.

Samantha Adams: Why on earth would you *help* him?

Deborah Taylor: Simple. To keep him.

Samantha Adams: [pause] I'm sorry?

Deborah Taylor: It was the only way.

Samantha Adams: Can you explain that, please?

Deborah Taylor: John started his . . . wandering . . . precisely eight years ago. Cynthia, our youngest daughter, had just left for her freshman year at Berkeley. There we were, John and I, alone together in the house for the first time in nearly twenty-five years. Our days consisted primarily of long silences punctuated by bursts of temper. It made clear what both of us had suspected. The marriage was dead.

Shortly after, John took up with a nurse at the hospital. He tried to do it surreptitiously. As if I couldn't tell from Day One. I confronted him. We discussed it, openly. We didn't argue about it. But I was adamant. He could see his nurse. Have his sordid little affair. But no divorce. Never would I agree. If he tried I would fight it, take everything he had, would do my best to ensure the children never spoke to him again. I don't think I'd have had much luck making that latter threat come true. The children—well, at least Cynthia and Evan—worship John. Charles is more difficult to read.

It was the threat of taking away the children's affections, rather than the money, that got to John. He felt his own betrayal of me more than I did, couldn't believe that others wouldn't judge him as harshly as he was judging himself. John didn't have much confidence in his ability to command affection from people. Ironic, when he was one of the most beloved of men. Truly. Ask around at his clinic. He had warmth, a vulnerability even, that was tremendously endearing if you were susceptible in that way. I wasn't. Not anymore, at least.

I monitored the situation with the nurse. As I suspected, it soon turned serious. John would never be satisfied with a casual affair. He would always need more. I put an end to it. I don't want to go into the details now. Suffice it to say I scared her off. My tactics may have been heavy-handed, but they worked. John was in despair. "I must have love," he said. "If you won't love me, I need to find someone who will."

I didn't mind him having cheap flings. "You may indulge yourself if you like," I told him. "But nothing that threatens our marriage, nothing that prevents you from coming home every night to me." But he didn't want fleeting affairs. He wanted the real thing. And I wanted to continue being Mrs. John Taylor. Younger women may mock me, may think me lacking in character, or ambition, or dignity—I know my daughter would—but that's the way I was raised.

We were at an impasse.

This lasted for a year. To say we were both unhappy would be an understatement. I had always run a harmonious household, needed things to be regulated, to run smoothly. And they weren't anymore. John was drinking, he was depressed, we were having real fights for the first time.

Late one night after a particularly bad fight we worked out a deal. He could have a serious relationship. He could seek love. He could even get married again, if he found someone he loved who loved him back. But whoever she was, she was not to know about me. She was not to have entrée into his public, professional life—he had to choose an outsider to our world. *I* was Mrs. John Taylor. And he had to be home by 5:30 every morning, to shower, dress, and eat breakfast in our house before going to work, before making his rounds. His car would be parked in our driveway as our neighbors roused themselves and left for work. How he managed that was his business.

It took him a year before all the variables lined up right for him. He met that MJ creature in some Silicon Valley bar, and courted her. With my permission. Eventually they had some hippy wedding, but legitimate as far as she knew. I continued to organize his life. I controlled the household, paid the bills, and kept his calendar. I kept him straight. I even booked his flights down to LA when he found someone there, too.

Samantha Adams: So you were an accomplice to a crime. Bigamy. Or whatever it is when three wives are involved. Didn't that bother you?

Deborah Taylor: Why, are you going to charge me?

Samantha Adams: [Silence]

Deborah Taylor: I thought not. Well, to get back to your question, why would bigamy bother me? If anything, it made me feel safer. The bigger the deception on his part, the more inexcusable his crimes against these other women—and, not incidentally, the law of the land—the less chance he would be able to come clean and make an honest man of himself. He would most definitely be hoist with his own petard if he tried. I had rigged the situation admirably. It would have worked. Even after he died, under normal circumstances I would have been able to negotiate deals with MJ and Helen to keep everything quiet. I would be John Taylor's widow, just as I had been his wife. And in return I would make sure they didn't suffer financially.

It was perfect until you prevented me from burying my husband. By the way, if anyone finds out that coffin was empty, I'll be the laughingstock of the town.

Samantha Adams: We told you that we needed to do an autopsy. You needn't have scheduled the funeral quite so quickly.

Deborah Taylor: People would have wondered why the funeral was delayed. I couldn't risk that. I needed John safely buried.

Samantha Adams: As it turned out, someone let the cat out of the bag anyway.

Deborah Taylor: Yes, that was unfortunate.

Samantha Adams: Was it you who tipped off the reporter?

Deborah Taylor: Why on earth would I do such a thing? My goal was that no one ever discover the truth. Now my own children are furious at me. They're not stupid. They know John. They know me. They figure I must have known about the deception, even suspect that I masterminded it.

Samantha Adams: Who else possessed this information other than the three wives?

Deborah Taylor: No one. I'm sure John would never have confided in another soul. By the way, you've not yet told me why you sent the body for an autopsy. Isn't that done only when there's a suspicious death?

Samantha Adams: Not necessarily. It's performed when the cause of a sudden death is unclear.

Deborah Taylor: What was unclear about my husband's death? From what I gather, the medical examiner believes it to be a heart attack.

Samantha Adams: Perhaps. We'll have to wait on the results of the autopsy.

Deborah Taylor: All right, but patience isn't one of my virtues.

12

Samantha

IT TAKES TEN LONG DAYS for the toxicology report on John Taylor to come back. It is inconclusive. According to the pathologist, the levels of potassium in his body were high, but then they would be after a heart attack. Nothing else—not a trace of any substance that would explain his death. Jake says the results of the forensic autopsy are also inconclusive, but that he believes enough questions have been raised by the evidence for a verdict of wrongful death to be issued by the coroner at the inquest.

Jake is sitting at his desk with the Taylor reports in front of him, frowning. As precise and neat as Jake is in person, his office is the opposite. Files strewn over the desk and floor, articles cut from *Forensic Magazine* and *Academic Forensic Pathology* taped to the walls, a whiteboard with indecipherable scribbles on it, and a decent rendering of a cartoon rodent sniffing suspiciously at a half-erased line drawing of a cadaver.

"The high levels of potassium by themselves would mean nothing," Jake says without lifting his head. "But when you put them together with the needle puncture and the bruises, that's when the jury at the inquest will get interested."

"So what actually killed him? Was it the head injury when he hit the desk?" I clear some papers off a chair and sit down, take out my notebook.

Jake shakes his head. "No. The pathologist believes heart attack. The blow on his head was a nasty one, and could have knocked him out. But it wasn't what killed him. He was alive when he hit his head. He died some time after that."

"I thought you said the coroner would probably issue a wrongful death verdict," I say. "I'm confused."

"Heart attack it officially is." He pauses, then picks up one of the papers from his desk. "But there was the hyperkalemia," he says. "Serum potassium levels, when normal, are between 3.5 and 5.0. The victim's were 10. Now that can happen with a heart attack. Or the high potassium caused the cardiac dysrhythmia. It could go either way."

"What's that—hyperkalemia?"

"Excess potassium."

"So the pathologist thinks . . . what, exactly?"

"That our good doctor suffered a heart attack. That he banged his head on the corner of the dresser going down, but that what ultimately killed him was the heart attack."

I shake my head. I feel like I'm being run around in circles.

"Yet you believe the inquest will be wrongful death?"

"Yes," says Jake, a little impatiently. "Remember the bruises? The needle mark? Here . . ." and he pulls out of the file some photographs. This time I see what he was talking about that day in the Westin. The puncture. Very distinct.

"High amounts of potassium in the system can actually cause cardiac dysrhythmia as well as being a side effect of it. My guess is that the coroner will want a full investigation."

I nod. "So you're saying he could have been injected with potassium? And that the high levels in his body may have caused the heart attack. Not the reverse."

"Maybe. Why not. Could have, perhaps, who knows?" says Jake, shrugging. "That's what the inquest will try to determine."

I pick up copies of the paperwork he printed out for me and start reading.

Most of the language is unintelligible. *Myocardial infarction. Rigor mortis, livor mortis, skin slippage, malodor.* I grasp on to phrases I can understand. *Forehead trauma. Contusions on arms and neck. Wrongful death not ruled out.*

"What about fingerprints in the room?" he asks.

Now it's my turn to shrug. "Nothing. Not even the usual partials you'd expect from a hotel room."

"How about other evidence?" asks Jake. "Did he have anything on his person that was unusual? Anything in the room that was out of place?"

"In his pockets were his cell phone and wallet. Most of his clothes were still folded in the suitcase. Interestingly enough, they were all brand new—still had tags on them. What he was wearing also seemed new—hardly worn. There was a pair of pajamas still in the packaging on the bed, and a new toothbrush and fresh tube of toothpaste in the bathroom. Otherwise, the room was as clean as a whistle."

"Which of course is suspect. You'd expect fingerprints all over the place—his, previous guests', and the staff's." Jake pauses. "Anything *not* there that you'd expect to be?" he asks.

This stops me short. I hadn't considered it that way.

"Let me think," I say.

"Razor?"

"Oh. Yes, of course. There was a new razor and an unopened package of blades in his suitcase."

"Comb? Brush?"

"Just a comb, in the bathroom."

"Car keys? I assume he drove to the Westin?"

"Yes. His keys were on the dresser," I say.

"How about his house keys? Were they on the same ring?"

I have to stop to think about that one. "It was a big bunch of keys," I say finally. "But wouldn't that bust him? He wouldn't have keys to all three of his houses on the same key ring. Or would he?"

"He probably had other keys as well—keys to his clinic, keys to various rooms at the clinic, keys to his office on campus . . . having one or two others probably wouldn't make much difference unless someone was looking for trouble," says Jake.

Something nags at me while he talks on. What else would I possess if I'd checked into a hotel room? Clothes, check. Toiletries, check. Wallet, cell phone, and keys, check. But there should be something else . . .

"What about the room key?" I ask.

"What?" asks Jake.

"I don't recall seeing a room key in the evidence bags. I'll have to double-check of course. It's not that I was looking for it."

"It's probably there," says Jake. "He had his key to get into the room. It was probably such an obvious thing that you didn't register it."

"But it doesn't hurt to check," I say.

"It never hurts to be thorough," Jake agrees as I take my leave.

13

MJ

OF COURSE I REGRETTED SPEAKING to that reporter the minute I hung up the phone. But something puzzled me. I didn't blab *that* much, drunk as I was. And that reporter definitely had information I didn't give her.

I never would have figured that the story would get as much attention as it did. And how that would lead to other reports, to TV and radio segments about my situation, to television vans with satellite receivers on their roofs congregating outside my door. As my grandma would say, *well butter my butt and call it a biscuit.* Because the circus that followed! Reporters calling so fast and in such volume that I'd answer the phone (that was when I was still answering it) and before I could say *hello* I'd hear the beep that signaled another call trying to get through. I eventually unplugged the phone from the wall.

But today my cell phone started ringing, and only my closest friends know that number. Someone has betrayed me. I turn it off and go into the garden. To weed is to close my mind to anything else. Kneeling in the dirt among the lavender, surrounded by the twelve-foot fence that safeguarded our privacy, I'm safe. I sit back on my heels and breathe in deeply, the way I've learned in my relaxation tapes. *Breathe in.*

Breathe out. Again. Again. After an hour of alternately doing my breathing exercises and pulling out the crabgrass that has been accumulating, my heartbeat has slowed and I can think clearly again.

I go back into the house to get a drink of water. I'm worried about the state of my Hummingbird Coyote Mint plants (Monardella macrantha), they are showing brown spots on their leaves and the bright red blossoms are drooping. I wash the dirt from my hands in the kitchen sink, and without thinking, move to the front door upon hearing a knock. I open it (stupidly).

Pandemonium. People leaping from cars and running toward me, camera lights flashing, yelling for statements. *When did you know, MJ?* And, *How are you taking it?* I slam the door quickly. Still, they keep coming. At first it's just the local channels. KGO, KTVU. Then CNN and the national news teams from CBS and NBC. I go to the AT&T store and change my cell phone number, but they somehow sniff that out. The story apparently has legs. Every entertainment and gossip rag runs with it, keeps publishing follow-up articles, digs up all sorts of things I wouldn't have thought anyone would remember. My sneaking out on the rent of the apartment on Pine Street in San Francisco back in the 1980s when the boys were small and I needed a clean slate to start over. Which I did, in Santa Cruz, living in a tiny box of a house that had obviously once been someone's summer vacation home scraped together using two-by-fours and plywood. The reporters find that part of my life, too, including getting busted for growing and selling weed in the early nineties, for which I had to do community service. Well, *shit,* I say out loud when I hear that on the radio. *I was just trying to make a living.*

Naturally the reporters find out where I work, and interview my co-workers who anonymously and predictably comment on my clothing and hair and general state of disarray. No one disparages the quality of my accounting work, that's the one good thing. The bad thing is seeing John, and by extension, myself, made the butt of jokes on David Letterman and Jay Leno. *Do you know the punishment for three wives? Three mothers-in-law!* And, *I take care of all my wives. Isn't that big of me*

(bigamy)? And, *Why did the polygamist cross the road? To get to the other bride.*
DJs speculate on John's sex life on crude radio shows. One newspaper
prints that John had to eat three turkey dinners on Thanksgiving and
Christmas. That is nonsense. Or is it? John always worked Christmas, or
so he told me, so we had our dinner early—at 1 PM, so he could go into
the hospital. But now that I think about it, a plastic surgeon needing
to go into the hospital on a holiday? What, just in case someone needs
an emergency face-lift? The obviousness of his lies is the truly shameful
part. Thinking of him in Deborah's house with relatives and friends eating his second turkey dinner makes me turn a hot and painful red. The
third turkey dinner must have been a fantasy of a reporter or neighbor,
as he would hardly have flown down to LA for dinner on the same day.

Call me naïve, but I didn't realize my neighbors were that *interested*
in us. How else do they know so much? Did our gardeners, our house-
cleaners, gossip? The plots in our neighborhood are large, the trees and
foliage mature, you can't see other houses from ours, the garden is protected by a fence. John liked his privacy. Yet someone knew that we
spent most of our hours back there, gardening or sitting under the sun
umbrella drinking sweet tea, even in winter. They somehow knew the
price we'd paid for the house; they knew the color of bougainvillea
we'd planted. One especially alert neighbor even heard John's car leave
every morning right after five. *Even on weekends. How could she not have
known?*

Which is, of course, the million-dollar question.

14

Helen

I SPECIALIZE IN THE TREATMENT of T-cell childhood acute lymphoblastic leukemia. The smaller the patient, the less time we have. The cells multiply and move so fast that it's a fierce race, the opponent impossibly swift. I typically treat the children and infants with a combination of chemotherapy and targeted therapy with a tyrosine kinase inhibitor. *Inhibitor.* That's what I am. An introverted inhibitor. My job is to prevent, to discourage, to put up walls and deterrents against the cancer cells. I was pretty good at doing that in my personal life, too. John vanquished all my defenses, though. I still don't know how he managed that.

I've built a name for myself over the years. Professionally, I let my work speak for itself, and it's gratifying in a small way that my practice calendar is full. Although distressing in a much larger sense, because it means a waiting list of sick kids, many of them hopeless cases, nevertheless hoping for a chance, any chance, I might offer. The fact that I often publish my research—my articles in the *Journal of Adolescent and Young Adult Oncology* and the *Journal of Pediatric Hematology/Oncology* have won awards—and increasingly speak at conferences has intensified the attention on my professional life. But I've always kept my personal life—what little there is of it—*personal*. That is now proving impossible. For the media uproar has been frankly astounding.

I'm not sure if it's just a slow news month, or whether the idea of a man with three wives is simply so titillating that it pushed everything else off the front page. I take some satisfaction in the fact that no one has yet managed to take a clear photo of me and no usable video. I cover my face every time I go outside. Most publications and TV shows are running my official photograph from the hospital's website. It's not particularly flattering, with my brown hair in a neat, sterile bob and a fake half smile plastered on my face.

The PR director of the hospital has been working with security to keep the reporters at bay at the front entrance. Still, some Judas on the hospital staff must have left a side door strategically open because a news crew managed to almost reach my office this morning. I was in there explaining to the distraught parents of a ten-year-old girl who had presented with excessive bruising on her legs and arms that it was probably not due to soccer practice. My assistant caught sight of the cameras and called the PR director, who then roused security and rooted the crew out of the building before they got to me. Even so, one particularly clever reporter bandaged her young daughter's two kneecaps and almost managed to make it to my office before being stopped by an alert aide. Since then, a security guard has been posted at the doorway to the pediatric oncology clinic and no one is allowed into the waiting area unless they have a child with them *and* a scheduled appointment.

I give the reporters nothing, and still they have the facts. So delicious are these that even the *LA Times* has run with the story. As have *Newsweek, Time, People, inTouch,* and a score of less reputable magazines. I don't listen to the messages on my voicemail inviting me to appear on *Good Morning America, Morning Joe,* and other radio and television shows. I think about my fellow wives, wonder if they're talking. I haven't seen any comment from either of them in the press after that first, disastrous, *Chronicle* piece—the hole in the dam that turned into the flood.

It's salacious stuff. People are repeating it in the elevators, in the break room of the hospital. There are sudden silences when I walk into the cafeteria, or past the nurses' station. One poor out-of-the-loop orderly even whispered the gossip to me. "Did you hear?" he asked, to the amused horror of everyone around us, as I filled my coffee cup. "This doctor was married to three women! And one of them works here!" I managed an "Imagine that!" before someone hissed the truth to him. He turned bright red, but I didn't resent his words. Only a handful of people at the medical center understood that John and I were in a relationship. Even fewer knew we'd actually gotten married. But with the press going wild, I'm resigned that everyone is privy to the most intimate details of my life.

Then there's the hush as I enter an examining room. The pity in the eyes of my patients' parents. Pity—from them, who are going through so much themselves. There's probably even a slight sense of schadenfreude there. I don't blame them. I have to leave the hospital by a side door to avoid the reporters and photographers. I push through hordes and protect my face against the flashing bulbs when I get home to my condo in the evening. I stop seeing friends. I spend longer in the hospital every day so that all but the truly tenacious of the reporters have gone home by the time I emerge.

These reporters are damn good at their jobs. They've found quite a number of people willing to talk. All anonymous, of course. *Sources say. A source close to the subject.* That some of my colleagues have no qualms about discussing me, dissecting me and my habits down to the tiniest minutiae, shouldn't be as much of a shock as it is, given human nature. The reporters have ferreted out our favorite restaurant on Broadway. The vintage of the red wine we drank. That we occasionally attended the opera. Compared to what is being printed about MJ—Wife No. 2—what's written about me is positively flattering. *Highly respected. Quiet and hardworking. Can be a bit standoffish.* But still, I flush when I read the purple prose describing our relationship, when I see how nothing has escaped scrutiny. *Clearly deeply in love, they were often seen holding hands at the Three Roses coffee shop in the early morning before reporting for duty at the medical center. And: They were once caught kissing passionately in the parking lot. And: She drives a Prius, which was a little too small for his bulky frame, but they didn't seem to mind being so intimately close with one another.*

It hurts to find out things about John from these media reports that I hadn't known before. I was astounded to discover he had once been a passable jazz pianist. The photo used in the obituary was from an actual professional gig. He'd played in jazz bars throughout Chicago. *Birdhouse. The Velvet Lounge. Andy's.* The John I knew eschewed music, turned off the radio when he got into my car, shook his head when I asked him if he'd like me to put on a CD at home. I thought he was tone deaf, even teased him about it. I offered to share some of my favorite recordings with him. Classical stuff. I never acquired an ear for anything but the music my father played. Beethoven. Bach. Brahms. In retrospect, I'm ashamed at my glib assumptions about John, about my certainty that I had a grip on the situation. Clearly, I'd been had on all sorts of levels.

The day after the *New York Times* article is the worst. The biggest crowds ever are waiting at the side exit to the hospital—they've discovered my trick—and at the entrance to my condo. I finally reach the safety of my apartment, double lock the door, and lean against it in relief. I have half a bottle of red wine left over from John's last visit. I pour a small amount in a water glass and open the large sliding doors onto my wraparound balcony. I had especially wanted this end unit for the views of both the hills and the city. John had loved it, too. Especially the mature palm trees that edge the street on this part of the property, leftover from an old-style 1930s apartment block that had been torn down to make way for the condo complex. I settle into a deck chair with my wine when I smell smoke. Cigarette smoke. It seems to be coming from the balcony next door, which is odd because I haven't been troubled by that in the three years since I'd moved in. Our condominium association's bylaws forbid smoking outside the walls of the individual apartments, especially on balconies, where secondhand smoke can drift into other units. Through the plants I'd deliberately placed upon the stucco divider for privacy between my balcony and the next, I can see a young woman sitting with her feet up. As I watch, she releases a lungful of smoke into what is essentially my face, given the direction of the breeze. Rather than simply call out, I decide to be civilized and knock on her front door.

After thirty seconds, the door opens. The young woman stands there, cigarette in hand.

Feeling awkward, I introduce myself as her neighbor. I don't mind being authoritative in places where I have actual authority, but this is a gray area. I can hardly tell her not to smoke in her own condo, and it seems petty to begrudge her the use of her own balcony. But before I can begin she says, "come on in," without asking what I want. Afraid of being thought rude, I step inside although I would have preferred to have the conversation in the more neutral territory of the hall.

"Excuse me," she says, and fumbles with her phone, then puts it in her pocket. Holding her cigarette in her left hand, she sticks out her right hand to shake. "Beth," she says.

"Helen," I say in return. There is an uncomfortable silence, then I gesture toward her cigarette. "If you don't mind not smoking on the balcony," I say. I hesitate a moment before adding, "It comes right into my living room."

A strange look comes over the young woman's face. Almost satisfaction. "I'm sorry," she says, "I hadn't thought of that." She doesn't make any promise to stop, though. Instead, she takes another long drag on her cigarette and releases the smoke off to the side. "Can I get you something to drink? Some wine?" I resign myself to the interruption, thinking of the importance of unpolluted balcony time. I calculate that it's worthwhile to have a short drink.

She doesn't wait for my reply, but disappears briefly into the kitchen. The condo is the mirror image of my own, only furnished in a modern style, with uncomfortable-looking leather furniture and bright primary colors. She emerges with two glasses of red wine. She's finally abandoned her cigarette.

"You're a doctor, right?" she asks, handing me one of the glasses. She gestures me into a bright red sofa.

"Yes," I say. Then, after sitting down on the cold slippery surface, "How did you know?" Bruised as I am by the day's events, I'm suspicious and alert.

"I've seen you leave the condo," she says. But that doesn't make sense, because I don't put on my lab coat until I get to the office. In the morning, I resemble any urban professional. When I mention this—probably sounding a bit paranoid—she laughs and says she must have seen my name on medical magazines in the lobby. Given the large numbers of journals I subscribe to, I think that plausible.

"How's Mr. Helen?" she asks, casually. When I look askance, she adds, "your husband. What's his name? I've seen him in the hall, but we've never introduced ourselves."

"John," I say, and decide not to explain that John is no more. And really, once I think of it, he had never actually existed. Not the man, not the life I thought I had.

We both sip our wine in silence for a few minutes. Casting my mind about for something to talk about, I ask, "So what do you do, Beth?"

"Typist," she says. As if anxious to shut down that line of inquiry, she quickly adds, "How long have you been married?"

"Six months," I say, thinking this wasn't too hard. Not telling lies, but omitting the truth.

I take another sip from my glass, and realize to my surprise that it's nearly empty. "Let me fill that," she says, and goes back to the kitchen, returning this time with the bottle. She tops both our glasses.

"So you're still newlyweds," she says rather than asks.

"You could say that," I say, and find myself mimicking what's being written about us. "Just getting to know each other. Still mostly strangers, but in an exciting way."

I don't recognize the person uttering these inanities, which is good because I want no connection with this woman, nothing to make me feel guilty about spinning falsehoods. I briefly wonder how a typist can afford a condo in this building, but shrug it off. She must have a well-off partner.

Another protracted silence before she attempts to speak again. "Aren't you the doctor who's been in the news lately?" She asks this casually, looking at her wineglass.

I shrink back and she quickly says, "I'm sorry. I heard some of the other residents talking in the elevator. You know. All the reporters hanging out at the front door." I must cringe even more because she adds, in a warmly sympathetic voice, "It must feel terrible, to be talked about. On top of the actual betrayal, I mean."

"Yes, pretty damn terrible," I say. I find my glass has been filled again. I've spent my life running under people's radar, only emerging to surprise them with my test scores, or my skills, or my insights. Now I'll forever be known as that woman who was married to the guy with three wives. I contemplate where I might go to escape. New York? Chicago? Houston? I could easily find another teaching hospital, another clinical appointment. But even so, I would never escape, not fully. I know better than anyone how eagerly medical interns Google their teachers and prospective teachers—virtually stalking them to find what research grants they've been awarded, what publications they've achieved, how often they speak at medical seminars, plus any nugget about their personal lives. No, no point moving. The stain is there. It will never be erased. "I'm done for," I say aloud, and the woman eagerly pounces. "Done for, how?"

I just shake my head without explaining. Why should I? I'm ashamed of my previous pride—my pride at living what in many ways was an austere life. Now my armor has a hole in it, and anger is leaking out.

"From what I've heard, you were duped," says the young woman. She leans forward, her wine apparently forgotten, is fiddling again with her phone.

Through the fog of several glasses of wine, I hear her talking on.

"I would want to kill him," she says.

"Don't think it didn't cross my mind," I say. Then I correct myself. "He was already dead by the time I discovered the truth." I retreat onto safer ground. "I never had the chance to confront him, to ask *why*, to find out *why me*." The girl nods, as if I've said something especially clever.

"You must have wondered why he picked you of all the women he met every day. Given his profession, I mean. He must have met tons of women."

I dismiss her suggestion. "John didn't do cosmetic surgery. Only his partners did. He never would have fallen for someone who came to his clinic for that. If anything, it would have turned him off."

"And he died of what . . . a heart attack? In a way, don't you think that's appropriate? For a man with three wives?" asks the girl. "His heart overloaded? Stressed to the limit?"

"Perhaps," I say. "That indispensable motor, broken." And mine, in sympathy, aching. Occupying such a tender position in my chest. I had an Egyptian professor during my cardiology internship. He said that in his home country it was sometimes said of the dead that their hearts had departed, and that it was the heart that was weighed against the feather of truth in the hall of Ma'at during the divine judgment of the deceased. A heart unburdened with the weight of sin and corruption would balance with the feather and its possessor would enjoy the eternal afterlife. But I know my heart is not light as a feather. The afterlife I am fated for is not one that will be enjoyed.

I often encourage my patients to describe their symptoms using metaphors. They are incredibly illuminating. Once a child said, "I'm being pecked by a tiny bird with a very sharp beak. His beak must be bloody." I looked, and sure enough, there were the telltale petechiae, the flat pinpoint dark-red spots under the skin that are one of the signs of childhood leukemia.

What are my metaphors? All clichés. Heavy heart. Burdened heart. Gandhi, my hero, saying, *It is better to have a heart without words than words without a heart.* What about neither words nor heart? I have nothing more to say. And it's this that saves me. Because suddenly it becomes clear, this young woman's constant fiddling with her phone, her probing questions, even her so-called profession. "You're a reporter," I say. She only hesitates a moment before nodding. "The *Star*," she says. "They promised me fifty grand for an exclusive. I bribed your neighbor to go out for the evening."

"You lured me over here with the cigarette smoke?" I ask, incredulous. Then I start laughing at her ingenuousness.

"I can't stand to smoke myself," the young woman says, "but it works nearly every time here on the West Coast. People who would be suspicious of a knock on the door are incredibly protective of their turf when it comes to secondhand smoke."

I point to the cell phone she's holding. "Have you been recording this?" and she nods.

"You gave me some good stuff, but not enough for you to feel embarrassed," she says. "You'll come across as heartbroken but dignified." *Heartbroken.* Metaphors again.

"I don't suppose there's any way I could persuade you to respect my privacy?" I ask. She shakes her head. But I seem to detect some true regret in the gesture.

"I don't like my job very much sometimes, but I'd like unemployment worse," she says. "But, like I said, it wasn't too bad. You didn't spill your sex secrets."

"That's because I don't have any," I say. And for a moment that seems true, that I have lived my life out in the open, with nothing to hide and few regrets. Then I remember, and am quiet.

"False face must hide what the false heart doth know," says the girl. I must look startled because she says, "Macbeth. I studied English literature in college." I don't think I'm imagining that she appears slightly ashamed. "We all end up in places we didn't expect," she says.

"That we do," I say, and somehow find the door and leave.

15

Helen

I CAN'T HELP THINKING FOR once that it's a good thing my parents are out of this. My mother. She would have fought with editors and written letters in rebuttal, fiercely protecting me, her only surviving child. But she's now locked in a memory unit in Indianapolis and no longer knows what a fork is used for, much less that she has a daughter. My father, on a good day, would have gathered me to his chest and wept with me. His tears a potent balm. On a bad day, he would have slapped my face and told me to get a grip. Still, I would have had to restrain him from tracking down those reporters and crippling them. Toward the end of his life, heavily medicated, he wept less. On the rare occasion when he felt the urge to break a piece of furniture, or hurt another living being, he simply took a special pill and went to bed for the rest of the day. He'd rise the next morning changed from Mr. Hyde back to Dr. Jekyll. We know now that Stevenson's antihero could have done with a prescription for lithium or valproate. How much of our great literature has modern psychiatry rendered quaint and obsolete? Someday they'll have a diagnosis and a pill for someone like John, something to render him less charming and beguiling, less of a risk to the women of the world. And there will be a pill for me, too. Something to keep my guard up. The world will be a healthier place. But even so, despite all that's happened, I think it will be a far less interesting one.

16

San Francisco Chronicle

Coroner Returns Verdict of Murder in Much-Married Doctor's Death

June 1, 2013

PALO ALTO, CA—The death of the Stanford doctor who had three concurrent wives was classified as a wrongful death by person or persons unknown by the Santa Clara County Coroner yesterday. Reasons given for the suspicions of foul play in the death of Dr. John Taylor were bruises on the body as well as a needle puncture in the back. Sources say that the police suspect Dr. Taylor was injected with potassium, which then brought about a heart attack. The police have questioned numerous witnesses, including the three women he had married, two of them illegally. Other persons of interest are also being brought in for questioning, sources say. A large funeral took place at Stanford Memorial Church, complete with closed coffin, but the body was never present, due to the suspicious circumstances of the death. "It was all for show," said one funeral attendee, who asked for anonymity.

17

Samantha

SO. THE VERDICT OF THE inquest was what Jake had predicted. Wrongful death by person or persons unknown.

The next step is establishing the time of death. Always done so effortlessly on television, but in actuality extraordinarily difficult to do with any degree of accuracy—as I'm learning. According to the pathologist at the inquest, John Taylor could have died anytime between 2 PM and 10 PM on that Friday.

However, we know he checked in to the room at 2:30 PM, and was alive and well. There was the fact that he ordered room service at 6:35: a steak, medium rare, roast potatoes, and a glass of white wine. Chocolate fondue for dessert. The young woman who had taken the order remembers it well because of their discussion about the chocolate fondue. "I told him it would take at least fifty minutes, and asked if he wanted his meal first, and for us to bring up the fondue when it was ready," she said. "He was very clear that he wanted everything at the same time." It wasn't until 7:50 that the room service waiter knocked on the door. No answer. He knocked again, and again. No one came to the door. "It happens," the girl said. At least that bookends the time we know he was alive (6:35 PM), and a time he was likely not alive any longer (7:50 PM).

I tell Peter at dinner. Mussels, so he must have paid another visit to Cook's Seafood and decided to buy the makings for a meal while he was there. Don't get me wrong, I love his cooking, but he should be working on his dissertation. I tell him that Taylor's bruised upper arm and neck coupled with the needle puncture and high levels of potassium were sufficient for the coroner to demand an investigation.

"But even if you have this wrongful death verdict, isn't there something called motive?" Peter asks. He pries a mussel out of its shell with his fork, places it delicately in his mouth. He is as fastidious as a young child when he eats, tastes everything as though he is prepared to throw it onto the floor in a tantrum. But the truth is, he is quite the epicure, and a terrific cook. The mussels are plump, fresh, tasting of garlic and white wine. Peter definitely didn't get much work done this afternoon. "I've watched my share of crime dramas," he says. "Motive is always the showstopper."

"A man with three wives?" I ask. I find I'm speaking more impatiently than I want, so I calm my voice down. "Enough was happening in this guy's life. Every place we poke around we find motive." Without thinking I swallow the mussel in my mouth whole. I have to gulp some wine to get it down.

"How do you figure?" Peter asks when I've recovered.

"Anger. Jealousy. Payback time," I say. "All the stuff that accumulates in romantic relationships, but times three."

"But the only wife who knew the situation was the original one," he reminds me. "And she accepted it. More than accepted it. She ran the show, right?"

"Right," I say, but again impatience creeps into my voice. I'm tired. I take a deep breath and tell myself to enjoy the moment. The food, Peter's presence—it's been more than a week since we've had a meal together—the relief of having the inquest over. I try to relax my shoulders, move my head from side to side to get the knots out of my neck. My body just tenses up again. This used to be enough, us together at night, over simple but good food. Though it has been growing less satisfactory. Something left wanting. Something about the John Taylor case and its web of love and deceit is souring what used to sustain me.

Peter is still intent on the discussion. Possibly because he hasn't noticed my shift in mood. Or possibly because he has. He's hard to read sometimes, that Peter.

"Who do you put your bet on?" he asks as he breaks off another piece of garlic bread. Mounds of fresh-chopped garlic spill off the toasted loaf. I calculate the time he must have spent chopping it. This annoys me further. I put my fork down and take another gulp of wine. "When do you defend your dissertation?" I ask.

Peter waves the bread in the air. "End of fall quarter," he says. "Plenty of time."

So get to work, I think, but don't say. Instead I ask, "So how's it going?" and despite my best efforts there's an edge in my voice.

Peter shrugs and ignores my question. Typical. Then, as is also typical, he goes into attack mode. His way of doing this is to push me into a corner with questions.

"Tell me who you think did it," Peter says. "Tell me what you're going to do next."

He's put his finger right on my vulnerable spot. "I don't know," I confess. "I suppose I could interview the wives again. Try and get a better sense of the lay of the land there." I am suddenly unhappy.

Peter then drops his attack mode, and turns into the comforter.

"You don't have to have all the answers now," he says in a soothing voice, and helps me to more wine. This is also quite typical. As soon as he suspects he might have hurt me, or really that I'm hurting for any reason, he turns gentle. It's as if he doesn't believe I can take it.

"People do crazy things for love," I tell him. "Or for what they think is love." I'm thinking of Helen Richter, speaking of her passion for John Taylor in that flat, professional voice, yet somehow making you believe in it. Like that C. S. Lewis book we read in an undergraduate

English class on romantic love. *Surprised by Joy.* That was definitely Dr. Richter.

"Do they, now? And how would you know?" Peter isn't smiling as he says this. He is staring at the pile of shells on his plate. This is getting perilously close to the discussion we agreed not to have.

I lay my hand on Peter's hand. "Good mussels," I say, and he looks up and smiles.

"I'm useful in the kitchen," he says. "Whatever else you might think of me."

18

Samantha

LOOKING AT SOMEONE'S CELL PHONE records and emails is like looking in their underwear drawer. Their whole life is laid out in front of your eyes. John Taylor mostly made calls to his voicemail, and mostly received calls from his office. There were a lot of outgoing calls to different numbers that belonged to patients' families. Dr. Taylor apparently took the trouble to personally follow up after his young patients left the clinic. There were fairly frequent incoming calls from Deborah. Just as she'd said, she organized his life, paid his credit card bills, booked his trips to LA and other places. He even depended on her to make restaurant reservations for him and the other wives.

Occasional calls from MJ, but not as many as I would have expected. Then there was a call every night to Helen's cell phone. At exactly nine like clockwork. She never called him, but emailed every day to his jtaylor3@taylorinstitute.com account. Deborah emailed jtaylor1@taylorinstitute.com, and MJ emailed jtaylor2@taylorinstitute .com. No subtlety there.

But nothing suspicious in any of the content itself. Nothing at all. No anger or hostility expressed. Most of the email communiqués to and from the wives were brief logistical notes: when he'd be home, when he'd be out of town. Deborah gave me access to John Taylor's Google calendar, which was a virtual map of his life to the quarter hour. Small wonder this guy had trouble being spontaneous—he was locked into a lifestyle that gave him little room to maneuver.

Still, I hit pay dirt when I check John Taylor's cell phone records for the forty-eight hours before he was found dead at the Westin. Everything just as the wives had said—almost. A call to MJ Thursday morning that lasted about ten minutes—likely enough time to chat with her about domestic items and explain that he had to go down to LA. Deborah began calling his cell phone frequently starting Friday morning at around 6 AM. Calls of short duration—just one or two seconds. Clearly she'd failed to reach him or have a real conversation. That, I calculate, would be when John Taylor failed to show up for his usual early morning shower and breakfast. Man, that woman was tenacious. She kept calling, emailing, and texting—multiple times per hour all day Friday and Saturday until 3 PM. That would have been approximately when Mollie appeared at her door with the news. It all fit.

I've never endured that kind of harassment. Peter is my only relationship, and he's usually pretty mellow. I see that anxiety though in some of my friends' relations, the perpetual hounding if plans aren't followed as expected. I wonder, not for the first time, what relationships were like before email, before cell phones, hell, before answering machines. My generation cut its teeth on this technology, but earlier generations? They must have had a lot more air, and a lot more mystery. Perhaps more doubt? Although I can't imagine doubting Peter. And it seems as though neither MJ nor Helen had any doubts about John Taylor. So far, the records reflect their stories. Were they stupid or blissed out? Some combination of the two, I decide. Whereas Peter and I are just boring.

Then I see two unexplained outgoing communiqués from John Taylor's phone on Friday evening, right in the window we'd identified as when he'd died. I sit up straight. At 6:47 PM he called MJ's cell phone.

It was only five seconds in duration—he must have hung up when voicemail clicked in. Certainly not enough time for a conversation or a message. Then, thirty seconds later, he texted MJ. *Urgent. Come to Palo Alto Westin, room 224. Now.*

Then nothing. So John Taylor had been alive at 6:47—and had summoned MJ to his secret hotel room. This requires some serious follow-up. I pick up the phone to summon MJ myself.

19

MJ

AT LEAST THEY HAVE AIR-CONDITIONING here at the station. I hate this hot weather, it reminds me of Tennessee, and of the silly things people used to say about the heat. *Hot enough to make a prostitute sweat in church. As hot as a goat's butt in a pepper patch.* It's also not good for some of the more delicate plants in the garden. Yesterday the temperature reached 99 degrees and today they're forecasting more than 100. At ten in the morning, I'm already perspiring. Of course, it's that time of life. And stressful situations make the flashes more frequent, and more intense. I've taken to wearing sleeveless shirts, even on cool days. At the office I wear short skirts (probably shorter than my figure can now bear). But the discomfort of being hot outweighs my sense of vanity. I heard a couple of the younger women snicker last week as I bent over the copier. All the sympathy and kid-glove treatment after John's death lasted exactly two weeks. Let them. So what. I've got more important matters to worry about.

This time I know why I'm sitting here in the interrogation room. I'm a suspect. In a case of wrongful death. Meaning murder. I would expect (well, would hope) anyone who knows me to laugh at that, only I haven't been able to face anyone since the first article named me as a "person of interest." Other published reports quickly followed, of course, along with the announcement that this was officially a murder investigation, which fired up the media circus again. *Person of interest!* It sounds flattering. Yet I know how serious this is. Last night I couldn't sleep, but wandered through the dark house, so nervous even my feet were sweating.

The door opens and that same young detective comes in. She holds out her hand and I extend mine shakily. "MJ," she says, "good to see you again," and I nod and say, "Detective," but she smiles and says, "Remember? Just call me Sam." It all feels very civil, would she be treating me like this if she truly thought I was capable of murder? I relax a bit, then recall what I've seen on television—the good cop/bad cop thing. Sam is the good cop? I tell myself to keep my guard up. Her next question only confirms that I should.

"So you decided not to bring your lawyer?" she asks. She walks over to the wall, and pushes the button on a machine connected by a cable to the video camera mounted high on the wall. "Do you mind?" she asks, and points to it.

I shake my head no, not trusting my voice. She settles back in her seat, and looks at me questioningly.

"I don't have a lawyer," I say. This is true. I don't know anyone who does. Who needs lawyers except rich people and criminals? We'd gone to a lawyer to draw up our wills, but that woman wasn't *my* lawyer in any sense of the word.

"As I told you on the phone, people usually bring their lawyer to an interview of this kind," she says, and her voice is gentle as she adds, "I'd really advise you to get one."

"I don't have the money," I say, and am embarrassed at how much my voice quivers.

"Oh," she says. And then, seemingly genuinely, "I'm sorry. I understand you're in a difficult position. But," she clears her throat, "You have the right to remain silent. Anything you say can and will be used against you in a court of law. You have the right to speak to an attorney, and to have an attorney present during any questioning. If you cannot afford a lawyer, one will be provided for you at government expense."

She says all this in such a normal voice that I only afterward grasp that she's read me my rights.

She stops and looks at me. "Do you want me to put you in touch with the public defender's office? It's your right."

"No," I say flatly. "I have nothing to hide. I can't say anything that can be used against me because I didn't do anything wrong." I hope she can't see how tightly my hands are clutching each other under the table.

The detective nods.

She then begins asking me questions again, but mostly they are the ones I've already answered. I slowly begin to relax, even begin to feel a little bored. Some water would be nice, but she doesn't offer me any. No two-way mirror, unlike all the cop shows I've watched. Just the cinder block walls. And the chair is comfy. Where did they get it, from someone's living room via the Salvation Army? It's so out of place here.

And this detective is very young. I know it's hot outside, but hair in pigtails? I've never seen a grown woman wear them before. But they somehow suit her. And there has been nothing ridiculous about her manner. She's very professional. Surely, though, she already knows everything about my marriage and life with John to write her report. And I've missed half a day's work. I look at my watch and take a series of deep breaths. In and out, in and out, that's what my shrink recommends in times of stress. Or clenching my fists, then releasing them— first one hand, then the other. It does something to both sides of your brain to help you relax. I do that, but it doesn't help.

The detective tells me to take a break. I go to the bathroom, grab a drink of water from the fountain in the big open room filled with desks. I notice that the officers stare at me. Even to them I'm an object of curiosity. I return to the examining room before the detective does, feeling acutely the strange mixture of boredom and anxiety that has plagued me since John's death.

Then, "Ready?" the detective asks after coming back in and seating herself. Really, she's young! She has a habit of fiddling with her little finger, twisting it around as though winding up her hand like some sort of child's toy.

"When was the last time you saw Dr. Taylor? John?"

"I've told you this. Several times. It was Thursday morning. He'd gotten up early as usual to make his rounds"—I stop briefly before I'm able to go on—"and left a bit after 5 AM. All as usual. Why don't you ask Deborah? According to her, that's where he headed every morning, their deal was supposedly sacrosanct." My voice betrays my bitterness. Resentful that Deborah had deprived me of the kind of lazy mornings in bed with John that I had always cherished as the sweetest part of a relationship.

"But you heard from him later in the day." The detective consults her notes.

"Sometime late in the morning. Here, I'll tell you the exact time." I pull out my cell phone and scroll down the calls. "At 11:07 AM precisely. I was at work."

The detective nods. She really hadn't needed to ask that question. She applied for—and received—a subpoena to vet my phone records and emails. I think of the dancing cats and poop jokes and other things I share with friends, and am resigned to looking like a fool in front of everyone assigned to the case.

"Your office is in. . . . Santa Clara."

"Yes. At WebSys. On Tasman Drive."

"Tell me again what he said in that phone call."

I sigh impatiently. And I can feel another hot flash coming on.

"Just that he had an emergency case in LA. That he was flying down that evening. He thought he'd be back on Friday, but he wasn't sure."

"And this was unusual?"

"Very. But not that he was going to LA, since he had an adjunct appointment at UCLA for the academic year and was there twice a month for a few days at a time."

"So what was unusual?"

"The disruption to our routine. He was very regular, and hated any disorder in his schedule. I wasn't allowed . . . well, he preferred . . . that I didn't surprise him with social events, or spontaneously suggest outings. That sort of thing made him extraordinarily anxious. He thrived on routine. He did travel, but everything was always meticulously planned ahead of time."

"What did he consider spontaneous?"

"He needed to know a full week in advance," I tell her. "His rationale was that he needed that time to process any changes to his plans." I realize how strange that must sound. And how foolish (and downtrodden) I must seem for catering to such unreasonable demands. I quickly elaborate. "When we first started dating, I would make the mistake of asking people over for drinks on the spur of the moment. You know, you run into friends at the grocery store, you don't think about it, you just invite them round. But it upset John terribly."

"Didn't that strike you as odd?"

"No. Yes. Maybe." I curse myself. "Well, John *was* odd."

"What was his reasoning?"

"The nature of his work with trauma victims was such that he led a very unpredictable professional life. He often didn't know what was waiting for him when he showed up at work in the morning. He demanded utmost regularity in the rest of his life as a result." I pause. "So he said."

The detective nods. I've told her all this before, why is she going over the same ground? She even has it on videotape. Did the reading of my rights make some sort of difference in how she can use what I say? I suddenly feel chilled.

"And then you didn't see him again," she says.

"No." Despite myself, the tears well up. Those first few days after John's death I'd been inexplicably calm. Since then, I haven't stopped crying. My boss told me to take a week off, but what would I do with that time? Sit in the house alone? Much better I'm with my precious financials, making order out of chaos. John and I weren't so different in some respects. We both thrived on routine.

"And you didn't talk to him either, after that 11:07 call on Thursday morning?"

"No. That was unusual, too. We'd talk every night whenever he was in LA. He made a point of it. He said ..." and here I break down again. The detective wordlessly hands me a Kleenex. "He said he didn't want us to get in a pattern of not communicating."

"What did you make of that?"

"Of course it made me wonder about his previous relationships, about whether he'd had communication problems. It made me wonder if that was why he hadn't married. He had always explained it away by the demands of his job, by never finding the right woman. And I ..."

"And you wanted to believe him." The detective smiles sympathetically. Really, she is a pretty little thing. No wedding ring. Then she is so awfully young. But it's clear I'm the simpleminded one in the room. My naïveté must seem preposterous.

I take another Kleenex and begin systematically shredding it into long thin strips. Another stress-reducing act. But the detective doesn't seem to notice. Although she has a notebook and a pen on the table, she isn't taking notes, is letting the video recorder do all the work. She is winding up her hand again. Another question is coming.

"What about the text John Taylor sent to your cell phone Friday evening?"

I try to keep my voice steady. "What about it?"

"At 6:47. Perhaps the last thing John Taylor did before he died was send you that urgent text. *Come to the Palo Alto Westin, room 224.* But you didn't respond until 7:45. Then you started calling his cell phone at frequent intervals—every twenty minutes or so well into the night and the next day. We tallied forty-three calls total between 7:45 Friday night and 11:30 Saturday night. You also called the Westin thirteen times during that same time period. Then all the calls stopped. What was going on?"

I sit up straight. "I went out Friday evening to run errands," I say. I am careful to be precise. "I went to both the grocery store and the drugstore. I left my cell phone at home, I frequently forget to take it with me, it drives . . . drove . . . John crazy. So I didn't get John's text or see that he'd tried to call until I got home. Around a quarter till eight. Then, of course, I was alarmed. What was he doing in Palo Alto? He should have been in LA! I started calling him. When I couldn't reach him, I called the Westin, asked for room 224. No one answered. I also asked the receptionist if John was a guest there. She said no. She couldn't tell me the name of the guest in room 224, but she could say it wasn't John Taylor."

I'm wondering if it's apparent how much I'm sweating. I can feel my shirt sticking to my back, and the drops of perspiration rolling down my sides. This girl is making me as nervous as a june bug on a string.

"Why did you stop calling Saturday night?"

"I went to bed, finally. And the next morning I saw the obituary in the paper," I say.

"Why didn't you volunteer this information earlier?" the young detective asks. She looks genuinely puzzled rather than suspicious.

"No one asked. I was questioned about the last time I talked to John, but not about what happened afterward." I know this sounds lame, but what can I say? That I was frightened? I felt responsible that John had apparently reached out to me for help, and I wasn't there for him? I wipe a damp strand of hair off my face, tuck it behind my ear.

The young detective is silent for a moment. Then she asks, "Did it seem usual for John Taylor to do such a spontaneous thing as fly to LA at the last minute? And then suddenly surface in Palo Alto?"

I'm eager to answer this one. "Oh, it was highly unusual! We had no surprises in our lives. Everything was carefully planned." *By Deborah,* I think.

"And that worked for you?"

Do I detect a hint of scorn in her voice? The superciliousness of the very young, who believe that spontaneity is the spice of life.

"We made it work," I say. I sound defensive.

"How far did this go?"

"What do you mean?"

"This lack of spontaneity. Were you allowed to change the television channel, for example?"

I look at her to see if she's kidding, but she's not. "If it wasn't one of *his* shows, yes." I hate how pathetic I sound. As though I was under John's thumb, but it wasn't like that (not really). We had a rhythm. It worked.

"What were his shows?"

"Mostly PBS. News. He enjoyed *Antiques Roadshow*. Documentaries. Although he hated so-called reality shows. They had no structure to them, he complained."

The detective allows herself a smile.

There is a brief silence as she winds up her hand again. But before she can come at me, I decide to try to take control. "Why are you asking me these questions?" Then, as a kind of joke, "You're not planning to charge him with bigamy beyond the grave?"

"No."

Silence.

"Are you asking his other . . . wives?" I pause. "Or are you singling me out?"

"We're questioning all of you."

"Why?" My voice comes out louder than I intend.

"We have some concerns about the death."

"Yes, obviously. But no proof."

"What do you mean?" she asks.

"You don't have proof he was murdered. Only suspicions."

The detective nods. "That's right. We don't know for sure. We have suspicious circumstances." She doesn't say anything more.

"And?" I prompt her.

"Some definite irregularities," the young detective says. She shifts in her seat as though she's uncomfortable. I derive some satisfaction from that, and from her obvious lack of experience. "So I'm afraid I'll have to ask you again where you were and what you were doing Friday afternoon and evening."

I feel relief. "That's easy. I was at work until 4 PM. I took off a little early. My work was done, and it was Friday after all."

"And then?"

"I went home, took a nap for an hour, dallied about until around 6:30."

"Can anyone verify that you were there?"

"Not at first. Later, my brother, Thomas, could. He lives in the city, but visits frequently. Given that John was out of town, he came down to spend a couple nights in the guest room."

"Was this usual?"

"Yes, when John wasn't around. We're very close, my brother and me."

"We'll talk to him," the young detective makes a note of it. "What did you do while waiting for your brother?"

"I went out at maybe 6:30, 6:45 to Trader Joe's to do some grocery shopping. I'm pretty sure they'll remember me there. I'm a regular. They always comment on my hats." Here I flush a little with shame. "Actually, I'm sure they'll remember me, because I accidentally knocked over a display of cereal boxes."

"And after that?"

"After that I went to Walgreens to buy some shampoo and stuff. I forgot I had a prescription ready until I got to the car. I didn't feel like going back into the store, so I used the drive-through window. It was probably 7:30 by then. I imagine they'll have a record of both those transactions."

The detective writes these times down in her notebook. *Trader Joe's 7:15 PM. Walgreens 7:30.* I see her draw a little happy face next to those numbers. She looks up, and it's her turn to blush when she sees that I've been watching.

"And after that?"

"Why, I went home. My brother Thomas had finally arrived. We went to dinner. They'll probably remember us at the local Chinese restaurant—we go there all the time. And we must have got home again by 9:30."

"And all through dinner you were calling John Taylor."

"Yes. When I got home at 7:45 and found the text, I was obviously worried. So I kept calling. But never got an answer."

"Thank you, this is all very helpful," the detective says. Then, suddenly, the interview is over. "You're free to go now." Despite her words, she remains seated, seemingly waiting for me to leave first. I clumsily extricate myself from my chair and stand, towering over her.

I have so many questions, so many anxieties. I leave the police station infinitely more distressed than when I went in.

20

Deborah

TONIGHT, FOR THE FIRST TIME in many years, I find myself thinking of Gerald. He was one of John's colleagues when we first came to Stanford, before John founded the clinic. John had just finished one residency at UCSF, had started another one at Stanford, and what with paying back his tuition, a four-year-old, a toddler, and another baby on the way, we didn't have much to spare. We were living in married student housing at the time, surrounded by the shrieks and wails of newborns and toddlers. No one even bothered bringing in the toys from the outdoor common area, they just let the kids out in the morning to pick up where they'd left off the previous afternoon. It was before all the fuss there is now about abductions; that anyone would steal one of our babies was the furthest thing from our minds. The kids wandered in and out of each other's apartments, and at mealtimes you could hear the mothers up and down the sidewalk outside the complex calling for Sean or Dorothy or Steven. And if they were at your house, you simply sent them home. Life was simpler then.

Gerald and Joyce lived one floor down. They were about the same age as John, and, instead of having one child in nursery school, one in diapers, and one in the womb, they had two who were in the campus nursery school across the street. I used to walk with Gerald and our kids over there in the morning. Joyce was also a resident, in OBGYN, and between the kids and her job had a pretty grueling time of it. Gerald wasn't one to do much of the dirty work. I wasn't working and I was exhausted all the time. God knows how Joyce did it on a resident's schedule.

I disliked early childhood parenting. My character wasn't suited for it. I overheard a couple of other mothers talking about me once. *She has no sense of whimsy, no sense of play,* said one. *And no sense of humor,* said the other. I wasn't hurt. What they said was the truth.

I wasn't well suited for pregnancy, either. Mine were difficult—not healthwise, but I was nauseated throughout all three trimesters for all three children. People complimented me on not gaining much weight, that's the way people thought then. But it was simply that I couldn't keep anything down. And even in the privacy of my own bathroom, I hated the indignity of retching into the toilet, the foul taste in my mouth afterward. I'd brush my teeth vigorously and then scrub the toilet bowl to erase any hint of what I considered my weakness. John honestly didn't notice. He'd pat my tummy affectionately the way men will, not seeing how much I despised that.

But Gerald. We were actually thrown together quite a bit. I was president of our apartment association, and he was on the management committee. He was poised to grow into one of those doctors who sit on the boards of the symphony and the ballet—civic-minded, and, once comfortable financially, looking to expand and enrich his mind. As it was, you'd hear classical music playing whenever you went over to Joyce and Gerald's apartment. He subscribed to some sort of record collection series, *the world's greatest music,* and was listening seriously to each track as he read the notes. Even I recognized the music, it had the familiar tunes from the Boston Pops concerts my parents used to love. But Gerald thought it was High Art.

He wasn't a handsome man, Gerald. Not like John. He didn't command a room, either. If anything, he was shy, and hung back from social encounters. I would have dismissed him as soft if it wasn't for a streak of cruelty in him. A less-than-endearing habit he had was to catch flies—he was amazingly dexterous and swift with his reflexes—and pull the wings off, almost absentmindedly. He mostly repressed this streak, though, and refused to let it color any of his words or actions. This was, in my opinion, highly commendable. Unlike someone with a natural wellspring of kindness like John, Gerald had to work at it. He was also studying to be a surgeon, but with a cardiovascular specialization, and, he confided in me once when we were both a little tipsy at a party, that the biggest thrill of his life was cutting through the breastbone, opening the rib cage, and seeing a beating heart underneath, knowing he could stop it if he wished. "I make a point of studying my patients' records, meeting with them more frequently than other surgeons, not because I'm more caring, but because I need that to cushion me from my instincts. I'm tempted, every time, to end that life, just because I can," he told me that night. He was a much more admirable man than my husband.

The night I'm remembering lately, I was babysitting Joyce and Gerald's children while they went out to dinner. They were loud children, even for three and four years old. I disliked their clamoring for story after story, but they knew they had the upper hand with their vocal chords, and I ended up reading until they finally went to sleep. I was quite pregnant by then, at least seven months along, and felt huge and clumsy as I walked around Joyce and Gerald's tiny apartment, too restless to settle down and read or watch television, just willing them to come home so I could go to my own bed. When they arrived, Joyce was uncharacteristically drunk—usually she only drank soda water—and Gerald steered her straight to the bedroom. I wanted to leave, but felt it would have been rude to just disappear. As he left the room, Gerald said to me, "Stay for a moment, Deborah."

"What is it?" I asked.

"I want a couple moments alone with you," he said. "Is that all right?"

But when we sat there he didn't seem to have much to say. Suddenly he reached over and took my hand in his. He didn't appear to have been drinking, and Joyce was always a stickler about having a designated driver. "Are you flirting?" I asked him as a joke, but he didn't smile. "You are!" I said, and laughed, pointing to my belly. He still didn't smile. But I saw that calculating look that I'd glimpse when he was operating on flies, and he reached out with his free hand, pulled my face to his and kissed me. It was a hard kiss. Just a hint of tongue and enormously erotic. I was astounded. I had genuinely thought passion was behind me.

Then Cecilia stumbled out of the bedroom and whatever might have happened stopped cold.

Whether or not things would have progressed further turned moot a week later. Gerald was in a head-on collision on University Avenue. Both he and Cecilia were killed outright. We heard the sirens that night, heard them keep coming, so many, so near to us, we knew it had to be bad. We listened to the shrieking and the silence that followed. John crossed himself, something he's never been able to shake from his youth, and said "God help them." We found out later it was Gerald and Cecilia, their car had gone over the yellow line and straight into a delivery van. They didn't have a chance. The kids got spirited off by one of their grandparents, there was a quiet memorial service at the medical school, and that was that. But I often wonder what might have happened, had Cecilia not disturbed us, or had death not taken them.

Death. Always interrupting things.

21

Samantha

ALIBIS. JUST LIKE IN THE cop shows, almost everyone has one. There's MJ's—she was indeed accounted for at both Trader Joe's and Walgreens. *That odd-looking chick with the hat*, was how one Walgreens employee remembered her, and she had in fact knocked down a cereal display at Trader Joe's, shortly after 7 PM. Even if she had responded to John Taylor's text at 6:47, she would hardly have been able to get to Palo Alto, much less there and back by the time one hundred boxes of Honey Nut O's got knocked over.

Deborah was at a meeting of the Women's Auxiliary for the children's hospital, in Menlo Park. She had arrived at the house of the vice chair promptly at 6:25. "Deborah? She's always five minutes early," the vice chair had said.

These stories were backed up and verified by multiple persons who would have no reason to lie.

Helen was the exception. She didn't have an ironclad alibi for Friday night. She'd gone home sick from work at noon on Friday—a fact verified by her administrative assistant—and stayed home the rest of the evening, she said. She wasn't seen again until the next morning at

9, when she bought a cappuccino at her local Starbucks. The barista remembered her because she was a regular: showing up promptly at 6:30 AM on weekdays, and 9 AM on weekends for the same drink. "She always gives a two-dollar tip," he told me. Yet between noon on Friday and 9 AM on Saturday certainly left enough time for Helen to get on the plane for an hour and a half flight to San Francisco, rent a car, and get to the Westin in time to inject John Taylor with potassium chloride. In fact, she's the most likely candidate to have known about the effects of a potassium overdose, and to have had access to a supply of it. Hell, she could even have driven from LA to San Francisco and back in that time.

I'll have to make the rounds of the airlines and car rental companies. I'll enlist Mollie for that. Yet Helen is so small. Could she have caused such bruising? And then her personality: so cool, so level and logical. Would she really be capable of murder? And what would be her motive?

Yet it's MJ's name that remains underscored in my notebook. There was something skittish about her in our most recent interview that went beyond what I thought was her typical scattiness. And the brother, this Thomas. I didn't like the sound of him, not one bit. And there was a weak link in MJ's alibi: a gap of approximately two hours between her coming home from work and being seen at Trader Joe's.

So with the possible exception of Deborah, the wives remain in the running. I still have lots of work to do.

22

MJ

YOU CAN'T GROW UP IN Gatlinburg, Tennessee, and be unappreciative of either beauty or the grotesque. We're the self-proclaimed Gateway to the Great Smoky Mountains, and have the very special distinction of being home to one of the oldest Ripley's Believe It or Not! Odditoriums in the country. I was six years old when it opened in 1970, but long gone by the time of the Great Fire of 1992 that destroyed the mummified cat and Abraham Lincoln's death mask, and the other wonderful and terrible objects of my childhood.

My brother and I were entranced by that Lincoln death mask. One hot summer day when we were bored, we decided to make our own. We oiled our faces with Crisco, and slathered them with plaster bandages we'd saved up our allowances to get from the Buy-Rite pharmacy on Main. I was thirteen, Thomas was eleven, and we were astounded to see from the masks that without my long blond and his short dark hair, our different clothes, and other superficial distractions, our faces were almost identical. Mine was perhaps constructed on a slightly larger scale, but we shared the same long cheekbones, the same bump in the nose, the same heart-shaped face.

Shortly after that, I lost him to the parish priest. We were close, but I was no match for the pot and pornography that could be found every night at the rectory. I was the one who blew the whistle, after Thomas broke down and confessed what went on there. My mother was furious at me for spreading lies. "My cow died last night, so I don't need your bull," is what she said when I told her,. Eventually she grew to believe me, and wrote to the diocese headquarters. Eventually the priest was transferred without punishment. But not before a generation of Gatlinburg boys had been ruined.

Thomas had changed. I never knew whether the priest had gone as far with him as with some of the other boys, but I lost my little brother and an angry stranger took his place. I hung his death mask on my wall, its sweet expression forever banished now from its living owner, but infinitely precious to me, especially as Thomas grew older and got into his various troubles.

What were his troubles? Oh, the usual for Tennessee teenagers of a certain class. By which I mean *lower,* as my family wasn't exactly high on the social ladder in Gatlinburg. Petty shoplifting. Possession of marijuana, of course, but small amounts, nothing to get him jail time. Thomas came home wired and irrational a couple times, and admitted to me privately that he'd gone out to the country with some friends and bought some meth (easy enough to find around there). Luckily, he didn't take to it, preferred the gentle dullness of weed to being hopped up to the point of bursting. Then he did some significant vandalism to the church, break-ing the large stained-glass windows behind the altar. He and a friend accumulated a wheelbarrow full of large rocks and stood in the woods behind the church and hurled them upwards, until the tall windows were completely shattered. He got caught (go figure), the shards of glass in his clothes that he hadn't bothered to wash, but by then he was on the list of usual suspects for this kind of thing anyway. It's a relatively small town, after all. Poor kid. He didn't have much of a chance.

I watched Thomas throw his life away and knew there was noth-ing I could do to help while I was on the inside. I was smart, and knew it, and determined to get through school and out of Gatlinburg, but got entangled with a local boy when I'd barely finished my second year at Carson-Newman Junior College over in Jefferson City. Our two children were born when I was twenty and twenty-one, and when I was twenty-two I packed them up while their father was working the afternoon shift at the Odditorium. I turned the car away from my parents' house and headed straight west. My only goals were to put my feet in the Pacific Ocean, make sure my babies didn't have the Tennessee twang—and help Thomas escape one day as well. How I ended up in Northern rather than Southern California was the result of a wrong turn onto the I-5 outside Bakersfield. The babies were squalling, it was two in the morning, and I got on the ramp heading north rather than south to LA like I'd intended. Nevertheless, it worked out okay.

San Francisco blew my mind. I remember arriving at Ocean Beach at about four on a Sunday afternoon in June. I didn't know it then, but it was one of those rare sunny days over on that side of the city, and I thought I'd died and gone to heaven. I stuck my feet in the frigid water for about two seconds, splashed a little on my babies' faces to make them laugh, and set out to build us a new life. Three years later, after bartending nights at various local joints while subjecting my kids to a series of mediocre babysitters, I finally had both my divorce and my degree in accounting from San Francisco State. People tell me I still have a bit of the Tennessee twang, especially when I get tired or excited. But both my boys talk like the native Californians they almost are.

The boys are good boys. Though the one dark spot on my marriage to John was that he didn't get on with them, or they with him. I think after having me to themselves for more than twenty years they didn't like to share.

They've both been calling a lot since the news got out. They're worried about me, whether I'll get by okay. But I stay up nights concerned about them. Especially Jackson, the younger one. He's a little too keen on get-rich-quick schemes, and has more avarice in his bones than I like to see in a son of mine.

My brother's another matter, another one to worry about. He eventually followed me to San Francisco a couple years after I escaped. He's still what I would call broken. He's had his share of relationships, some with women, more with men, but none of them seem to last. I think the last boyfriend had a bit of a temper. On the one occasion I had them to dinner they were both injured, Thomas with the remnant of a black eye and his boyfriend noticeably limping. I took Thomas into John's office and read him the riot act. "I don't care who you sleep with as long as you treat each other well, and I just don't see that happening here," I told him. Thomas shuffled his feet and mumbled, and then on the way out put his fist through our front window. That's how things take him.

For Thomas, John had a surprising amount of patience. Perhaps he could tell how important Thomas is to me. But he was generous and forgiving in many instances where he didn't need to be.

Thomas has a lot of natural talent as a graphic designer, is self-taught on the computer and doesn't have any trouble finding work when he puts his mind to it. I wish he'd put his mind to it more often. He's a bit of a lost soul. But he's my baby brother, and I love him dearly. I would do anything for him, and he knows it.

23

Samantha

THE COMPLETION OF MY FIRST interviews for this case since the inquest excites me and agitates me both. Weeks have passed, but I find I can't concentrate. I look at the calendar and realize we're in June already: Summer is flying by. I leave work early, go home and change, and head out on my bike despite the fact that the sky looks threatening.

The sun won't set until after eight, so I'll have plenty of light. I never ride after dark, having had to fill out too many accident reports from my years on the campus beat. But I got a new bike from Peter for my twenty-eighth birthday, so I've been riding a lot lately, even though I don't even understand how to change the gears; it's so fancy. I take it down Palm Drive to Campus Drive, and under the 280 overpass, back into the Alpine Road loop. For some reason, squirrels know enough to stay out of your path there, it's only on campus that their brains are addled enough to commit hara-kiri.

As I pedal, I barely notice the landscape. I'm sweating profusely, and it's not because of the heat or the exercise. This case is getting to me. Last night Peter came out of the bedroom at 3 AM to see where I was, and found me facedown on a diagram I'd drawn under the label, *the usual suspects,* but which made absolutely no sense to me the following morning.

I'm on a popular bike route. Passed by dozens of riders, outfitted in identical uniforms, looking fierce and determined in their helmets and wraparound sunglasses. The men, in particular, disturb me when they're dressed like this, it seems so aggressively sexual, the tight black pants with the genitalia outlined front and center. A bunch of them are lounging outside the Alpine Inn, drinking beer, strutting in and out of the pub, pelvises outthrust, in their special clip-on shoes. I ignore them and keep going. I'm not dressed appropriately in their eyes, they scorn me as the amateur I am, I'm wearing some old cutoff sweats and a PAPD T-shirt, and despite my angst over the case I feel strong as I pump my way into the countryside and escape from suburbia. But just as I hit the Portola–Alpine junction, the sky opens and I'm drenched. Ten miles from home and the rain seeming here to stay, pouring down, soaking my hair and clothes, which now hang heavily off me. I decide to keep going. I'm not going to get any wetter, and it's a warm rain, so I'm not uncomfortable. And the drops splattering against my face and neck, the dark clouds overhanging the hills exhilarate rather than depress me, seem to open up something in me that has been stubbornly closed lately.

I catch a flicker of a memory. Playing in the rain at my grandmother's house on the Jersey Shore. The warm wind gusting through the open windows, the rumblings of distant thunder, the spattering of rain as the storm descended, my grandmother pushing me out the door to get the laundry off the line before it got wet, then staying outside myself once the clothes were safe inside. The house doesn't exist anymore, it was destroyed in one of the mega storms that have been plaguing the East Coast over the past few years, but it was my favorite place in the world when growing up. We always spent at least a couple weeks there in the summer, my parents, my younger brother Gregory, and me. I lived there with my grandmother the entirety of one summer, when I was eight. That terrible and wonderful summer. Those days were genuinely glorious: the salty sea, and the sun, the cold ginger ale waiting for me when I got back from the beach, the sharp tangy scent of the Noxzema my grandmother would spread on my sunburned face to cool it down. Me having her all to myself, my parents back at home in Brooklyn tending to Gregory. Although they hadn't told me yet, they knew he was dying, and they sent me off to miss as much of it as possible.

When I got home that September, there was Gregory, on the hospital bed in the living room where he would spend his last days. He'd been an annoyance and an infuriating shadow on my life for years, the snot-nosed younger brother always wanting to bust up my games of dress-up with my friends and bother my parents with his aches and pains and bruises and, eventually, visits to the doctors and stays in the hospital. I was home in time to witness his horrifying end. Never a large boy, he was wasted and waxen, tubes snaking around his bed, into his mouth and wrists and under the covers. Then one day I got home from school and it was over. My parents must have been all cried out by then because they were simply sitting in chairs next to his bed, quietly talking. I think they were even laughing as I came through the door and stopped at the sight of that poor limp body, so clearly not Gregory any longer. He had been there, in all his infuriating physicalness, and then he wasn't.

To say there was a hole in my life would be imprecise. To say I missed him would be giving me more credit than I deserve. More humanity than I had back then. We'd had cautious truces, but they were too rare to give me much regret that Gregory was gone. I'd never given any comfort to him while he was around, even after he got sick. Once I'd made a fist in frustration and punched one of the larger bruises on his thigh, causing him to howl with pain. I showed no remorse, and lost a month of playtime after school when I stubbornly refused to apologize.

I think of Helen, Wife No. 3, and wonder how many Gregories she sees every year, how many she buries. And whether she likes them all, or whether she would also have been as annoyed by my brother Gregory as I'd been.

My parents divorced the year after Gregory died. Both decent people, truly desiring to be good parents, they did what they could to ease the pain of separation for me. I got my own therapist, as well as regularly attending a family counselor with both of them. My therapist showed me lots of pictures and asked how they made me feel: happy, sad, angry, joyous, pitiful, etc. It was easy to guess the right answers, but occasionally I'd throw her by saying a picture of two people shouting at each other made me happy, and a sleeping cat made me angry. My childhood in retrospect consisted of crowds of well-meaning people trying to do the right thing. I didn't always react appropriately. In fact, I could be a little brat.

My inability, or my refusal, to make commitments began back then, I believe, if I can indulge in some amateur psychology. My parents pushed me to decide whom I would live with. I chose my mother, and moved cheerfully enough with her into a new apartment in Manhattan. Then I cried, predictably enough, day and night for my father, who stayed at our family apartment in Brooklyn. So we started alternating weeks for visitations. I couldn't help but see how sad my parents were when it was their turn to hand me over Sunday nights. My father would drive into Manhattan, and there was always a short but emotional parting in the hallway outside my mother's door, sometimes because I was staying, and sometimes because I was going.

Most of the tears shed during that difficult era are ancient history. But that back and forth for nine years until I went away to college took its toll. I learned to compromise, but never to commit. I couldn't even decide on whether to have a cat or a dog, so, predictably, I got both. I never had to choose. I didn't even choose Peter. He chose me, and somehow that was easy.

Still, sometimes I find myself yearning for more. To give myself over to something. Not to waver. To embrace passion. Whatever John Taylor lacked in his life, whatever hole he was trying to fill by marrying multiple times, he certainly had passion. And I'm not sure I ever did. This is the conversation that Peter and I agreed not to have. It makes him miserable.

The rain drives into my face, nearly blinding me as I make my way back down Sand Hill Road. *Passion.* I decide it must be the root of everything in life. And I feel that it will be at the root of the John Taylor case.

24

Deborah

I KEEP SEEING GHOSTS. Or rather one ghost, in many places. At the grocery store, John walks by pushing a cart containing nothing but a dozen avocados and two gallons of skim milk. But it's just a portly man of John's age, probably going on some sort of fad diet, something John would never have done. I see John driving the Volvo behind me, and I'm so intent on looking in the rearview mirror I almost crash into the back of the yellow Toyota idling at the red light on Cowper. I come downstairs every morning at 5 AM, a habit I can't break, and find myself listening for the sound of his car, that noisy muffler he should have fixed months ago. His inattention to details like that enrages me. Or I guess I should say enraged me. Except that I'm still angry. I find myself raging over his words, spoken so long ago, about how he'd found love with someone else.

That would have been MJ. I paced through our living room all night, then when the sun came up got in my car and drove to where she lived in south San Jose. I parked in front of her rental house, a flimsy stucco construction with aluminum windows—the ones in the living room barely covered by torn shades, Batman sheets hanging over the bedroom ones. I was relieved when a tall and thin, almost gaunt, woman came out the door. Her shirt was loose and untucked. She had blowsy hair and a ridiculous straw hat with cherries on it, like a dissolute Mary Poppins. I actually vomited from the release of stress—with a total lack of dignity, opened my car door and retched, right outside the house. MJ noticed. She came over, concerned, asked if she could help. *Hay-elp.* She had a more pronounced accent then than she does now, gave each word more syllables than strictly required. She meant her offer, wasn't just hoping to be told it was all right, to move on. She was that kind of woman. You could see it from the small lines that edged upward from the corners of her eyes, her mouth surrounded by lines of genuine concern. Her large hands already reaching out, committed to the idea that help was needed, and that she would give it. Not my type of person at all.

But although certainly compassionate, MJ was apparently not intelligent enough to ask why a well-dressed middle-aged woman was sitting in a top-of-the-line BMW at her home early on a Tuesday morning. She spoke very kindly, offered to get me a glass of water, and when I refused, went back into her house to get one anyway. I took the opportunity to drive off. I don't believe she remembers, or associates me with that long-ago incident. If so, she hasn't said anything. Perhaps her life is made up of too many of these random acts of kindness to remember this time when her kindness was rejected.

I wasn't sure if the visit made me feel better or worse. Among women in my social sphere, it is tacitly recognized that any favor involves a contract, and to be a contract there must be quid pro quo: this for that. Value for value. Payback. When MJ offered to help me, I felt instinctively that to accept her help would result in me owing her something. That would have been an untenable situation. I am known for being quite generous with my time, for my willingness to help others. But I take my social contracts seriously, and always ultimately demand my quid pro quo. This has gotten me quite satisfactorily through years of dealing with women in organized groups. But my encounter with MJ left me uneasy.

What would it be like to offer up a gesture of goodwill with no expectation—realistic expectation, I should say—of it ever coming back to you? Planting a seed and not claiming the fruit or the flower that grew from it? That's why the people who believe in karma are such hypocrites. They live by the same rules as I do, only they expect the universe to even the score. Or some benevolent being. Not bloody likely, as my British friend Josephine likes to say. *Not bloody likely* that I was going to let this woman, this MJ, prevail. Neither would I owe her anything. So I drove off. Yet in fact she did do me a favor—a huge one. With her relative lack of intelligence, she took on John without asking many questions, thus saving my marriage. So if I act in accordance with my own value system, quid pro quo, I owe MJ. And my debt is not a trivial one.

25

Helen

MY PREVIOUS INTERVIEWS WITH THE detective had been over the phone. The woman had a low, melodious, and mature-sounding voice. So I am surprised to find this young person—barely in her twenties, it seems—waiting among my patients on Wednesday morning. She is dressed casually in jeans and a button-down blue shirt. She'd be a little overheated in our LA midsummer, but I remind myself she comes from Northern California. Her red cowboy boots are stenciled with stars and moons. I can see multiple piercings up the sides of both ears, and detect the remnants of a nose piercing, almost grown in. Today she's wearing just a single pair of conservative stud earrings of blue glass that match her shirt.

"How can I help you?" I ask as I gesture her into my office.

She seems more nervous than I am, drops her notebook, then when she bends to pick it up, tampons and a recorder fall out of her purse.

She laughs, a bit shamefaced. "So much for appearing the seasoned professional," she says when she's collected her possessions. I like her immediately.

I tell her again that although she's flown in from San Francisco, I have very little time. It was hard enough finding this half hour. When she says that she might need more, perhaps tomorrow, depending on how this goes, I shake my head firmly. She also says I can have my lawyer present—a suggestion I disregard.

She removes a stuffed lion and a plush brown bear from one of the chairs in my office, and sits down, turns on the recorder. "First of all, I'd like you to again give me a complete statement of where you were and what you were doing on Friday afternoon and early evening, May 10, 2013," she says. She places the recorder on the chair next to her, but then, like one of my patients, sees something interesting on the floor and pounces. It's my office mascot, a stuffed replica of a huge horny toad, so realistic in color and expression that everyone—adults as well as children—is drawn uneasily to it. The only thing not authentic is its size. It's as large as a basketball, and nearly as round. She places the thing on her lap and strokes it, appears delighted with its softness.

"As I told you before, I was home alone. Not feeling well. I'd even canceled my afternoon appointments to go home early," I say, while she makes the toad hop and trill and laughs to herself. She's quite charming, really. Certainly not coplike. I bring up my calendar. "Yes, I saw my last patient of the day at 11:45." The detective nods, I know she's already verified this with my admin assistant. "I then drove back to my condo. Spent the rest of the day and night in bed."

"Can anyone verify that you were home at that time?" the detective asks.

"No," I say. "I live alone." I stop for a moment before continuing. "I suppose another resident might have seen me enter the building. But if you're asking if I can prove I was home that evening the answer is no."

I hate canceling appointments. I can't remember the last time I've done such a thing. I remember that afternoon and evening. But I don't share all of it. I'd been nauseated and vomited until my stomach was empty. Then I continued with the dry heaves well into the night. Not pleasant.

"Thank you, that's helpful," says the girl. She has finally abandoned the toad, it is back on the floor. She is writing in her notebook. She looks up and smiles, and it is a genuine smile. "I'll need to follow up on this," she says, almost apologetically. The criminal element in Palo Alto must have an easy time of it. "But I'm afraid that until I do some investigating, you're still on the hook."

"What kind of hook am I on?" I ask. "Just curious."

She hesitates. "As you've probably gathered from the media reports, we're not completely satisfied about John's ... your husband's death," she says.

"And I'm naturally one of the suspects," I say.

"Naturally," the girl agrees. I'm amused to see that she blushes when she says this.

"And what motive would I have?" I ask. I'm curious to hear what she comes up with. Probably something banal, like jealousy. But she surprises me.

"That's what we'd have to determine," the girl says. "Your husband was a complex man. He probably died for complex reasons. When we understand why he died, we'll have a good handle on who did it."

I am impressed by this. I try to look serious despite the fact that this girl, this *woman* in a position of authority, is again playing with the toad, pressing down on its cloth eyelids to make them close over its ominous black plastic eyes. She catches me watching her and blushes again. She puts down the toad firmly, at a distance, as if trying to avoid temptation.

"Do you mind if I ask you some more questions?" she asks. "I'd like you to fill in some pieces of the puzzle."

"Not at all," I say, with what I hope indicates my respect and willingness despite my suspicions that the interview is being modeled on those she's seen on television. "Although at most I have twenty minutes left today. I may be able to squeeze you in tomorrow if you're not finished."

She nods, picks up the recorder and points it toward me. "What was the state of your relationship with John Taylor?" she asks in a slightly louder voice, I assume for the benefit of the recording.

"Very amicable. Very . . . harmonious," I say. The latter word is not quite appropriate, but I want to communicate the solidity of my relationship with John. I feel surprisingly calm talking about him. I've been avoiding the subject, worried about flailing emotionally in public. But I feel grounded and logical speaking on the subject today—that could be because of the hospital setting, the fact that in no time I will have to go back to reviewing charts and lab results of dying children. I've put myself in self-protective mode.

"When was the last time you saw John Taylor?"

"Two weeks prior to his death," I say. It had been a bittersweet visit, or perhaps I'm only remembering it that way because of all that has happened since. I'll never know, now. My most precious memories, corrupted by events beyond my control.

"He flew in Friday morning, so we had dinner at La Scala, our local Italian restaurant near our—my—condo. Then went home to bed," I say.

"Were you intimate that night?" the detective asks, and looks away, not making eye contact.

"Is this really something you have to know?" I ask, and when she nods, I tell her "Yes, in fact we were." Then shut my mouth. No one need know what went on between John and me in private. I am not being sentimental when I say I don't believe I'll ever see the like of those nights again.

She goes to speak, then hesitates. "Did he . . . did he act differently in any way? Say anything unusual?"

"No," I say. "But if I'm not mistaken, his mood was tinged with melancholy. Mine was, too." I remember now that was the week the

Meekle boy finally died. "I had lost a patient the morning he arrived. That might account for my associations."

"I'm sorry," says the detective, and she sounds like she means it.

"It had been coming for a while," I say. But these things tend to depress me despite my best efforts. I always analyze cases for anything I could have done differently, anything that might have changed the outcome. It's a sobering habit, but it keeps me honest. In the Meekle case, however, the poor child wasn't diagnosed until he was stage 4 and metastatic. Just sixteen. His father was one of the what-won't-kill-you-makes-you-stronger types and had forced his son to keep playing football despite the dreadful pain he was having in his legs, didn't take him to a doctor until after the season was over. "I could just kill some of these parents," I say, and then, "Oh, don't take me literally. Only an expression."

"And the rest of that visit?" she asks.

"We had a quiet, if short, weekend," I tell her. "Typically, John would come down on a Wednesday or Thursday. He taught a seminar that met every third Friday for a full day, and he'd stay until Sunday night. This time we only had Saturday together. He came in Friday to teach his class, and flew back to San Francisco Sunday morning. That was the last time I saw him."

I remember, although I don't tell her this, the sense of anticipation, mournful anticipation, that had been building all weekend. I had a feeling he had come down specifically to see me, his seminar notwithstanding, and that he had something important to say, but he couldn't quite bring himself to do so. By Sunday morning we were both somber, the mood having taken a decided downturn for no reason I could put my finger on.

The detective is watching me. She's sharp, this one. I see her making a mark in her notebook.

"Saturday we went to the Getty. Not for the art, which is wretched, but to wander around the buildings, have coffee in the café," I say. "That night we stayed in. I cooked a chicken curry, we each had our journals to read, and we did what doctors like us rarely do—nothing."

She nods but doesn't say anything.

"I'm not being much help to your investigation," I say, breaking the silence. Then, "I don't believe John was murdered. Maybe I don't want to believe it. He deserved a better end."

What do I want to believe? I wonder. That I wasn't such a dupe. All of us, dupes. Each woman thinking we had a man when we only had a piece of him. If that. The most mortifying part is that having just a part of him suited me fine. I suppose I'm easily pleased.

"You said, before, in our first telephone interview, that you hadn't anticipated such intense emotion—I believe the word was *ecstasy*— when you got married," the detective says. I cringe. Did I really say that? I must have been in a state. "Can you explain that further?" she asks.

"You have to understand, I said that right after the . . . incident," I say. Then more firmly, "Right after John died, I wasn't completely sane. Not completely myself."

"What would you say now?"

I think, but all I can come up with is, "Our relationship was cordial."

The young detective looks disappointed.

"Would John have described your relationship that way?" She seems to be hoping for something, and I'm afraid I disappoint her again when I say. "It was mutually satisfying." This is even worse than *cordial,* but I let it stand.

"How do you reconcile your experience with the fact that Dr. Taylor had two other wives?" she asks.

It takes me much longer to answer this one. I frankly don't have the words. When the silence grows too long, I tell her the truth. "I can't," I say. "I'll never be able to."

It's my turn to reach down and pick up the toad. The trilling sounds in the quiet room until I hold it firmly to my chest with both arms like I teach my youngest children. *When you hold it to your heart it stops its crying.*

The detective hesitates, then says, almost shyly, "So the hurt. It's bad?"

I stall for a few beats. How much of myself to reveal? The detective isn't looking at me; she is giving me some privacy. "Almost terminal," I say, finally, echoing words I'd spoken to a mother and father only two hours earlier. I put the toad down and the minute it is released from my arms it shrills its high wail. The children adore this; they think it signifies the power of their love. Only I know it doesn't feed on love but pain.

26

Helen

IT'S ABOUT TO STORM OUTSIDE, the wind blowing so hard against the sliding doors to the living room that I fear the glass is going to crack. The palm trees edging the property whip back and forth on their slender trunks. The clouds have yet to break, however—there's not a drop of moisture in the air. A dry despair to the landscape.

I've never thought of myself as an insomniac despite the fact that I rarely get more than four or five hours of sleep. I stay up late and wake early. Rather, I tell myself I don't need much sleep. I've simply got too many things to do to waste precious time unconscious. When John was with me, we'd go to bed together, then, after he was safely snoring—he was a terrible snorer—I'd quietly leave the bedroom to read my journals or do paperwork. Whatever my marriage did to me, it didn't change my sense of urgency that there is work to be done, data to absorb, knowledge to acquire.

But since John's death I've been ghosting at night in a different kind of way. Not able to sleep even three hours, yet not being productive with the extra time, either. The urgency *not to waste a moment* completely dissipated. There are still sick children's charts to review, journal articles to read and write, as many emails to sort through, prioritize, and answer. Only now I am realizing that all these years I've worked my way into exhaustion out of fear. Fear of the void that only sleep or work can fill and which stretches out in front of me now. The nighttime has turned into a deep empty vessel that I must fill drop by drop.

I sit in the armchair, John's favorite, the one he would drag onto the balcony. The curtains are open. Light from the window illuminates the palm trees and their contortions in the wind. Beyond them, inky blackness.

I stand, and walk to the kitchen to make myself a cup of hot water—I don't even bother steeping a tea bag in it, my inability to taste grows worse in times of stress. I sip it as I move to my office, sit down at my laptop, open a patient's file, then leave it there. I go back to the armchair, calculating probabilities, couching the odds, wondering whether to get dressed and make a trip to the twenty-four-hour Rite Aid on Mulholland. Back to the kitchen for another cup of hot water. Then to the bathroom for the twentieth time this evening, staring at the white stick lying on the counter, at the pink plus sign displayed at one end of it.

I go to my computer, and click to the manufacturer's website again, to the FAQs, looking for the chance that the birth control pills I have been taking every day since I met John could fail. The label was very clear. *Less than 1 out of 100 women will get pregnant each year if they always take the pill each day as directed.* That should be reassuring, except for one word. *Always.* I read the next sentence. *About 9 out of 100 women will get pregnant each year if they* don't always *take the pill each day as directed. Don't always. Don't* now being the operative word.

As a physician, I understand the importance of the words, *as directed.* And from my own medical studies know that this means taking the pill at the same time every day. Which I always had done. Except once. One inexplicable day when I left the house without turning the wheel around and popping out the little pink pill. Thinking of John arriving that morning for his twice-monthly stint. Looking forward to seeing him in my ward, where he had agreed to consult for a child with a benign but disfiguring facial tumor. I realized about halfway through my rounds that I had forgotten. So I took the pill that evening when John and I finally got home after dinner out. Assuming that what every medical intern would recommend is good advice—take a missed medication within twelve hours and you are probably all right. *Probably.* Compared to *always.*

I've seen so many test results that spelled death for a child, and now to have one that means life.

But a surprise this isn't. I've always been regular, can predict my period almost to the hour every twenty-eight days, since I was fourteen. So I've known for almost two months. I knew the week before John's last visit in late April. Yet I said nothing, and put off taking the test. Deniability. Isn't that what lawyers call it? After all, that last weekend John was here, I didn't officially know, so I couldn't tell him. Now I do. And the landscape has altered, is full of strange eruptions and abruptions. I may as well be on the far side of the moon for how it relates to life as I have always known it.

27

MJ

DEATH. I'VE BEEN CLOSE TO it several times. My grandparents. My mother. Now John. But my first encounter with death was also my strangest. It was also my first tangle with the law.

I was twelve, Thomas was ten. We were in and out of the woods all the time, like the other kids were. We had our secret paths and hiding spots and remnants of forts we'd been building and tearing down since we could barely walk. The Smoky Mountains weren't the near-holy grounds that the hikers and campers and environmentalists worshipped, but one huge playground for our games. None of their dark corners held any fear for us, and we'd laugh at the hikers laden with gear who wouldn't go near the forest without being completely provisioned with the right hiking boots, the right jackets, the latest high-tech tents. *So dumb they couldn't pour piss out of a boot with the instructions written on it.*

One day, Thomas came home terribly excited. He and his friend Andy dragged me into the woods to a homeless man's camp. The poor old guy had died sitting half propped up against a tree. There was a rudimentary home, a shelter made of branches, the remains of a bonfire, some tattered odds and ends. My brother and Andy were absolutely entranced by the whole scene. They made a point of raiding the dead man's provisions, looking at his dirty magazines, cooking a can of his beans in his fire pit, eating it using his utensils. Pretending they were outlaws, and that he was one of their gang who had been shot. I was disgusted. Among other things, it stank to high heaven, but they just wrapped cloths around their noses, and kept going, the dead body an incredibly exciting addition to their role-playing games. They kept this up for a week or so. Then, I don't know whose idea it was, it could well have been Thomas's, they decided to bring home an arm. Halloween was a few weeks away, and what they did with this arm you can imagine, two boys of a certain age with such a prize.

I remember most trying to stand up to Thomas when he came home with that gruesome limb, urging him to take it back to the woods, to forget about the whole business. Instead, I helped fill the huge pot that my mother used to stew squirrels my father shot, put it on the outdoor fire pit, and boiled the flesh off the arm. I even dried the bones with paper towels for them.

What does this tell me? That I was capable, even back then, of doing anything Thomas bade me do, no matter how obscene or unlawful.

When the police came by later (it was inevitable that someone would call them with Thomas and Andy waving that grotesque thing around town) I was taken to the station for questioning with the two boys. They eventually let the matter drop, but not before scaring us with talk of the legal penalties for the desecration of bodies.

Our parents grounded us for a month. Thomas obeyed for about half a day; then he was off, climbing out his window to run around town with Andy and his other friends. As usual, I dutifully kept to the terms of my punishment (even when my parents were at work and I could have done whatever I wanted). Despite the fuss, Thomas managed to save a finger from the hand, kept it in a jar on his desk. For all I know, he still has it, a grisly trophy from that early misadventure. And, as always, he came out on top whereas I paid the full price for his escapade.

28

Helen

I'M A NATURAL BRUNETTE. I'VE always been one. You might say I pride myself on the *ordinariness* of it, the honesty of it. Brunettes are down-to-earth. We don't dazzle, not like blondes or redheads. And we're not striking, not in the way truly black-haired women are.

When I was young I wanted black hair, real black hair. I would have cut it bluntly against my neck, with bangs, so I resembled the pictures of the ancient Egyptians in the books I got at the library. I was looking at my dull brown hair in the mirror last week when I remembered from reading those books that the Egyptians of both sexes cut off their hair to mourn. So I booked an appointment with my hairdresser this morning. The lovely, the fabulous, Simon. He's wanted to color my hair since the first gray strands began appearing at age thirty-four. When I tell him I am ready to make a change, he claps his hands. "Streaks," he says. "I think we'll put in some golden-brown streaks." Instead, I shock him by demanding that he cut it short, very short, androgynous-style. I also instruct him to bleach it blonde. I want an overhaul, a total overhaul. I want, no need, to shock myself into accepting that my life has now irrevocably changed. As the hair-dye commercials promise, I want a *new me.*

Of course I'd read the literature on hair dye and pregnancy. Although a 2005 study suggests an association between hair dye and the childhood cancer neuroblastoma, a host of other studies on the use of hair dye before and during pregnancy haven't reached the same conclusion. Rats fed a composite of a series of commercially available hair colorings from days six to eighteen of gestation with doses of up to 97.5 mg a day exhibited no teratogenicity. Five oxidative hair dyes were administered by gavage to rats with up to 500 mg/kg daily on days six to fifteen and again no adverse fetal effects were observed. So I feel safe proceeding with my makeover.

I make a point to avoid the mirror until Simon finishes blow-drying what is left of my hair. I watch his face instead. He has a dubious expression, like he's being forced to eat something he doesn't enjoy. I finally look at my reflection. I don't recognize myself. It's as if an ageless boy, a blond Peter Pan, is staring back at me. Someone with inner power and magical secrets. I walk out of the salon feeling considerably lighter.

Perhaps now my mourning for John can conclude. Perhaps I can begin to celebrate my new life. Because although I've certainly lost my much-valued personal privacy—perhaps even the respect of the greater world—haven't I gained something significantly more important? My new self is reflected in shop windows as I walk down Mulholland Drive, and I almost laugh out loud I am so happy.

29

Samantha

I'M SITTING IN THE WAITING room of the Taylor Institute, a beautifully constructed square building, just off campus, with a façade of flesh-colored stone. Only a façade, because in California real stone buildings wouldn't have a chance of surviving a major earthquake. I actually drove around the block three times before I understood that this building was the clinic. Oddly, there's no sign, only the street number in small gold lettering, so discreetly placed among the ivy covering the stone that I had trouble locating it. When I finally figured out that this was my destination, I was stopped by a security guard hidden in a special booth off to the side of the entrance. I showed my badge, and he let me pass.

Inside, the sofas are green velvet brocade, the carpet is rich, red wine–colored and deep enough that your feet sink down into it as you walk. A smell of rose water. The hush of a library, or a church. And everyone on staff is so damn beautiful, from the receptionist, to the "intake counselor" who comes forward with a clipboard after I told the receptionist I was there to see Drs. Epstein and Kramer, John Taylor's partners in the clinic.

"Detective," the intake counselor says. She's what one would call a natural beauty, with a creamy complexion and the kind of shiny hair my mother used to promise I'd have if I washed my hair with egg yolks. I'm not sure what natural means in a place like this. Was this woman's nose her own? How about her cheekbones? "Dr. Kramer will see you now."

She gestures at an ornate doorway with large oaken doors. I hear a low hum as the receptionist buzzes me in. I wonder at the security of the place. Are they afraid that the masses will come bearing pitchforks and demanding face-lifts and nose jobs? I've done my research, though. You don't call them that anymore. *Rhytidectomy* and *rhinoplasty* are the terms they prefer. And a boob job is a *breast enhancement*. Right-o.

A man in an exquisite tailored suit waits for me on the other side of the doors. He is everything that Dr. John Taylor had apparently not been: tall and fit, in his midforties, impeccably turned out.

"I'm Dr. Kramer," he says. "Please come to my office." He leads the way to more of a sitting room than an office. If it weren't for his medical diplomas hanging on the wall, you could have mistaken it for an exclusive men's clubroom, complete with black leather chairs and a marble-topped coffee table. I almost expect him to offer me a fine cigar and brandy. "You're here to talk about John's death," he states in a low voice, as if afraid to be overheard. It is not a question.

"Do you know of anyone who might have wished John Taylor harm?" I decide to be blunt and plainspoken. After his gentle tones, my voice sounds rough and boisterous.

"No." The answer is given in a soft but emphatic voice. "John was the kindest, most generous man I've ever known. No one could want to hurt him."

"What about his three wives?" I ask. "Did that come as a surprise to you?"

"Absolutely," he says, but so mildly that he could have stated the opposite and I would have believed him. He straightens his already-straight tie, picks an invisible piece of lint off his trousers. Then he sees that I'm waiting for more.

"I'm sure they might be upset, very upset," he says. "But to harm him? That seems extreme."

Dr. Kramer gazes at me now and smiles. I could hit him for that, and for what I know he is going to say next. Sure enough, out it comes. "Samantha," he says. "How old are you?"

"It's detective," I say. "*Edward,* how old are you?" To his credit, he seems embarrassed.

"I'm sorry," he says. "But you look like one of my daughters. Playing cops and robbers."

"This isn't a game."

"I apologize."

I decide to pretend our last exchange hasn't happened, and plunge back in.

"What I don't understand is how Dr. Taylor was able to live openly with his Los Gatos wife when his real one was so close by," I say. "How could someone not have spotted them together—at the movies or the mall? What about work functions?"

Dr. Kramer nods. He's more eager to help now after offending me. "It's possible because John kept his personal life under wraps. None of us had even met Deborah. If we'd seen John with a woman, we would have naturally assumed it was her."

"Never met your partner's wife?" I ask. "That seems odd."

"He told us she didn't care to socialize," Dr. Kramer says. "We had no reason to disbelieve him." He hesitates a moment. "It's not like we were friends in any meaningful way. We were business partners, and colleagues. Dr. Epstein and I see each other socially, but John made it absolutely clear he wasn't interested—he wanted to keep his personal life separate from work."

Just then, a soft knock on the door, and in walks a truly spectacular young woman. She stands out even among the other beauties here—both men and women. What a surreal place. She might be my age, or a year or two younger. It's hard to tell because of the extraordinary whiteness of her skin, especially when contrasted to the black of her hair. These days of course we know to keep our babies covered up with hats and long sleeves, and to apply and reapply sunblock. But who would have been so obsessive about it twenty-five years ago? This woman's parents—or whoever raised her—sure were. With her white skin and black hair she looks like a modern-day Snow White.

And it's not just her looks, but her bearing that makes her stand out. For someone so young she is extraordinarily assured. She nods to me, but walks straight to Dr. Kramer and hands him a folder. "The photographs you wanted," she says. Her voice is deeper than I expect, and raspy, almost a smoker's voice, although I doubt she would deign to pollute her perfect body, her perfect skin, by inhaling such poison.

This woman's black hair is cut straight across her jawline, and swings in one motion as she turns to leave the room. She is wearing a white lab coat over plain black trousers and white blouse, and some very kick-ass spectacles.

"This is Dr. Fanning, Dr. Claire Fanning, our newest resident," says Dr. Kramer. "She's been with us four months while completing a fellowship at Stanford. Claire, this is Detective Adams, who is following up on John's tragic death."

Claire flashes her black eyes at me. "What is there to follow up on?" she asks. "My understanding is that his death was due to cardiac arrest."

"Myocardial infarction," I correct her, and smile. She doesn't smile back. My guess is that although she ranks a ten in beauty, her sense of humor is sadly underdeveloped.

"Detective Adams isn't satisfied," says Dr. Kramer.

Claire's eyes behind the spectacles widen. The result is comically theatrical. "No?" she asks.

"No," I say. "It's been all over the news. The coroner's verdict was murder by person or persons unknown. Too many unexplained factors for us to let it go."

There's a moment of silence. I turn back to Dr. Kramer. "Speaking of publicity," I say, "How's business here at the clinic? Has it been impacted by the media circus?"

"Not at all. Business couldn't be better," he says. He speaks louder than before, almost boisterously. "We have a waiting list for procedures that goes for months." I notice Dr. Fanning looking at him steadily, but he seems to be avoiding her gaze.

"Who will take over the children's cases now that Dr. Taylor is gone?" I ask.

"We haven't yet decided. It's obviously a big part of our brand here at the Taylor Institute. We can't let that goodwill lapse," Dr. Kramer says. There is no mistaking it now: Dr. Fanning is sending a message with her steady stare.

"What do you think?" I ask her.

She startles at my question, but answers quickly and decidedly. "Although the money is in the adult cosmetic procedures, we owe it to John to keep our pediatric practice going."

"But is anyone qualified? I understand that he was uniquely talented at his work."

"Of course he was," interrupts Dr. Kramer. "But we mustn't confuse the mystique with the man. There are other surgeons who are just as qualified, just as adept at the procedures. I don't anticipate much will change in that regard."

"Except the mix of patients and procedures," says Claire. Dr. Kramer frowns.

"What do you mean?" I ask.

Dr. Kramer says, "I don't think we need hold Dr. Fanning here any longer," but I motion for him to let her speak.

"There was a growing consensus to throw the children under the bus," she says. "So to speak." I look for a hint of a smile, but there is none. Definitely no sense of humor. "Management meetings were becoming very contentious," she adds.

Dr. Kramer picks up a pen on his desk and begins making little stabbing motions at a piece of paper.

"Why is that?" I ask her.

She significantly rubs her thumb against her index finger: the universal sign for money.

"John was facing a mutiny," she says.

"That's too strong a word," objects Dr. Kramer. "The detective is going to get the wrong idea."

"Maybe she should," says Dr. Fanning.

"Or perhaps the right one," I say at the same time. We glance at each other.

"What made the meetings ... contentious?" I ask.

"Do the math," she says. "The adult cosmetic patients are, for the most part, cash customers. No worries about insurance, Medicaid, waiving of fees, just a rich influx of cash. The children are a different matter altogether. Wrestling with insurance companies—even when they have insurance. Scrounging for donations. Trying to constantly find innovative ways to fund the pro bono cases John was committed to."

"Exactly how much money was at stake?" I ask.

"Annually? Millions," she says. "John wasn't interested in expanding the cosmetic side of the business. And John had veto power. Something he'd held on to when drawing up the partnership agreements."

I turn to Dr. Kramer. "Is this true?"

He shrugs, trying to appear casual, but there's a tenseness to his shoulders that wasn't there when we started. "Business partners often disagree," he says. "It's the nature of the relationship." Then he pauses before continuing, "Hardly a motive for murder."

I nod, but in a neutral way. "No one said it was."

"It's where the conversation was leading," he says. "I thought I might as well name the elephant in the room."

I decide to change the subject. "Curious question: Why don't you have a sign out front? This place is almost impossible to find."

Dr. Kramer looks relieved at the shift in direction. "Our clients prefer it that way," he says. "It's more discreet."

"What he means," says Dr. Fanning, "is that the cosmetic customers prefer it. Heaven forbid they're seen going into a plastic surgeon's office. Or seen leaving it. Did you see the rear exit? So our *clients* can make quick getaways." She walks over to another door on the other side of the desk, and opens it. Through it I can see a dark hallway. "Every doctor's office and recovery room in the clinic has a door like this," she says. "It goes out a back way, through an alley that's even more obscured than the front entrance. This way, our cash customers can escape unseen. Whether they've just had a consult or a procedure done, their identity is protected."

Dr. Kramer stands up. "Dr. Fanning, I'm sure you have work to do. Don't let us keep you." He turns to me. "I understand you also want to speak with Dr. Epstein."

"If possible," I say. I already have much more information than I expected.

"Of course," says Dr. Kramer. "Follow me."

I hold out my hand to Dr. Fanning. "Thank you," I say. "It's been . . . illuminating."

30

MJ

MY BROTHER IS DUE TO come by at ten this morning. Knowing Thomas, he'll be half an hour to forty-five minutes late. He'll also be hungry, in need of a shower and a change of clothes. Only two years younger than me, he's never learned to take care of himself, instead choosing partners who take him on, though always for the short term. He is between lovers right now, so I expect to see a run-down specimen when he shows up. I asked him once, how do you always find these ... not sugar daddies, because they're not necessarily flush with money ... but men with an excess of compassion, and a desire, no, really a *neediness*, to tend to others, to serve them. To serve *him*, Thomas.

He says it's a dog whistle that he can hear when these men talk, or even when they're not talking. Something in their body language. "I can really sniff them out," he'd boasted. "What about love?" I asked him. "Oh, I love them," he immediately said. "How could I not? They take such good care of me."

He's always the one to leave these relationships, to break up with some of the nicest guys I've ever met. But he moves on. Usually quite suddenly. It's like a stray cat you've been feeding and sheltering, and you think you have a relationship, an understanding, but then it disappears and you find out months later that it easily transferred its affections to a neighbor down the street. The stray has a different name, and a different affect to its walk, and pretends not to recognize you.

"You give out that signal, yourself," Thomas once told me. Perhaps. But something else about me must send a correspondingly forbidding signal because I haven't exactly been deluged with men over the years.

First my boys were small, and I was too busy raising them and earning an income. When the boys began to need me less, as teenagers, I ventured into a couple of ill-advised relationships. There was Jonah, a neighbor whose wife had just left him, taking the kids and leaving him the rental apartment and the dog. I was his rebound relationship. I knew it at the time, but still, to be touched like that after all those years. To be a sexual being again, however unequal the exchange of affection. He moved on eventually, leaving just a note taped to my backdoor handle, to which the dog was also attached.

After Jonah was Mike, who owned the gas station down the road where I got my aging Subaru repeatedly patched up. That turned out okay. Mike took my oldest, Paul, under his wing and taught him car repair at the shop. Not that he had to do much teaching, Paul was a natural. It was never something I could get excited about as a profession for him, but he has nevertheless done well, today operating his own repair shop at the age of twenty-nine. I'm proud of him.

My youngest, Jackson, is more ambitious, wants to forge his way. He went to junior college and then dropped out to get a programming job at a start-up. He's got the bug for what they call *entrepreneurship,* which I call greed. Yes, I'd call Jackson greedy. He sees all the wealth around him, and wants his share. *Pigs get fed and hogs get eaten,* that's what I'd tell him when he was a kid and wanted more than his share of pancakes. That first start-up failed, as did the next two. You only hear about the Facebooks and the Googles, but not about these other small businesses that rent cheap space in industrial parks east of the freeway in Santa Clara and come and go. I had to do a little protecting of

John from Jackson, I'm afraid. Smelling the presence of money, Jackson hoped John would invest in his latest scheme, don't ask me what it was, it involved some kind of software to *solve a pain point in the medical device industry*. He wanted John to give him a couple hundred thousand dollars as seed money. "You'd be an angel investor," Jackson had said during the sales pitch that I ultimately couldn't prevent from happening. "You'd get every cent back plus a fat return." John said no, and Jackson never forgave him. He hasn't stopped asking me for money either. Between Jackson and Thomas, my salary went pretty fast every month. It'll have to stop now that I'm on my own. I've even decided to rent out the back guest bedroom, and with that, I should be able to scrape by, make the mortgage and still have enough to eat.

I hear a car pull up outside, and Thomas is finally here. He walks into the house an hour and fifteen minutes late, much more confidently than he ever did when John was around. "Hey sissy," he says, and gives me a peck on the cheek. He accepts a cup of coffee and a plate of bacon and eggs. He wolfs that down, asks for another. I start cooking again. I'm glad to have the company, glad to have something to do for someone else. It's been almost eight weeks now, and I am nowhere near acceptance of John's death. A friend came over and packed away his things because confronting them every time I looked in the closet or in the bathroom proved too devastating.

"So the gravy train got derailed," he says, and motions around the kitchen. "Have you figured out if you'll be able to keep all this?"

I nod.

"Let's go into the backyard," I say, and he follows me. It's getting a little scruffy because I fired the gardening service that trims the grass and carts away the debris. Too expensive. I'm doing what I can, but the weeds grow faster than I can pull them. Like everything else in my life, the once-gorgeous garden appears a shambles. I am going down fast.

We pull out chairs from under the sun umbrella, bask in the warmth of the June morning.

"You look terrible," I say, noting his bloodshot eyes.

"So do you," he replies sharply. I hadn't meant my words in a hurtful way; I was just concerned. His words, however, sting.

We sit for a moment in silence.

"Well, what do you expect?" I say, finally. "After all that's happened."

"What's the verdict," he says.

"About what?" I ask.

"How much money is left?"

"It depends."

"On what?"

"Not on what, on whom," I tell him. "On Deborah. She said I can keep the equity in the house. That's the good news. Now I'm waiting to see if there will be any more."

"Will there be?"

"It's possible," I say, then, half drowsily in the sun. "It's possible," I repeat.

Thomas smiles. "My big sister," he says. "Who would have thought she'd have it in her?" I can tell he's on edge, though, despite his smile. I see him go in and out of these phases (mood swings would probably be a more accurate way to describe them, except they can last weeks or even months) and he seems to be accelerating into the anxiety stage. He stands and starts pacing back and forth before me.

Then he changes the subject. "They've made a movie about the woods," he tells me. "Actually, it's an old movie, but I've only just seen it for the first time. A movie that really captures it."

"Captures what?" I ask.

"The terror," he says, simply. I'm astonished, that he's talking about this, the thing he never talks about.

When very young, Thomas had spent much of his time in the woods, both alone and with his friends. He had a little pup tent and would sneak out of his window with it in a backpack (a backpack not dissimilar to what he carries his belongings around in now). He'd take it into the woods and sleep there. He had his secret places. I never asked, and never told on him. In fact, many times I'd cover for him, especially in summer months, when sometimes he wouldn't come home until lunch or even dinnertime.

That changed when he was twelve, when he started going to the rectory with the other altar boys. It was when the mood swings (for lack of a better word) began. Then the woods became a place of unease (no, worse, terror) for him. I'd ask him to come play there with me or even go for a walk. He'd refuse. He never explained why, but I noticed that he started sleeping with his curtains drawn over the window that faced the edge of the Great Smoky Mountains National Park, which ran up to our property. Then, right around that same time, there was my own . . . experience . . . that rendered the woods inhospitable to me as well.

"What is this movie?" I ask.

"Three kids go off into the woods to shoot a film," he says. "And bad things, terrible things, happen." He shudders as he says this. "It was frigging hard, but I watched the whole thing last night. Jesus, it brought up a lot." He didn't have to say whether what it brought up was good or bad.

"I was always scared shitless out there alone," Thomas says, after a pause. I decide not to say anything, but to see what comes next. Better late than never, these revelations. "And sometimes frightened even more when other kids were there, given that my friends were such fuck-ups. I always thought it would make me stronger, able to deal with the real things that were going down." He didn't tell me about the real things until it was too late.

I stand up and walk over to where he is pacing, and still him by putting my arms around him, rest my cheek against his. Both of us damaged goods, needing to take care of each other. "There's nothing to be afraid of," I say. "Absolutely nothing. I'm here, and always will be for you."

31

Helen

I JUST LEFT THE OBSTETRICIAN. Funny, after an illness-free life, all these doctors' appointments, all these blood tests and checking of blood pressure, and now, today, the ultrasound. I didn't sense that wonder at seeing the shape of the child—perhaps I'm too inured from my residency in OB-GYN. Besides, I feel her already. I know it's a girl, and will know for certain in a month when I have my amnio. I debated whether to have one—there are certain risks—but have discovered a deep well of worry that shouldn't have surprised me, given my line of work. There's so much that can go wrong, too many toxins in the air and water, and too much hazard in our DNA. I'm already protective of this child, determined to *do this right*. As if sheer willpower will bring forth the perfect physical specimen from my womb.

I've added four hundred more calories per day to my diet. More reds. More greens. More yellows. I can almost taste the colors. I'm filling out, and my pants won't fasten around my waist. My scrubs have gone from extra small to small.

I return to my office and see child after sick child. At three months I am barely showing, but on my thin frame it's enough for many of these balding and listless children to comment on it, pat my belly and ask if I have a baby in there. *Yes,* I reply, *there's a baby in there. Do you want to feel her kick?* I ask even though it's way too early for that. And I let their little hands rest on my belly.

I'm finding it difficult for the first time to do my job; my dread grows from the minute I step through the hospital door. And there is guilt, too—not an emotion I am overly familiar with. Because I know that if John had lived, this child would not have. It was in our agreement: no children. How can you weigh one life against another? Yet that is what I have done. And decided.

32

Samantha

"I CAN'T HELP BUT THINK that people are laughing at me, and I resent that," I tell Peter. It's after dinner and we're lounging in our living room. That's a grand name for the ten-by-ten-foot box that barely holds our sofa and CD collections. "I want to be taken seriously for the first time in my life, and it just ain't happening."

"For starters, lose the pigtails," Peter says. "People will naturally disrespect you if you don't act a little less like an ingénue."

I try not to show how stung I am by his remark. I really need to be less thin-skinned. Certainly in my job there's no room for hurt feelings. Then I have an idea.

"You be Deborah," I say. "I'm interviewing her tomorrow, and I'm a bit weirded out by the prospect. Let's do some role-playing." I move to a chair that is facing Peter as he sits on the couch. "Go on," I say. "Hit me with the worst you've got."

Peter thinks for a moment. Then he dramatically arches an eyebrow. "Child, how dare you step on my precious carpet!"

"Seriously, dude," I say. "I'm asking for your help here."

"Okay, okay," says Peter. He pauses, obviously considering what I've told him about the case.

"Why question me *again?*" he barks.

I'm startled, but I try to come back fast. "Because I have more questions," I say.

"These sound like the same questions to me," he says. "Doesn't the Palo Alto police force have a more . . . mature . . . officer they could send?"

He manages to say this with the exact right mixture of scorn and anger to rile me.

"I'm it, baby," I say. "Get used to it."

Peter frowns. "Not professional. Try again."

His curtness is getting to me, but I comply. "I am the detective assigned to this case," I say.

"Most detectives would have collected all the information they needed in the first interview," Peter says next. "Why do you keep calling me in? It's sheer incompetence. Or laziness. Or lack of purpose."

He spits out those words, putting special emphasis on the last phrase. *Lack of purpose.* It hits me in the gut.

"I'm doing the best job I can," I say, and immediately regret it. I sound weak, almost pleading.

"'I'm doing the best job I can,'" Peter mimics. I'm uncomfortably aware of how accurately he has captured my pathetic facial expression, my tone. "Well, your best isn't good enough," he says.

"Answer my questions or . . . or . . ." I say. I can't think of what to threaten him with, my arsenal is so poor.

"Or you'll *quit?*" asks Peter. "That would be pretty much par for the course. We'd get to close another chapter of Sam Adams's not-so-young-anymore life."

Silence. I find I can hardly breathe. Peter is sitting back with a smile on his face. He knows he's scored.

"Peter?" I ask finally. "Where's all this coming from?"

"What?" he says, opening his eyes wide. "I'm Deborah. Being a bitch. Like you wanted me to." He is still smiling.

"No, you were being Peter. And I had no idea you were this angry." I am genuinely shaken.

"Deborah's the angry one," he says. He won't look at me.

"I don't think so," I say. "And the scariest part isn't that you meant what you said, but that you were enjoying yourself. That hurt, dude. Seriously."

Peter doesn't say anything. We are both exhausted and ashamed. Bad idea on my end, to open the door to honesty. Destructive stuff. Such behavior, such words, even if said in jest or role-playing, have the potential to poison.

33

Samantha

THE WALKWAY FROM THE SIDEWALK to Deborah's house is constructed of perfectly positioned stones that fit into each other like puzzle pieces. That, as well as everything else I see when she opens the door, screams money. From the beautifully buffed wood floors, probably something exotic and doomed from the rain forest, to the scent of fresh roses in profusion arranged in a crystal vase on a small table in the hallway, I see a world that will always be out of my reach. I am suddenly furious. I don't really understand why. I'm not a covetous person. But some of Peter's bile from last night seems to have left its mark on me.

The Oriental carpets must be genuine and quite valuable, but to my untrained eye they're more or less the same as the machine-made ones Peter and I bought secondhand at a yard sale. Same colors, same patterns. Although when I examine them more closely I can see the delicacy of the woven flowers, the subtlety of the colors. I hope to find the obviously pricey furniture uncomfortable out of pure spite, but I sink into an armchair that I would happily trade for our lumpy bed. Money very well spent. Oil paintings on the walls, mostly portraits of peculiar-looking men and women, but they must be by artists worth collecting. Nothing else would do, for this house.

Deborah is dressed in a simple blue sheath, and even though the July day promises to be a hot one for the Northern California summer, she is wearing stockings. And despite the fact that I would have pegged this as a shoes-off-at-the-door house, she's wearing shiny black pumps with modest one-inch heels. Our shoes are always left in a jumble at the front door, not because, as in this house, the floor or carpets need protecting, but because both Peter and I hate shoes and take them off as soon as possible. Bare feet in the house, always. We even divide up the people we know into shoe-wearers and barefoot-goers. Deborah is clearly a shoe-wearer of the extreme kind. She probably puts them on straight out of the shower.

Deborah offers me an iced tea, which I accept because I'm thirsty, and then instantly regret it when I see her triumphant air as she carries the glass into the room. It is complete with a fresh lemon slice and long-stemmed iced-tea spoon—who keeps special iced-tea spoons on hand but the super privileged? Of course she brings nothing for herself to drink. Somehow she has seized advantage by going to the trouble of serving me. Not that she didn't have it already. I am in her territory, after all. I am her plaything. I take the glass, but look around, unsure if I can put it down on the exquisitely polished oak coffee table. She sees me searching, but makes me ask.

"Do you have a coaster?" I finally say when the silence goes on too long. "Indeed," she says immediately, and pulls one out of a drawer in the table and puts it in front of me. Power games. Bitch.

"Now, what can I do for you?" Deborah asks me. She crosses her hands in her lap, seemingly quite at ease.

"You're sure about not wanting your attorney here?" I ask as I turn on my recorder.

"Quite sure," she says. I don't urge her to reconsider. This chick knows what she's doing.

"For the purposes of the record, I need you to state where you were the night of Dr. Taylor's death," I say. "Especially between the hours of 6:47 PM and 7:50 PM."

"That's easy," Deborah says and smiles. "I was at my Women's Auxiliary meeting in Menlo Park. We met at the vice chair's house. Usually we convene here but I had asked to move locations as I wasn't feeling well, and I was worried I might have to cancel the meeting entirely. If it were at Gail's house it could go on without me."

"From what time to what time?" I ask. I know she'll have the right answer.

"The meeting lasted from 6:30 to 8 PM, and I stayed an extra hour to work on some numbers we needed to turn in to the finance committee the next day," Deborah says. "I got home around 9:15 and was home for the rest of the evening. I'm afraid I don't have a witness from that time on, but my committee members can validate my earlier presence."

I ask for the names and numbers of her committee cohorts, but know they'll hold up. Even if this woman did commit murder, she'd have everything so carefully plotted that I'd never smoke her out.

"Tell me who might have wished your husband harm," I say next. How lame.

She lifts her hands and holds them out, palms up, in the classic sign of bewilderment. "Besides one of the other wives, in a jealous fit? I can't imagine. Although I think they'd want to murder *me,* if anyone."

"Why is that?" I ask.

"Well, as the legal wife, I was certainly in the way," says Deborah, as if speaking to a two-year-old. I feel my face growing warm.

"But both MJ Taylor and Helen Richter claim they had no clue about the other, or about you," I say. "Are you saying you don't believe this?" I'm genuinely curious.

"Although Helen is the more intelligent of the two, even MJ should have had enough brains to figure out something was wrong," Deborah says.

"So you *are* saying that they knew," I say.

Deborah sighs, gently, "Either that, or they were highly motivated to believe in the fantasies John fed them," she says. "I'm inclined to believe the latter. Everyone has their vulnerable points, and John was especially good at finding them."

She says this casually, with a touch of scorn, as if everyone should know these things. But I'm determined not to be bullied.

"And what's your vulnerability?" I ask.

"You can hardly expect me to reveal it to *you*," she says, and appears amused. I curse my tendency to blush when embarrassed or angry.

Deborah, hands still crossed, is smiling, waiting for the next question. I get the impression that she's playing a part; there is something about her affect that doesn't feel quite genuine. Every once in a while around Palo Alto you see some poor rich woman who's had too much plastic surgery and you pity her tight expressionless face. Deborah has that. I don't mean that she's had work done. Her face is as a fifty-four-year-old woman's should be. She looks good for her age, but she does look her age. Still, there's some immobility of features that suggests she is being guarded. I also feel that she's not taking me seriously.

"But why do you want to hear all this? Surely my opinions are irrelevant."

"Everything is relevant," I say. I pick up my iced tea. It's not like any tea I've ever had before. It's bitter and aromatic at the same time. Although sweetly fragrant, the taste is sour and puckers my mouth. "If I understand John, and his relationships, perhaps I'll understand his murderer."

"That seems to be taking the long way around to your goal," says Deborah. "As I've said before, a goal with an erroneous premise. No one killed John. He was in terrible shape, wouldn't take care of himself. You know the phrase. 'Doctor, heal thyself.' John should have done so."

What she says sparks a question I'd meant to ask.

"By the way, did John have life insurance?"

"Yes, of course. I insisted, from early on, John being our sole source of income."

"How much was the policy worth?"

"Ten million dollars."

I must have involuntarily made some sort of noise because she adds, " I know that might sound like a lot to someone like you"—I keep my face frozen to avoid giving her a reaction—"but you have to understand John brought in quite a bit from his share of the clinic. And we've put away quite a bit over the years, invested it well. So actually, I'm financially secure enough without the insurance money."

"I understand from MJ that you aren't going to make any claims on equity in the Los Gatos house, although you'd certainly have a case."

"Yes," says Deborah, almost indifferently. "As I said, we invested wisely. I can spare a few hundred thousand for that poor creature."

MJ. Poor creature. I wonder how Deborah refers to me when I'm not here.

34

Deborah

WELL, THAT YOUNG DETECTIVE IS gone. A relief. No, more than a relief. A liberation. Liberation from emotions I don't wish to feel. She reminds me too vividly of a way of living, of a milieu I am very anxious not to be in contact with. I saw how hungrily she looked around. Although I'll say to her credit that I don't think she hungers for things, but rather for beauty. I don't imagine her life has much of that in it. And when one has a taste for beauty, the lack of it is a deep hunger indeed. I doubt she fully understands this. To my mind, that must be even worse, to have such an acute ache and not enough self-knowledge to know what part of the body or mind is in distress.

I could sympathize, if I let myself. I won't. I grew up in a world without beauty. My parents were failures. *Losers,* as the kids today would say. Forever changing jobs, changing houses, changing lives. Not exactly criminal, because they were never caught doing anything wrong, but my father always had schemes, always had partners with whom he was going to strike it rich. I never really understood how he earned a living, but when he talked on the phone, he spoke of "opportunities" and "prospects" and offers that "wouldn't last." For a while we'd have money to pay the rent, the electricity bill. Then the partners would disappear, the money would evaporate, and we'd move on. Once I came across an old passport of my father's—but with a different name. I took it to my mother, who just shrugged and said he had his reasons to not be that person anymore. She said it as though it was of no importance.

My mother, she could find work wherever she went as a court stenographer. She was good, could type 150 words a minute without a single error. It was all about focus, she would say. And she was utterly focused on the present. Because the past was over, and the future yet to come. *Why worry?* she would say. Character by character, word by word, she eased through life, always disappointed but sanguine when my father's latest scheme failed and it was time to move again.

I determined early on I would have nothing to do with that sort.

They're long dead, of course. My mother first, of breast cancer, which wasn't caught until late since they didn't have insurance. Then my father killed himself about a year after that. I hadn't talked to him for at least six months when I got the call. He blew his head off with a gun. Always the dramatic one. I'm not sure how they tracked me down to tell me the news. I'd pretty much erased the traces that connected me to them. I was into my twenties, already a wife, already a mother, a new name with a new life attached to it.

I met John at a church dance on the south side of Chicago. Not that either of us was religious. He was just finishing his final year of medical school at the University of Chicago, and I was still in high school in Franklin Park. Seven years difference between us. I went with a friend, as her church was sponsoring the dance, and John tagged along with some medical students to meet some "nice" girls. Funny, how they still thought that way then.

I was about to graduate high school. A year late at age 19, but even that was something of a miracle given I'd gone to eight schools in five years. College had never been in the cards for me. I never even considered it; higher education was out of my league. As was John, really. But I was a looker then, and caught his attention at that dance. My goodness, was he *attentive*. We were married within eight months, and the babies followed after that. I was 23 when I had Charles, 25 when I had Evan, and 28 when I had Cynthia. I told John that I'd had enough at that point although he wanted to keep going. My thought at the time was he loved the admiration of his tiny fan club. They were crazy about their father. Still are. Just because someone is dead doesn't mean you stop having a relationship with them.

John and I were good together for many years, and tolerated each other for some years after that. John was always lively and idiosyncratic, although he slowed down and sobered up considerably as he aged. If I hadn't seen it for myself I wouldn't have believed he'd have the energy for three wives. I had been telling him for some time that he needed to cut back on work, get more rest, some exercise. In typical John fashion, he brushed me aside.

I don't know why this sticks in my mind, but in his midtwenties, John imagined himself a bit of an artist. He had some rudimentary sketching talent that had served him well in medical school. I had seen his notebooks, filled with scribbled quick sketches of parts of the human body that had helped him get through anatomy classes. I often saw him surreptitiously sketching people, friends, neighbors, strangers at the coffee shop, on the El. He told me that if he could manage to capture even one human being on paper, he'd be satisfied.

We moved to San Francisco so he could complete a plastic surgery residency at UCSF, and we'd go to Golden Gate Park on the days they closed the road, sit there on the grass with the children—there were just two of them then—letting them run and crawl. They, and everyone around us, were our entertainment in those cash-strapped days. San Francisco in the eighties was a colorful place. Or perhaps it always is. John would sketch the people, sometimes quite adequately. Once he drew an elderly couple sitting on a bench outside the arboretum, and was so pleased with himself that he showed it to them. They were excited, and asked him if they could buy it, assuming he was a professional artist. He was flattered and simply gifted it to them, but not before they insisted on him signing it. This made him blissfully happy. But although drawing was a talent of his, it was a small talent, and I told him so, that day, as we walked home. I've never seen him so cut up. He stopped pushing the double stroller on the corner of 15th Avenue and Geary, and stood there, blinking tears from his eyes. He admitted then that he had registered to take drawing lessons at a night class over at San Francisco State. He'd been afraid to tell me. For good reason. I said absolutely not, that I could not have him fragmented in that way, I needed him to *focus*, and he said, "Deborah, one day you will kill me." We didn't speak for three days. Unusual for us, as those were our good times. At least in my mind. Anyway, he never drew anything again, or if he did, never showed it to me.

Piano playing was another minor talent he had. Previously, before we moved to San Francisco, while still in medical school in Chicago, John played around town in jazz clubs, anywhere that needed an opening act for a headliner. He'd walk over his audition tapes, and got a surprising number of gigs. Leaving me home alone with Charles as a baby. John never slept, or hardly slept in those days, between his surgical residency and piano playing. God knows what was keeping him going. Sheer adrenaline. But his piano, like his sketching, was not his life's work. Medicine was. And if he hoped to excel at it, he had to devote himself to the study of it. I told him. Repeatedly. He needed to be reminded, was easily distracted, and I kept him on track. I was not going to have an adult life that in any way resembled my early one.

John would have been happy as a general practitioner, would have stopped his education there. I insisted he proceed into surgery. And once we were there, I insisted he specialize. He was the one who chose plastic surgery over neurosurgery, which is what I wanted. He was surprisingly forceful about this. "You don't think much of my artistic talent," he told me, "but I could use it in reconstruction work." From the beginning he was determined that he wouldn't do cosmetic plastic surgery, only medically necessary procedures. He endured the six additional years of residency required to be board certified at UCSF, and then got a fellowship at Stanford, after which he was almost immediately hired.

About ten years ago, he opened the Taylor Center for Pediatric Reconstructive Surgery, as it was originally called. Against my wishes. His goal was to treat children only, victims of fire or birth defects or other traumas. He hoped that some insurance payments coupled with grants would be enough to allow him to see a substantial number of patients who couldn't afford to pay, who didn't have insurance. But, as I predicted, that was harebrained from a financial perspective. So about six years ago he took on a partner who specialized in cosmetic procedures, and changed the name of the clinic to the Taylor Institute of Plastic Surgery. Three years ago, they took on another partner due to the great demand for what John called vanity procedures. He would have nothing to do with that side of the business.

Whether John was happy or not in the later years is a difficult question to answer. He was a complicated man. He still smiled at me over breakfast. Still sang or talked to himself in the shower. In fact, that's how I usually gauged his moods, by listening outside the bathroom. He gave away a lot in his discussions with himself, in his brief bursts of words and song. Once I heard him say, "Oh MJ, don't be silly, that's a zone 12 flower." In fact, when MJ's name came up it was usually in the form of a fond reprimand. Helen's name appeared less frequently, but when it did, it was only her name. *Helen.* Spoken almost dreamily.

I think the three of us together added up to the perfect marriage, and he needed all of us in order to have a balanced life. Of course, he paid a high price for achieving that balance, for attempting to satisfy the needs of three women. I know I'm echoing the jokesters when I say I'm not surprised he had a heart attack.

Now that John is dead I have to admit that I was tired, too. Tired of being the puppet master. Tired of playing God of John Taylor's world. Even God needed the seventh day to rest. Every once in a while, amidst the chaos, and grief, and guilt, I feel a deep sense of calm. I was—am— ready for the next phase of my life to begin. Without John.

35

Samantha

WE FINALLY HAVE A BREAKTHROUGH.

All parking lots and street parking in downtown Palo Alto, near the Westin, have two-hour time limits. I'd instructed Mollie to dig up tickets given to cars that had exceeded the two-hour limit on the afternoon and evening of May 10. It was a long shot, but you never know.

Mollie found forty-three tickets from that Friday starting at 4 PM and ending at 10 PM for the streets surrounding the Westin. I go through the painstaking work of tracking each ticketed car to its owner, and calling each of them. Mostly I get voicemail, and leave messages. But one of the names sounds familiar: Thomas Johnston. A city address, in the Mission, in San Francisco. Then I realize: MJ Taylor has a brother named Thomas, and her maiden name was Johnston. We have a match.

Thomas Johnston has a full head of bushy black hair and black eyebrows, deep brown eyes. He strides into the police station clearly incensed. I notice him immediately. Despite his dark coloring, and darker expression, the resemblance to his blond sister is striking: the same long face, the widely spaced cheekbones, the pointed nose. You'd know they were related without being told.

He does not meet anyone's eyes as he's shown to my desk, where I'm still going through the rest of the tickets. I lead him to an interview room, offer to get him a glass of water. He refuses, and sits down. He looks as if he hasn't shaved in a week. He is not unattractive, despite all this. With his delicate, almost feminine features he is a pretty, pretty boy.

"I don't know why you asked to see *me*," he says as I turn on the video recorder. He's slouching in the chair.

"You are your sister's alibi, at least for part of the evening that John Taylor was killed," I say. "Yet there's the matter of this ticket, which puts you quite near the scene of the death at 6:27 PM." I can smell his unwashed body. This is not a man who takes care of himself. Repulsive, really. Yet I think of MJ's lifelong devotion to him. The age difference must be roughly the same as the one between Gregory and myself. But MJ took on the role of protecting and nurturing her brother, whereas mine needed to be protected against me. My on-again, off-again shrink tells me this was because my parents had created a "safe" environment. *If the emotional situation had been riskier for either you or your brother, you would have clung together*, she's told me on more than one occasion. According to this philosophy, we would have been more devoted to each other if we'd had less love from our parents. I'm not sure I believe that. I still crush spiders with more force than I need to. I speed up when motorists are trying to merge. There is this streak in me that I must fight against, especially with Peter.

"So tell me where you were the afternoon and evening of Friday, May 10," I say.

Thomas glowers for a moment before answering.

"I came down to visit MJ," he says. "I knew she'd be at work until at least 5:30, but I didn't want to hit rush hour, so I started down early—around 3 PM. Since MJ wouldn't be home for at least another two and a half hours, I stopped in Palo Alto and walked around, went into a bunch of different stores. As it turned out, though, MJ was home, but I didn't know that, and by the time I got to her house, she was running errands. So I didn't actually see her until after 7:30."

"So can anyone verify your whereabouts between 6:30—the time you got the ticket—and the time you finally saw MJ?" I ask.

"I'm not sure. I wasn't watching the clock. It was probably after 7:30, but before 8," he says "And, no, no one. I was driving between Palo Alto and Los Gatos between 6:30 and 7:00. And after 7:00 I was waiting at her house, alone." He smiled at something then.

"What?" I ask.

"I had a key," he says. "It drove John crazy that I could—and did—walk into the house whenever I wanted. But MJ was adamant: Her house was my house."

"What about before 6:30? What were you doing?" I ask.

"I was just walking around downtown. I suppose you could ask in the stores if they remember me," he says. "I personally doubt it, but you never know."

We sit there a moment, looking at each other. I frankly don't know what to ask next.

"What was your relationship with John Taylor like?" I say, finally.

"Very friendly, the key notwithstanding."

"How friendly?" I ask.

"He was generous with money when I was out of work," he says. "I counted him as a true friend."

I'm surprised at this, at the thought that anyone would trust Thomas with money or friendship. "How much money are we talking?"

He pauses and appears to be calculating. Then he says, "Maybe fifty thousand over the years. More or less."

"John Taylor gave you fifty thousand dollars?" I ask. "It wasn't a loan?" Again, I'm incredulous. Such a ridiculously large amount of money—almost as much as I make a year.

"No," says Thomas. "Like I said, he was a very generous man." He then says, "All that generosity died with him, you know. I would be the last person to benefit from his death. Unfortunately, he was on the verge of giving me more money. Had promised me another 10k the week before he died. I've been kinda down on my luck lately. And I had an idea for a new business venture."

"Do you have any proof of this?" I ask. "Of the money given, or promised?"

"No," he says. "This was all a gentleman's agreement. John was that kind of person."

Something about Thomas, something about his sleek complexion and the expression in his wide-set eyes, makes him appear to be holding back, to have secrets. It makes me think that if I just poked him a little, in the right way, other stuff might come out, perhaps relevant to this case, perhaps not. So I decide to poke.

"Can you give me a list of the stores you visited on that Friday?" I ask. "Then I can check to see if anyone remembers you."

He smiles and nods before he speaks, apparently trying to give the impression of being eager to please, although he fails utterly. His affect has changed completely since he walked in the door. He's sitting straight up in his chair, is no longer glowering, but groveling. The very picture of a parasite, a weak stooge. I resist the urge to kick him.

"I remember, I can tell you now," he says. "The Apple Store is where I spent the most time. Then the bookstore. Then Starbucks, for a coffee. Then I figured it was time to go to MJ's, that she'd be home."

"Your ticket was given at 6:27 PM," I say. "If MJ got off work at 5:30, why would you wait so long to go to her house?"

"I didn't want to run into commuter traffic on 280," he says. "I figured I'd be happier sucking back a latte than sitting bumper to bumper for an hour and a half. I left Palo Alto at around 6:30. I must have just gotten the ticket when I got to my car. At that point, I whizzed to MJ's in twenty-five minutes."

"Only to find she wasn't there," I say.

Again, he nods. "Yes," he says. "She was out running errands."

"So between 7:30 and 8?" I ask.

He looks down at his hands and counts on his fingers. "Maybe around 7:45," he says finally. "Around then. I didn't look at my watch. But that sounds about right."

"But that makes no sense," I say. "Why not go straight down 280 from the city at 3 PM? You'd hardly run into traffic then. You had a key to the house, after all."

Thomas shook his head. "I didn't want to just sit around her house. Neither did I want to hang around Los Gatos. Palo Alto's more hip, more fun to hang out in."

"Tell me what you did in the Apple Store."

"I browsed the new hardware," he says. "I'm a graphic designer. I like to keep on top of it. That's partly why I needed more cash from John. To get the latest equipment."

"And after that?"

"I walked down the street to the bookstore—you know, the one in that converted movie theatre, with the courtyard. I love that store. So I roamed around the books for a while."

I lean forward. "And what kind of books do you read?" I ask. I'm going to take this slow.

"Mostly mysteries. Thrillers. Easy reads. Not like MJ. She reads the hard stuff, is in a book group that's always reading stuff that sounds incredibly boring. Actually, I ended up buying her a book while I was there, wish I could remember. Oh, I know! *Great Expectations*. She was thrilled."

He smiles, almost shyly. "Usually I'm on the receiving end with MJ," he says. "It was cool to be the giver for once." He sits back, looking pleased with himself.

"There's just one problem with that scenario," I say. I find, when it comes down to it, that I am genuinely unhappy at what I'm about to say, he seems so sincerely proud and affectionate when talking about his sister.

"What?" He sounds nervous.

175

I say, as gently as if speaking to a preschooler, "The bookstore closed two months ago. That amazing old cinema site is empty. For lease."

He's silent.

"So now can you tell me again why your car was parked in downtown Palo Alto from at least 4:30 PM to 6:30 PM?" I ask.

"I really did go to the Apple Store," he says, and he sounds desperate. He is pulling at his shaggy hair, you can see the tension in his shoulders, and how his feet are shuffling against the tile floor. "I really did look at the new iPad there."

"And then?"

"And then . . . I . . . I had an appointment," he finally spits out.

"With whom?"

"I can't say." This he says with a determined stubbornness.

"Even though it would give you an alibi for a murder?"

Silence again before he says, "Is there some way you can promise me immunity if I tell you what I was doing during that time?"

"Immunity from being charged with another crime?" I ask. This strikes me as funny and I involuntarily laugh, but stop when I see his face.

He doesn't answer.

"I think you better fess up. What were you doing on the afternoon and early evening of Friday, May 10?"

"At five o'clock I was in the Apple Store. Like I said. It was after that I had my . . . appointment. Then I went to MJ's."

I raise my eyebrow at this.

Then, in a rush, he confesses, "I was buying weed from a guy I know. My dealer in the city had run dry, referred me to a guy down here."

I'm quiet. And now he's sitting up, acting like someone who has confessed. I have to ask someone whether I can hold this statement against him. It's on the record. But really, I couldn't care less. We don't go out of our way to bust marijuana users. On campus, we'd have to lock up half the student population. I'd estimate that half the profes-sors have their own stashes. I'd naturally done my share of smoking at undergrad parties, but truthfully I didn't like the way it made me feel, and hadn't indulged for years.

"I'll have to determine what to do with this information," I say fi-nally. But it rings true to me in a way the bookstore story hadn't.. Much easier to see him scoring dope from a connection in some run-down student rental house. There are dozens of them downtown.

"Okay," I say, and start doing the math. "Even if your sister can vouch for you from 7:45 on, and even if it would take you twenty-five minutes to get to Los Gatos, that still leaves fifty minutes unaccounted for during the critical period. In almost the exact location of the crime, from 6:30 to 7:20."

He looks genuinely scared. "I didn't kill John," he says. "I have no reason to. You have to believe me."

Oddly enough, I do. He strikes me as cowardly, but not violent. I'm quiet for a minute. Then I get up and turn off the video recorder. "That'll be all for now," I say, and dismiss him.

I sit in the chair he's just vacated, still warm from his body, and sigh deeply. I don't know what to think. But it's the first crack in the seemingly impenetrable walls of this case.

36

MJ

THOMAS WAS SUMMONED TO THE police department yesterday. They didn't say why. That worried me.

The thing is, Thomas doesn't know how to stop talking. When he was brought into the principal's office or police station as a boy on suspicion of something he hadn't done, he often confessed to another crime he *had* committed. The police in Tennessee knew that, and exploited it shamelessly. He also ratted out his friends frequently. Not on purpose, but because he couldn't stop blabbing.

What makes me the most anxious is that I won't know by questioning Thomas what he actually said. He always considered himself at the top of his game during talks with authorities, sort of a sly verbal Robin Hood who hoodwinks them at every turn. So when I called him this morning and asked him how things went yesterday, he said "fine," and believed it, too. Now I wait fearfully for the next call from that young detective. She projects the innocence of a fawn, but is quite sharp. Not much gets past her.

When I heard she'd called in Thomas I finally took her advice and hired a lawyer. I didn't know how to go about it, so I just picked the firm with the biggest ad in the Yellow Pages. This is costing me four hundred dollars an hour. I've already spent more than a thousand because he needed time "getting up to speed," and I told him my worries about Thomas going to the police alone. He asked if I wanted him to accompany Thomas, and I hesitated until I did the math. Given travel time, that would probably be another cool thousand dollars, so I said no. I need to conserve every penny I have for the mortgage.

Then the lawyer told me Thomas didn't have to go in, unless they issued a subpoena, but that it's best to cooperate as much as possible. "Unless he's hiding anything, of course," he said, as if casually, but he was probing, I could tell. "Thomas has nothing to hide," I said, and hung up. Another hundred dollars wasted, as he bills in quarter-hour increments.

37

Samantha

"YOU CAN'T BOOK HIM, YOU can't really touch him, without more evidence."

This is Grady speaking. I told him about the parking ticket, and he watched the video of Thomas's interview. We're sitting in Susan's office, conferring.

"I don't think he did it. But he's lying about something," I say. "You can tell. Look at the way he shifts around. And every time he's caught in a lie he makes up a new one. You can practically see him pulling these stories out of his ass."

"What do you imagine he knows?" Grady asks.

"I dunno. Something." I know that sounds weak.

Susan finally pipes up. She's been keeping me on what she calls a tight leash, asking for daily updates, and encouraging me to make use of Grady's expertise. "Sam, that's not how it works. We don't charge someone until we feel we have a good case. Otherwise, the DA's office is just going to throw it out. All you have are suspicious circumstances and weak circumstantial evidence. I'm afraid you'll have to keep digging."

I'm frustrated. I turn to Grady. "What would be compelling enough evidence to bring this guy in?"

"Fingerprints at the scene."

I shake my head.

"An eyewitness that places him *at* the Westin instead of only near it." Grady says.

I shake my head again.

"There was a major conference getting started," I say. "Registration was in the lobby, and a cocktail hour spilled out of the meeting rooms to take over the entire first floor of the hotel. No one saw anything. We've been going down the list of attendees and showing them pictures of MJ, Deborah, Thomas, even Helen, although supposedly she was four hundred miles away. Nothing. Everyone was half bombed and looking to get laid, not exactly a noticing mindset."

"What about the potassium chloride?" asks Susan. "Did that lead you anywhere?"

"It was just like Grady told me," I nod toward him. "Google it, and it's everywhere. Of course, you need a prescription, even for pets, but all the wives were in close proximity to prescription pads. I've checked all the local pharmacies. Nothing. . I've also put calls in to the top mail-order Canadian pharmacies online, but all are refusing to release customer records. And, since it's a different country, I don't have any leverage."

"Helen would have easy access to it at the hospital," Grady says. "Don't discount that. She would also have the knowledge."

"Yeah, but I Googled *murder* and *heart attack* and about a hundred sites came up that advised using potassium chloride."

"Either this country has a lot more murderers than I imagined, or everyone is writing a detective novel," says Susan. "I suspect the latter is true." She pauses for a moment, then asks, "How long does it take someone to die after they've been injected with potassium chloride? Did your research tell you that?'

"In sufficient amounts, it can cause nearly instantaneous death," I say. "Apparently, though, a person can survive for a little while if the injection isn't enough to kill them immediately. They'd feel pretty awful, though."

Susan taps a pencil against her Diet Coke. "Okay," she says, dismissing me. "Keep us in the loop, Sam. You're doing good work. But if we don't get a break on this case soon, I'm going to call in the Santa Clara County detectives. Those boys have been itching to get their hands on this since the beginning. This is too high profile to go unsolved."

38

Helen

THEY SAY THE PRESENT IS rooted in our past. Perhaps. Perhaps I was con-
ditioned from birth to fall for a fraud such as John. Me being so well
trained by my father to accept both abuse and affection from the same
person. It is a mortifying thought. But then I have this child growing
inside me. Yes, I keep reminding myself. *This is real*. It is a true source of
joy. Unlike the past.

When my mother was pregnant with my little sister, I was old
enough—there were nine years between us—to sense her ambivalence
about being pregnant at 42. My father would alternately rail at her to
get an abortion, and lay his head against her belly, even when it was
too early to feel the baby move. I wondered how she could take such
badgering, but she maintained her calm throughout.

My mother was a librarian at the Minneapolis public library, and
would take me to work with her. I was always a good child. She could
trust that I would do my homework, then safely amuse myself in the
stacks. Occasionally she would stick her head down the row of shelves
where I would be sitting cross-legged, reading, and smile. The legions
of homeless people who would eventually overtake the place had not

yet shown up. Those were magical hours. No worries about my father storming in, kicking the book out of my hands or, worse, appropriate it and force me to listen to him read it out loud. His voice was raspy, hard on the ears. John's voice was so different, so soothing, so *rational*. And yet John turned out to live the crazier life.

My father was highly educated, and charming, and loving. Most of the time. But then he would change. Something would trigger his temper and he'd rise and heave the kitchen table over while we were trying to eat. We'd have to wipe mashed potatoes and meatloaf from every crevice in the kitchen. Later he would weep and beg our forgiveness. Once I began my medical training, I realized that of course he could have been helped by medication. But back then I just accepted it—life had provided me with a gentle, caring mother and a violent, caring father. What I know now to be the toughest combination of all. What it has done to me is my own secret. I don't turn over tables, but I do have a temper. On those rare occasions when I lose it I am filled with remorse and suffer for days. I only allow myself one apology, though—I will not be my father, begging for forgiveness. Dignity is essential. I leave the room to prevent myself from groveling before the person I've injured, the unfortunate nurse or orderly or, on a rare occasion, the parent of a dying child.

But my father the weeping tyrant never exercised any restraint. He was president of a midsized pipe manufacturing company in north Minneapolis. I'm sure he was good at what he did; he exuded competence and authority outside the house, and seemed to have been able to control his moods while at work.

I prefer to remember my father as a reader. That was why my mother the librarian had fallen in love with him. He would rhapsodize about Proust or James or Wharton. He was always quoting poetry, and indeed I learned early on that reading to him from the poems of Emily Dickinson could calm him down, could delay or even prevent the fits of rage and melancholy. Studies have shown that a good dose of poetry, spoken at the right time, can impact the same parts of the brain as the pills we use to medicate bipolar patients today.

My father often slipped into quotations so easily and so naturally that you wouldn't realize he was quoting at first. Not that he was trying to fool you. No. His thoughts just moved so quickly that he sometimes had trouble footnoting them. Most of what he would recite was melancholy. I frequently had to fight back the tears. But I did fight because I knew it was important not to give in to the sadness—or the frustration for that matter. I would not, I was resolved, end up as my father.

So why did I choose pediatric oncology, what one professor in medical school said was the "saddest of all the professions"? Not out of any altruistic ideal to save children, although that is what I passionately try to achieve each and every day. No. It's about stopping the cancer. Winning the battle. A place to focus my anger. For it's always there, the rage, underscoring everything I do. You don't choose pediatric oncology without that rage. You'd die of sadness, otherwise.

About my poor mother, my father was fond of quoting Henry James:

Three things in human life are important: The first is to be kind. The second is to be kind. And the third is to be kind.

Yes, she was kind. Her kindness defined her, yet it didn't always come easily. She had her demons, too. You could see her struggling sometimes, not during my father's *temper tantrums*, as she called them, but at other times, when she fought against the tedium that was women's lot in those days. The librarian's role, although it kept her near her beloved books, was too limiting for her. She had a larger mind than that. Still, her familial challenges consumed most of her mental and emotional strength even though she dealt with those challenges with kindness and more kindness. The only sign that she was struggling was sometimes a slight hesitation before fulfilling the demands of my father, and, I'm now ashamed to say, me. I was a selfish child.

Still, kindness, for my mother, was a discipline. That didn't make it any less authentic. She was not faking it, she was not manufacturing it, she was calling it up from some place deep inside her that otherwise never saw the light of day. My mother was a complex woman.

I say this because it all played into my decision to go into medicine. So my own deeply ambitious soul wouldn't feel thwarted. I also knew I needed a way to channel my anger against a more formidable foe than a bipolar husband. And to practice my own brand of kindness in the midst of my own rage.

My father once shared with me a quote about anger by Aristotle.

> *Anybody can become angry—that is easy, but to be angry with the right person and to the right degree and at the right time and for the right purpose, and in the right way—that is not within everybody's power and is not easy.*

That could stand for my life's work: to channel anger to its rightful spot. In the battle between anger and joy, to give joy the better odds. But all I can think of right now, as I lie here trying to sleep, trying to empty my mind, is a quote from *Medea:*

> *The fiercest anger of all, the most incurable,*
> *Is that which rages in the place of dearest love.*

39

MJ

JOHN ENCOURAGED ME TO GO visit my father—my mother was long dead by the time we married. But he always refused to come with me, said he couldn't get away. Didn't even let me send any photos of our wedding that included him. My father was puzzled by the beach ceremony. A marriage without a proper priest? Without a wedding dress? Without a dinner and dance afterward at the veterans' hall? To him, it didn't seem like John and I were married properly at all.

But I'd already done the priest, white dress, and potluck dinner and dance at the VFW with my first husband, Brian. It was where everyone had their wedding receptions in Gatlinburg. If you didn't know how to polka, you had the good manners to sit down until everyone had their fill of the Doghouse or the Bird Dance or was too drunk to stand any more. After the polka band put away their tubas and clarinets, the real party band (hired by the couple's friends rather than parents) would start warming up, and the older folks would let the younger generation take over the floor. This was what everyone expected, and me and my few friends from high school hadn't the courage to wish for anything more, or different.

My wedding to John, in comparison, was idyllic. On the beach in Santa Cruz, by a hippy friend who had gotten his minister's license from a crackpot website as a joke. My bridal bouquet was made of wild rosemary that grew out of the cracks of my apartment building's parking lot in San Jose, where John and I lived until we found the house in Los Gatos.

John always struck me as singularly upright. Except for the photo disagreement, he didn't give any indication that he was on the lam from his real life. He would look anyone in the eye, and give the sort of handshake that indicated he was as upstanding as they come.

These days, my embarrassment and guilt lay heavily upon me. A lifetime of sins accumulating. I can't look anyone in the eye, not even strangers. I have trouble swallowing, and drink gallons of water for my dry throat. I glance in my rearview mirror more than is necessary. I shake out my shoes to find out what's secreted itself inside them. Most of all, I hide from those who know me well.

I felt this way after I ran off with Paul and Jackson still in diapers. Ashamed of my cowardice in stealing away without notice, I stayed away, not corresponding with anyone but Thomas. I never saw my mother again. I always wondered what she would have thought of who I became when I reached California—the real me, I'm convinced. Braless. Shoeless. Free of ponytail holders and bobby pins and belts. My mother was so different. Everything about her screamed restraint, from her shellacked hair to her girdle to her closed-toe shoes; even in the summer, she wore heavy shoes, even in the shower she wore a shower cap, even out of the shower she wore a robe rather than run through the house dripping in a towel. She whisked away your clothes to the laundry the minute you took off a blouse or a skirt, and it would be washed, dried, and folded neatly in your drawer while you were still searching the floor for the last place you'd dropped it.

Then she died. Dying back home while the boys were twelve and thirteen, and we were scraping things together down in Santa Cruz in that house we shared with two guys who considered themselves surfers first and students second. Mother love. Gone like that. And it was years before John, before I felt loved again and redeemed by that love. All false, as it turned out, John as duplicitous as any run-of-the-mill adulterous husband. As for me, chalk up another failure to be ashamed of.

The surfers always had the radio tuned to one obscure Santa Cruz station that played coded music for the surfers on where to find the waves. That was the year of secrets. The secret waves. My secret affair with a married father I'd met while gassing up my car between taking the boys to football practice, soccer practice, swim meets. Thomas's secret boyfriend, who really wasn't such a secret. And the secret my mother kept of her illness. She had been prone to bouts of sadness her whole life, and I think the breast cancer diagnosis must have felt like a relief. Two months after burying her, my father moved in with a widow from Pigeon Forge.

That was my last experience with death before John, a mother so sedated that she didn't realize I'd been gone for eleven years when I called. She would say hello drowsily into the phone, her morphine dialed up as high as it would go, so I never really had a chance to say goodbye to her, either.

40

Samantha

SUSAN SAYS I NEED TO start showing some progress. Says she's seen this before, a growing obsession as success eludes, and that it's unhealthy for the officer and unproductive for the department. "Sam," Susan says, "another two weeks and I'm pulling you off this case."

I go back to my desk and click on one of the videos I found online of Dr. John Taylor. Educational videos on websites devoted to disfiguring birth defects or trauma: www.abeautifulchild.org and www.nomoredefects.org. I'm not interested in watching the surgeries themselves—surprisingly, a fair number of these have been videotaped. Rather, I watch and re-watch the classroom lectures accompanying them.

I fast-forward through the clinical scenes until I get to the point where Dr. Taylor is standing in front of thirty students, explaining techniques for fixing cheiloschisis in infants. It is a beautiful thing. He ignores the camera. He makes eye contact with students, and uses his large hands as a ballet dancer would use her whole body, to express what is inexpressible in words. I watch his face in particular. He doesn't look like a man who would lie to women. I hit pause and go to the Taylor

Institute website and click on another video. It is required viewing for all men and women undergoing cosmetic procedures in his clinic. Dr. Epstein, when I interviewed him on the same day I interviewed Dr. Kramer, told me it discourages almost 20 percent of prospective clients. He did not sound happy about it. I'd asked him if they continued showing it to prospective patients after Dr. Taylor died. "No," he said, firmly. "The partners agreed it was no longer ... expedient ... to do so."

"By partners, you mean yourself and Dr. Kramer?" I asked. "Yes, the remaining partners," he said.

In the video, Dr. Taylor is sitting at a desk. He looks directly at the camera. "Before you undergo this procedure, I want you to know some facts," he begins. He talks about the trauma to the body due to breast augmentation, facial sculpting. He talks about the odds of procedures going wrong. He talks about percentages of women unhappy with the results. He gives statistics about self-esteem: Only 29 percent of women feel better about themselves one year after the surgery. "Rhinoplasty is the exception," he says. "But body contouring, thigh lift, tummy tuck—the gratification is fleeting." He stares deeply into the camera for his wrap-up. "If you have confidence issues, if you feel unattractive or unlovable, plastic surgery is not for you. It will not change those basic personality traits. You will only see more imperfections, want more improvements. Your body is not clay to be molded to your specifications. It is a gift. Treat it as such."

The first time I saw this video, I described the procedures to Peter. He was repelled at the idea of a body lift, touched my insubstantial right breast and said, "But you are perfect the way you are" or some such nonsense. That is a lie. I am not perfect; I am not even *regular.*

Once you watch the *before* and *after* videos of Dr. Epstein's and Dr. Kramer's patients—the ones who saw the video but were not dissuaded—you do begin to look at yourself differently. This pinched inch of excess flesh, wouldn't it be nice if this disappeared? As you grow older, wouldn't it be nice to reverse the inevitable sagging? I am twenty-eight years old and imperfect enough to avert my eyes from the mirror when I get out of the shower. How will I feel when I'm thirty-nine? Fifty-nine? Peter and I rarely go to LA but when we do we're struck with the billboards advertising cosmetic procedures the way that Silicon Valley billboards advertise the latest technology advances. This is the future. Dr. Taylor had his finger in the dam trying to hold back the flood.

He appears to be a man you could trust. Here is a man who had your interests at heart. I would imagine that many of his patients' mothers fell in love with him. But as you watch the competent, straight-talking yet compassionate man in the videos, you know he would never take advantage of the emotionally charged situations, would never prey on his patients, or feed on their vulnerability. This is not a man who would cheat on his wife.

I wonder what I would feel, sitting in the clinic, considering an arm lift or body sculpturing, listening to Dr. Taylor's attempts to stop me. I think I might fall in love with this bear of a man, would gladly join his harem for his eyes to light upon me and stay there for even a moment. That would be enough.

I notice that he is not wearing a wedding ring in any of these videos.

The phone rings. It's Peter.

"What time you coming home tonight?" he asks. His voice is neutral, which is his way of saying he's sorry. We had a fight last night. He said I haven't been "present," that I'm not there in the room, not listening when he speaks, not responding when he touches me. Perhaps it's true. This case has cast a spell over me. I have the obituary from the *Chronicle* out on my desk. I'm looking at the photo of John Taylor as a young man. Very handsome. A light emanating from the eyes half closed in a mischievous smile that borders on lascivious. I've heard that women fall in love with their doctors, and now I see why. Really, who wouldn't have been at risk from John Taylor?

"I'm not sure," I tell him. "I'm working."

"On the Taylor case," he says flatly.

"Yes, of course. It's my case. Susan is already talking about bringing in homicide experts from San Jose. I want to solve this on my own."

"All right," Peter says and hangs up. I go back to watching videos. I understand now that Dr. Taylor had chosen a happy profession. The worried and anxious looks at the beginning of each procedure always gave way to smiles, hugs, and handshakes at the end as the parents viewed their sleeping but altered child. If Dr. Taylor had ever failed at surgery, it wasn't recorded. His failures lay elsewhere, apparently.

41

MJ

I'VE BEEN THINKING A LOT about our honeymoon, mine and John's. I realize now, of course, that it was done with Deborah's permission, that she must have even made the reservations. If she did, she chose well. I hate fancy hotels, chichi resorts. I've been to Hawaii, Honolulu, stayed at the Hilton, hated every minute of it. The chlorinated pools, the air of forced frivolity, the people chattering, not to each other, but into their cell phones. *Parallel play*, that's what it was called when I was raising my boys, all children go through it. Now it seems as though adults have regressed into it as well.

John and I went up north, to Ukiah, to Vichy Springs, a 150-year-old hot springs resort in the hills. The room was small but clean, no television, no electronics of any kind. You couldn't even get a signal on your cell phone, we were so remote. We sat on the deck outside our room and watched an ancient dog totter after the wild turkeys that ranged over the property. At night, after the other guests were asleep, we snuck down to the mineral baths and filled two of the iron tubs that are positioned next to the spring, under the stars, to the brim with the warm, fizzing water. It was like bathing in hot champagne. Against regulations we shed our clothes, no bathing suits, and lay in the tubs naked staring at the stars. Afterwards, we wrapped coarse towels around our bodies and ran through the cool air back to our plain but clean room.

The sex was okay. I mean, I've had better. John and I were more comfortable with each other fully clothed, preferably with garden implements in our hands and dirt on our knees from planting hydrangeas: mopheads, lacecaps. Whatever motivation John had for marrying me, it wasn't for the sex.

Did this bother me? At first, maybe. One does fantasize about passion, about being the object of desire. But I was soon reconciled to it. We were so happy! At least I was. *Happier than a hungry tick on a fat dog.*

How can I describe how it felt to be shopping for houses with John! Looking at places with price tags of one million, two million dollars and more, casually dismissing each until we found the special one in Los Gatos.

At a glance you wouldn't know why we loved it so. Just another California rancher, the pavement cracked from the Loma Prieta earthquake, the front yard a mess of brambles and tall grasses. A rat scurried out of the bushes as we walked up the path for the first time. But then we saw the backyard, encompassing two full lots, with hillocks and knolls that undulated to the property line. In the corner a legacy oak tree, at least two-hundred years old, spread its limbs in every direction. We counted two fig trees, a lemon tree, and two persimmons. In another corner, a tangle of blackberry bushes. All surrounded by a high fence covered in scarlet bougainvillea. John had tears in his eyes. Now, after seeing Deborah's tightly disciplined, clean-edged landscaping, I understand. No one would be invited (or tempted) to sit on her manicured lawn. No dog would dare shit there.

John and I rarely fought with each other, but I remember one heated argument about something silly. About all things, a hibiscus bush I had trimmed too closely. He came home from a Saturday afternoon grocery run, and I was helping him put everything away when he looked out the window at the area of the garden I had been working in. He released an anguished wail. "What have you done?" He happened to be holding a carton of eggs, which he lifted above his head and hurled with all his strength at the wall. Eggs spattered over the counter and floor. "I told you to leave that alone," he nearly screamed. I was in shock; I'd never seen this side of him before. I didn't remember him telling me anything about the hibiscus, and said so. This made him even more furious. He raised his voice, his face red. "I don't expect much of you, MJ," he said. "But I do expect you not to mess with my garden." I was crying at that point, but he just slammed out of the house, got into his car, and roared off. He was gone four hours, where he went, I'll never know. He was calm when he returned. He did not apologize, though. We never spoke of that incident again, but it made me tread more cautiously around him than before. And that he called it *his garden*. Not *ours*. Never ours.

42

Samantha

IN ONE OF JOHN TAYLOR's videos I spotted Snow White—that young doctor I met at the Taylor Institute—among the students in the lecture hall. Everyone else was furiously scribbling, taking notes, but not her. She simply sat there, her notebook open, her pen untouched beside it, her hands folded on top. Her eyes never left John Taylor. It could have been funny; instead it was creepy. Then there was one half second where he looked straight at her. His face remained expressionless, and he glanced away without haste though also without lingering. I thought *so that's the way it was.* And I picked up the phone and called the clinic to invite Dr. Claire Fanning to stop by. I kept my voice casual when talking to her, but I didn't feel that way. I knew I was on to something.

Snow White—Claire—said she couldn't meet me until 9 PM, when she got off her shift. So here I am still at the station house at 9:15, hungry and cranky and yet not particularly eager to go home and see Peter, either.

I don't like being alone here at night. Of course, I'm not completely alone. The night dispatchers are on duty in their office, but the door is closed, and they have their own isolated world that they reside in. At this time, the regular station house takes on an otherworldly feel, what with all the dark screens, the low lighting, the chairs left akimbo as if everyone had departed in a panicked stampede. Susan is usually the last out, but at 7:30 PM she sighed, packed her stuff, and left. I hate being at work this late. Actually, I'm unhappy to be most places after 9 PM, that's why Peter and I are such homebodies. Around 8:30 I start looking for a pair of pajamas to put on.

This Claire, on the other hand, I doubt she ever sleeps. Despite telling me she couldn't meet until after work, when she shows up, she is wearing workout clothes and has clearly been exercising, there is perspiration on her neck and arms.

"I thought I'd get in a run between the hospital and here," she says, by way of explanation when she sees me eyeing her getup, but she's not apologizing. In fact, it's more of a boast. "I'm preparing for the Hawaiian Ironman, so I have to grab every opportunity I can to train."

I find I'm in no mood to hear more about her exercise regime. "Please sit down, Dr. Fanning," I say, and point to the seat next to my desk.

"Call me Claire," she says.

I nod. "And Sam for me," I say. Even though we met previously we shake hands and it feels oddly formal, like we are entering into some contract.

"I have something to tell you about John Taylor and myself," she says, without preamble, and without waiting for me to ask anything. Despite the perspiration and her admission that she'd been "training," she's surprisingly not out of breath or showing any sign she has exerted herself.

"That I figured," I say, and then I nod and cross my arms. Clearly, this Claire is not stupid, so she must see the look on my face. Because I'm sorry. When a young attractive female mentions she has something to say about an older male colleague in a position of power, you just know what's coming. I didn't even need to have seen the look exchanged in the video to realize that. I say to her, "You're going to tell me you were sleeping with John Taylor."

She doesn't blink. "Yes," she says.

We sit there looking at each other.

"Why did you wait this long to tell us?" I ask.

"I didn't think it was relevant," she said.

I don't have to give this much thought. Her words hang between us, clearly false.

"What changed?" I ask.

"This did," she says, and holds up the copy of the *Chronicle* with the results of the inquest declaring John Taylor a victim of foul play.

"But that article, and the media firestorm, happened weeks ago," I say. "Why wait?"

"I wasn't sure I wanted to be involved," she says. "Precisely because of the . . . firestorm. I had to consider carefully what to do. I'd be involving myself in a mess that could impact my professional and personal life for years to come." She says this very coolly, without showing any emotion. This doctor doesn't have much of a bedside manner.

"Okay," I say, but I still don't uncross my arms. "So you finally decided it was your civic duty to talk to me. Fine. That means you believe that the fact you were sleeping with John Taylor was important in some way?"

"No," she says, and shakes her head emphatically. Her thick black hair swings across her cheekbones. I feel a stab of envy of her beauty.

I lay my hands down on the table. "Hello? Isn't that what you just said?"

"No, that's what *you* said. There's another reason you should want to talk to me."

"What's that?"

"I was John Taylor's fiancée."

Really, you could pick me up from the floor.

"What?" I say. "*What?*"

Claire nearly smiles, but composes her face. "Yes," she says. "And I knew about all the others."

"You knew?"

"Yes. Part of our deal was that he would divorce Deborah and sever ties with the other 'wives' to marry me."

I sit quietly, trying to absorb this.

"Did anyone know?" I ask.

"Only John and me," she says.

I attempt to gather my thoughts. Whatever else I'd figured might come up in this case, another woman was not among them.

"Don't you have some questions for me?" she asks.

If Claire is trying not to show disdain, she's not succeeding. What I mean is: I feel her disdain. She isn't hiding it. I notice again just how black her eyes are, how black her hair, against that pure white skin. And that extraordinary composure. Is there some injection that medical students take to get that damned mien of superiority? If so, she's been fully inoculated. I want to scream at her, curse, anything to break that composure.

Instead I speak calmly. "I'm still puzzled why you would hesitate to come forward with your fiancé dead under mysterious circumstances. Weren't you concerned to have justice done?"

"We hadn't yet gone public with our relationship," she says. "And it would have seemed . . . cheap . . . to have added to the circus. Not until it became clear that foul play may have been involved was I even remotely conflicted about that part of it."

When it's apparent she isn't going to say anything more, I ask, "And how long were you . . . lovers?" I hate that word, it sounds so smarmy coming out of my mouth, but I can't think of another one.

"Almost from the start. He was my professor. The nature of the relationship means we spent a lot of time together, with me shadowing him on cases. One afternoon it just happened."

"At the clinic?" I feel like a dirty-minded voyeur.

"In the beginning. There were private places there. Then we went to my apartment, off University Avenue. We couldn't go to his house, for obvious reasons."

"So you knew he was married?"

"Of course. Although for a time I thought Deborah was the only wife."

"I'm sure you understand that I need to know the details of where you were on Friday night, May 10, between 6:30 and 8 PM," I say.

"That's easy," Claire smiles. "I was at the clinic. I finished my last case at four, and I was catching up on John's paperwork. He'd been letting it slide. And he'd asked me to be a coauthor on a couple of papers. I was preparing them for peer review. You can ask the night guard in the building. He comes on duty at 6 PM, and I didn't leave until after 9 PM."

"I'll look into it," I say. Then I pause. I have to know.

"What, exactly, did you see in him?" I ask. "He was, what, well over twice your age? Not in the best of shape. Married. Why take him on?"

Claire laughs, a genuine laugh, the first true sign of emotion I've seen in her. "John Taylor was the most magnetic man I've ever met," she says. "He was genuinely interesting, and genuinely interested. In the world, in others. You inhabited a private space when you were with him. It was quite remarkable. *He* was remarkable."

"What was his rationale for having an affair? I mean, before you became engaged?" I hope my voice doesn't betray my . . . scorn? Envy?

"He spoke of his loveless marriage, of his wife needing to keep up appearances, and his need to protect her."

"The usual crap, in other words," I say, wanting to get a reaction out of her.

"Yes, the usual crap," Claire agrees. She is not disturbed by my words. I doubt anything would throw her off.

"So how long did it take to get beyond the usual crap?" I ask.

"Not long," she says. "He asked me to marry him after about a month. He said he loved me, that we could build a life together. I believed him."

"So when did you find out the truth?"

"What truth?"

"That he had more than one wife to dispose of?"

"Oh *that*," she says as though it was of no consequence. "When he proposed, he told me everything. It didn't matter."

"So you knew? Like Deborah?"

"No, not like Deborah. I knew *everything*. She didn't know about me."

"You're certain of that?"

"From the way John described Deborah, I can't imagine she would know and not want to get her hooks into our relationship, to stage-manage it the way she did the others. But our relationship couldn't be manipulated or controlled in that way."

"So when on earth did the two of you have time together?" I ask. The thought of three marriages, three households, was dizzying. But a fourth? Madness.

"On the job, between procedures. On weekends, when he wasn't in LA, or when MJ and Deborah thought he was at a conference, or on call. We made the time."

I am beginning to digest this news. It changes everything. Everything. I need to go over the transcripts, see what the wives told me, assess it in this new light.

Claire breaks into my thoughts. "There's something else you should know," she says.

"What?" She is driving the interview, not me. She's staying two steps ahead while I trail behind.

"I think I was the last person to see John alive. Other than the hotel people and the murderer, of course."

I snap to and realize that this is a valuable witness, and she is volunteering valuable information. I need to capture it instead of sitting here gaping. Better yet, I have to seize control of the conversation. I scramble through my bag for my recorder, raise it up to get her nod, and turn it on.

"Tell me about that last week, the week he died," I say. "We know his movements up through Thursday morning. When he left Deborah's house that morning. After that, no one could trace him."

"He was with me. We got into a fight. We'd met for coffee before going into the clinic, and I told him off. I felt he wasn't going to go through with it, that he'd lost his nerve. I threatened to tell Deborah myself. Later he called MJ and Deborah and said he'd been called down to LA. He didn't go in to the clinic that day or the next, but came to my apartment. He stayed Thursday night with me. And then Friday, when I went home during my lunch break, we got into another argument. We were both tired, it had been a long week. We weren't faring particularly well in my apartment, which is a small studio with barely enough room for a bed and desk. I left to go back to work, and when I came home he was gone. I didn't know where, but suspected to one of his wives. I was furious. And that was my state until I read about his death in the Sunday paper."

"So it was you who called the *Chronicle*, who spilled it to the press about the three wives."

Did I see a shadow of shame cross that perfect face?

"Yes," she says finally. "It was an impulse. I don't usually act on impulse. And I regretted it immediately."

I can't figure out Claire. The rest of John's women I have more or less fixed in my mind. I see the relationship that each of them had with him, and each one makes sense to me, in an insane sort of way. But not Claire.

I have this theory about people. I can't think of them as weak or strong personalities, I find that useless in terms of categorization. Under such a system, conventionally, Deborah would be considered the strongest, MJ the weakest, and Helen somewhere in the middle. But I don't think of MJ as weak; I think of her broad shoulders, her height, and her large hands and intensity. Underneath that scattiness is a real person. The same applies to Helen, and dare I say it, Deborah. Perhaps that's what I mean. *Real people.* John Taylor married three real women. He sure knew how to pick them.

But this Claire? I find I'm disappointed by John's choice. You look at her delicate beauty and you understand why any man might consider pursuing her. But it's still a disappointment. I've built an impression of John Taylor, I realize, and it doesn't have anything to do with marrying young china dolls less than half his age.

"Do you have a way to prove your relationship with Dr. Taylor?" I ask Claire.

She holds out her hand. An exquisite, and very large, diamond ring is on her fourth finger. At least that's what it looks like. It could have been just glass given my untrained eye. I have the feeling I'm supposed to *ooh* and *aah* at the size. I merely nod. I've found that being silent when I'm unsure goes a long way to making people think I'm not as stupid as I feel.

"I wasn't allowed to wear it in public before," she says. "Now it doesn't matter." She isn't expressing sadness when she says this. Odd. Her perfect face reveals nothing.

"You could have bought that yourself," I point out.

"I thought you'd say that," she says. She opens the small backpack she was wearing and produces a receipt. A credit card receipt for a diamond ring from Haynes Jewelers, in San Francisco. Even I've heard of them. *$75,000.* Paid for by John Taylor on his American Express. Talk about a sugar daddy. Fifty thousand dollars to MJ's brother Thomas. Seventy-five thousand dollars for a ring to a would-be fourth wife. This boy was leaking cash all over town.

"Do you have any witnesses who can verify what you're claiming?" I ask.

"Of course not," she says. "We were keeping things under wraps."

"No one from the clinic knew?"

"There were the usual rumors," she says. The disdain is back in her voice. I don't appreciate disrespect.

"Why *usual*?"

"I've found that office gossip often links me to the men I work with," she says. Then, interpreting my look correctly, she says, "Falsely." Then, as if describing her professional qualifications she says, "An attractive young woman in a mostly male field. This sort of annoyance comes with the territory."

"I wouldn't know," I say.

"Oh, it's true," she says, not wishing to acknowledge my snarky tone. "There were rumors about John and me simply because we worked together quite closely. But no one had any proof."

"So you believe," I say.

"Has anyone else even hinted that we had a relationship?" she asks.

She has a point.

"No," I admit.

I attempt to take back the reins.

"John was with you Thursday and then Friday morning. But why did things come to a head that particular week? What forced the crisis given things have been, if not calm, at least in equilibrium, for some time?"

"We were preparing to make the announcement to the other," she pauses, "women that Saturday. May 11."

Now there's emotion in her voice. It is definitely scorn when she says *other women.*

"How did you think these women would react? Helen Richter is a doctor with an impressive CV," I remind her. I don't know why I feel the need to defend the three original wives, but I do. "Deborah was his real wife for thirty-five years, and MJ"—I search for the right words and come up with "MJ is a force of nature." I've ended weakly and know it.

"If one of the wives had been suspicious, that would give you a motive to work with, right?" Claire asks.

"Do you have any reason to believe that one of them did suspect?"

"John was very jumpy Thursday night. He kept checking his phone for voicemail, texts, emails. When I asked him what was wrong, he just shook his head. He told me he was worried. But actually he seemed more scared."

"Why didn't he go to work on Thursday or Friday?" I ask her. "Was there anything going on at the clinic that he wanted to avoid?"

"I think he was just overwhelmed. His wives, and then there was this tension with his partners," says Claire. She says *partners* the same way she says *wives*: with what I now recognize as her trademark disdain. "They wanted to hire more surgeons, expand the cosmetic practice. John was adamant that the clinic stay true to his original vision."

"So he might have been avoiding them?" I ask. I recall Dr. Epstein's perfect cool demeanor. I wouldn't put much past him.

"I don't know. John canceled all his appointments for both Thursday and Friday," says Claire. "Highly unusual. More than highly unusual. Extraordinary. Unheard of. I think it showed how anxious he was about the pending announcement on Saturday."

"Did he pick up anything from either Deborah's or MJ's houses?"

"No. He was in hiding."

"What did he do about clothes?" I ask, testing her. "He didn't keep any at your apartment, did he?"

"No. He was never there long enough. When I got home Thursday night, he'd been to Macy's and bought some slacks and shirts, other necessities," she says. "That way, he would have a few things if it went really bad on Saturday. We were already looking at rental listings for apartments since we couldn't possibly live in my studio for long."

I'm at a loss what else to ask. I'm tired and my head aches. I reach out and turn off my recorder. "That's enough for tonight," I say. "But I'll almost certainly have more questions for you."

"Of course," she says, gets up from her chair, and leaves the station house, her pale shapely legs flashing in the overhead lights.

I pick up my recorder and turn it on again. "Holy mother of God," I say into it. "Do we have a situation *now.*"

43

Samantha

I RARELY GO TO STANFORD MALL, despite passing it every day on my way to work. It's full of high-end stores like Neiman Marcus, Bloomingdale's, and Ann Taylor, alongside the usual Macy's and Victoria's Secret. There's one fast-food joint: a McDonald's for the rich Palo Alto parents who haul their spoiled children around town in Mercedes and Lexus SUVs. Otherwise, no mall food, no hotdog or pretzel stands, no cheap jewelry stores for teenagers. Once I made the mistake of going into a tea shop. It had smelled heavenly from outside, and they were giving samples of some amazing-tasting pink-tinted tea. I asked for half a pound, thinking Peter would like it. Once wrapped and packaged as if it were a gift for the queen, it was rung up, and my jaw dropped. I had to decline. It was the end of the month, and I didn't have that much money in my bank account.

Mollie and I walk over to the Macy's men's store—and sure enough, easily find Jenna, the saleswoman who helped Dr. Taylor with his purchases. She turns out to be about thirty-five, dressed in the requisite black pants and white shirt, a little overweight, but carrying it well. Her posture is superb, and her outfit impeccable. She screams fashion know-how and good taste. On a different salary, I would take her advice to outfit Peter.

She remembers Dr. Taylor perfectly. "At first, he declined my assistance, but then after wandering around for about ten minutes, he came up and confessed he hadn't shopped for himself in years," says Jenna. "I took him for a recent divorcé, perhaps a widower, because he seemed rather sad. He told me he was looking for a couple of serviceable pairs of pants and shirts. His size being on the large side, I had to go to the back room to find items that would fit. He was grateful, easy to please. I actually tried to dissuade him from one of the purchases, I felt it wasn't exactly flattering, and suggested a pair of pants with a different cut. He said no, bought the other ensembles and left. He seemed to be in a hurry."

"What about the second Macy's charge?" I ask, looking at the Amex statement. "Same day, just after he bought the pants and shirts." The woman shrugs. "He probably had also purchased things from another department," she says. "Do you have the transaction number? I could type in the code." She scrolls through a screen. "It seems he purchased something downstairs, in our 'necessities and accessories' department."

"That figures," says Mollie. "He probably needed pajamas or underwear."

"So what do we do with this information?" Mollie asks.

"To a large extent, it bears out what Claire says. We know he was staying somewhere close by, although not going to work," I say. "And that he somehow felt the need to buy clothes rather than stopping by one of his homes to pick up a few things."

"But couldn't Claire be lying still?" she asks. "What if he just bought these on a whim? What if he *did* go home? To one of his wives? That Claire, and the wives, all of them, could be gaslighting you. They could simply be lying."

"All of them?" I ask, with my eyebrows raised. Then, without waiting for an answer, "We did check with Deborah's neighbors, and none of them remembers Dr. Taylor's car parked in front of the house after Thursday morning," I remind her. "Ditto MJ's, although I'm less inclined to think they would notice. The houses are further apart, and there's more foliage." Then I shake my head. "I think this goes a long way toward validating Snow White's story."

We walk slowly to the car, when we hear someone running behind us. It is the saleswoman from Macy's. She is out of breath, her chest heaving. "I just remembered something," she says. "When he was looking at himself in the mirror with the new pants and shirt on, he murmured, half to himself, 'need to get a haircut, too.' I teased him a little. 'A big day coming up?' I asked. 'You could say that,' he answered. He said Saturday. I told him I hoped it was something fun, but he shook his head. 'No,' he said. 'But quite momentous all the same.'"

44

Samantha

WITH CERTAIN ASPECTS OF CLAIRE'S story now confirmed, I decide to
confront the wives again. I settle on Deborah first, since she lives closest. Then I'll try to catch MJ. Unawares, I hope. I consider what to do
about Helen. I want to deliver this particular news in person to experience her reaction firsthand, gauge how honest it is. The sooner I talk to
Deborah and MJ, the sooner I can fly down to LA. But there is the risk
that Deborah or MJ will call Helen and preempt me.

Of course, I have no hard evidence the wives are in contact with
one another. But in my notebook, written at 2 AM, are the words *Are
the girls talking?* Some humming of wires seemed to connect them;
they each seemed to have soundlessly absorbed whatever information
I had given the others. There was nothing I could put my finger on. I
just had the feeling that resources were being shared, defenses mutually
bolstered.

Deborah is home. She answers the door, as always impeccably
dressed and groomed. I ask involuntarily, "Are you going out?" because
of her shoes: boots this time, elegant ankle-length leather ones. Then I
remember, she's a shoes-on-in-the-house kind of gal.

"No," she says. "Please come in." She doesn't actually sigh, but I keep expecting her to. I notice she skirts the edges of the rugs as she leads me into the living room. I deliberately step on them with my sneakers, mud-stained from a bike ride through the hills.

She offers me coffee, but I decline. I won't let her get the upper hand this time. Today Deborah has adopted a resigned air. Like some-one patronizing a small child.

"I was wondering if you know a woman named Claire Fanning," I say as I sit down. I pull out a photo of Claire that I had grabbed from the station house's security video camera last night. Even with the poor phone-quality image she comes across as an exotic. The concubine of an emperor.

Deborah shows no reaction whatsoever. "The name sounds famil-iar, but I've never seen this woman," she says.

"She worked with your husband at the clinic," I say. "She was doing a fellowship at Stanford, and your husband was her mentor and professor."

"That may be where I heard the name," Deborah says. She seems disinterested. "John may have mentioned her. He often talked about his students to me."

"Claire was more than a student, at least according to her." I'm watching Deborah carefully for any sign and am reading nothing. Ei-ther she is a tremendous actor or she genuinely has no idea what I'm about to spring on her.

"Such as . . . ?" Deborah asks.

"A fiancée."

"Impossible." Deborah is emphatic. She is so quick to react she almost speaks before the word is out of my mouth. "John would have said something. He told me everything."

"According to Claire, they somehow managed without you," I say. "They flew under the radar by telling you John was in LA a bit more than he actually was. They changed the tickets and the schedules. Not very often. But enough to get involved. Deeply."

Deborah is unmoved. "It's impossible," she says again. "John was not capable of fooling me."

"There's more," I say.

Deborah simply raises her right eyebrow.

"According to Claire, he was going to divorce you, tell MJ and Helen the truth of their relationships, and marry her," I say. "He was going to announce this on Saturday, May 11. The day after he was killed."

Deborah is stone-faced. "And what proof do you have other than the word of this . . . medical student?" she asks.

"She has the engagement ring, and the receipt for it, which was paid with John's credit card."

"Which card? I pay all the bills. I would have seen it."

I pull the copy of the Haynes Jewelers receipt and hand it over. Her face falls slightly as she sees the name on the receipt, the account number. "This is not a credit card I know about," she says, finally.

"Then, perhaps there are some things you don't know," I suggest. I get the feeling that I must tread more gently now. Deborah has projected nothing but strength since I first met her, but the façade may crumble if the blow is calculated precisely. I don't think that coming at her too forcefully will work. Easy does it.

"She also has an explanation for his disappearance before his death," I say. "According to Claire, he was with her from Thursday morning until Friday lunchtime. They argued both days, and on Friday he left and checked into the Westin. She didn't know where he went— just that he'd left her apartment. But she was in possession of other facts she wouldn't have unless her story was true."

I can see that Deborah's face is white under her makeup. Her hands are neatly folded on her lap, but I detect trembling.

"In one sense, all this is moot, of course," I remind her gently. "John is dead. He did not divorce you."

Silence.

"Still," I continue, "this provides me with motives that previously I didn't have."

Her eyes turn up to my face. She is expressionless again. "You mean me."

"Yes," I say.

"And how would that motive work exactly?" she asks.

"Well," I say, choosing my words carefully. "If your husband really intended to divorce his wives . . ."

"*I* was his only wife," she reminds me.

"Okay," I concede. "Divorce *you*, and break the news to the other two that they weren't really married, that would upset quite a few people."

"By *quite a few people* you mean MJ, Helen, and myself," Deborah says.

"No, others too," I say, thinking of Thomas, but I decline to elaborate.

More silence.

"Well, if you're asking if I did it, the answer remains no, and I presume my alibi still holds," she says. "Unless something has caused you to reevaluate the time of death."

"No," I say. "The physical evidence hasn't changed."

"Then I have nothing more to say," Deborah says. I take this as a dismissal, and rise to go.

"Wait," Deborah commands as I'm halfway out of the room. I stop and turn around to look at her.

"You might think you understand what's going on here," she says. "But you don't."

I open my mouth to protest, but she waves at me impatiently to be quiet.

"He was comfortable with our arrangement," Deborah says. "Me and the girls, that's how I thought of them. It wasn't a rivalry, it was a supportive network; we were his connective tissue. We were a living, breathing organism, one that was thriving. John would never threaten that, not something so carefully nurtured over the years."

I don't like not being treated like a grown-up. I make my face impassive. I don't go into my usual head-nodding routine that is a habit when people in authority speak to me.

Deborah frowns. "I expect to be believed in this," she says.

"*Whatever,*" I say. I walk out of the room.

45

Samantha

"THIS IS GOING TO SOUND strange," Grady says, "but for now I would ignore the alibis."

He's sitting on the corner of my desk. This morning, Susan came by and congratulated me on the case finally beginning to move. "A fourth woman, eh?" she asked. "Too bad this John Taylor is dead. I'd like to nominate him for Man of the Year." Still, despite my leads, she'd like me to consult with Grady before I take the next step.

"I'm confused," I say to Grady. "If two of the three most plausible suspects had absolute proof that they were elsewhere at the time of death, how could they commit the crime?"

"Alibis can be faked," he says. "Times of death can be manipulated. Motives are harder to cover up."

"But the alibis for Deborah and MJ are very solid," I tell him. "Multiple reputable witnesses in each case. Helen is a different story, as is MJ's brother."

"Then question the time of death," he says. "I'm always most suspicious in cases where the alibis are foolproof right when someone is supposed to have died."

He starts pacing the room. "So what about Helen? You haven't discounted her, then?"

"Well, Mollie checked, and no Helen Richter left LA on any of the airlines from any of the local airports on that date," I say.

"What about driving? After all, she had a twenty-one-hour window to do the twelve-hour round trip between LA and San Francisco and easily bump off her cheating husband in the process."

"I know," I say. "I've subpoenaed the security camera tapes from Helen's parking garage and the condo building's entrance. I should have those in the next few days."

"And even then, will you have covered all entrances to the building? Could she have gotten out a back way and rented a car or otherwise run off to San Francisco?" Grady asks. "Don't give up on Helen. She's my personal favorite front runner."

I laugh. "You wouldn't say that if you'd met her," I say.

"In the meantime, work on the other two," says Grady.

I'm not happy with his advice. "What should I do, keep calling them back in for questioning? Ask them where they were every minute of Friday? I've run out of questions, and they've noticed."

"Don't be shy about asking them the same things again," Grady says as he turns to leave, "and study the transcripts. Something will appear. Someone will crack. Something will shake out. It always does."

46

Samantha

I KNOCK ON THE DOOR. No one answers, so I knock again. And yawn, tired from last night. Peter's friends came over, we played Scrabble and drank too much wine, stayed up until 2 AM arguing about whether *armpit* and *brainpower* were valid words. Our version of debauchery: drunken wordplay. I woke with a hangover, and I welcomed the thousand tiny knives of a cold shower.

It's one of those days that you question everything. *Why am I in Palo Alto? As a member of the police, no less? Why Peter? Why not any other of the twentysomething males littering the valley?* The arbitrariness of stuff sometimes gets to me. *Why this car? Why this pair of jeans? Why this life?*

I knock again. Still no answer. Yet a car is in the driveway. It's 2 PM so I doubt MJ is sleeping. A bright Saturday, not too hot, the perfect early August Northern California day that is now becoming a year-round phenomenon thanks to global weirding.

The house is a nondescript California rancher, distinguished from the rest on the block only by its air of tired neglect. The grass on the front lawn is parched and yellow, the mailbox appears to be nearly falling off its pole, and the pavement leading up to the house is cracked and uneven. The car in the driveway is a late model Toyota Prius. Of course it is. And the yard probably hasn't been watered to conserve natural resources. I know my neo-hippies.

I also know that despite the outward look of this property, the price tag would be substantial. I'm standing on some of the most expensive real estate in the world. The fact that many of these aging multimillion-dollar ranchers are bought and then scrapped to make way for custom-built mansions—no prefabricated McMansions, not here—speaks to all the money that surrounds us.

I knock one last time, not expecting a response. Then, because I am loath to make the long drive back to Palo Alto without accomplishing anything, I begin exploring. Walking to the right of the house yields nothing, just a high fence. I get luckier on the left side. A gate is set in the wooden fence that apparently encloses the entire backyard. It isn't locked, so I click open the latch and pull.

And am stunned by what I see.

Talk about a garden of earthly delights. The colors: a wild profusion of deep reds, purples, yellows. The smells: subtle and soft and aromatic. And the sounds: bees and other insects humming quietly but insistently, the breeze causing slight rustling among the leaves.

A third of the garden is in shade from a magnificent oak tree that spreads its boughs for thirty feet in all directions. The ground underneath is carpeted in blue. Tiny blue flowers, as thick as grass. The other two-thirds of the garden enjoys bright sunlight, and the high fence that surrounds it is completely covered with a brilliant purple flowery vine. Trees bursting with lemons, oranges, figs. I've never seen anything like this. I'm in paradise before Adam gave names to any of the flora or fauna, before Eve bit into the apple.

In the middle of it all, kneeling, is a woman, at first glance almost naked, the muscles in her gleaming strong shoulders working as she plunges a trowel into the earth. When my vision clears I notice she's wearing a kind of flesh-colored sarong that leaves one shoulder as well as most of her legs and thighs bare. Her long gray-blond hair is down and in loose ringlets. Her breasts are spilling forward. A magnificent earth mother. She hasn't yet seen me. *No wonder John Taylor fell in love with her,* I think, and am ashamed that my opinion of her had previously been so small, so narrow-minded.

"Oh!" She spots me, and is rising to her feet, holding her sarong up to cover herself more thoroughly.

I hurry to apologize. "MJ, I'm so sorry. I rang the bell and no one answered."

She nods. The slightly anxious, guarded look I recognize from our first meeting appears and I feel terrible to have conjured it up in the midst of this beauty.

"How can I help you?" she asks. She is still holding the trowel, which is coated with rich brown soil. I can smell it from where I stand.

"I just have a few more questions," I lie. "Nothing important. Wrapping up loose ends." I see her visibly relax and again shame slices through me. I don't deserve to be trusted.

"Come inside. It'll be cooler there." I follow her into the kind of house I dream about. Comfy overstuffed chairs. Colored walls hung with vivid posters and old black-and-white photographs. No cut flowers, but lots of leafy plants.

"You went to Berkeley?" I ask, pointing to a classic protest poster from the 1960s, beautifully preserved and framed.

"Actually, San Francisco State," she says. "It didn't matter, though. By the time I got to the Bay Area all the fun was over," she laughs. "I should have been born a generation earlier." She motions me to sit at the kitchen table, which is of bleached pine, and pours me a glass of water from the tap.

"People still find plenty to protest today," I say.

"Yes, but there's a different vibe," she says, and is silent for a moment. "I grow flowers now. That's my protest against what's going on in the world."

"Your garden is amazing," I say, and mean it.

She relaxes more. Then she says, "Let me show you something."

I put down my water and follow her back outside, into the garden, past the oak tree to the sunniest corner. It is closed off by four-foot walls, with just a small gap to walk through. We enter the space. At first I think that the air is full of tiny scraps of paper, confetti perhaps. All different colors of paper, chaotically swirling around me. Then I understand: butterflies. Flitting amidst the bushes and flowers, arcing over our heads. One even alights on MJ's bare shoulder. A butterfly garden. I've heard of these, but never experienced it firsthand.

"This was John's favorite spot in the garden," she says, pointing to a bench in the midst of the riot of colors and beating wings. "He always said something I never fully grasped. Not until after his death." Her face clouds over. "He said he needed this chaos. That everything else in his life was too regulated."

I'm silent for a moment. "That's what happens when you take on three wives," I finally say. "Regulations."

I ease myself next to her on the bench in the sun. We sit in almost comradely silence. If I'm not careful, I could easily fall asleep here, drugged by the heat and beauty.

"What will happen to the house?" I ask. "Can you afford to keep it?"

She starts. I've touched a nerve, apparently.

"It depends," she says. A black and orange butterfly lands on her arm. She absentmindedly touches its wing and it flies off.

"Houses in Los Gatos aren't cheap," I say. "Did John buy it?"

"He put down the deposit. Then we paid the monthly mortgage out of our joint funds," she says.

I'd done a quick online check before coming here. This old 1940s unimproved rancher is worth a cool $2.6 million on the current market. They'd bought it for $2.2 five years ago. Not a ton of appreciation compared to the boom real-estate years here in the Bay Area a decade ago. But not too shabby a profit for just living in a place, either.

"So how much is your mortgage?" I ask her.

She visibly squirms.

"About 500 k," she says, not looking at me.

I can't help it. I whistle. "John made a $1.7 million down payment?"

"Yes," she says. "He wanted the mortgage to be manageable in case anything ever happened to him."

"Well, is it?" I ask.

She avoids my eyes. "Pretty much," she says, but I'm thinking that accountants, even in Silicon Valley, don't end up at the high end of the wage scale.

I admit to being fascinated with money. Well, not for money itself, but how people acquire and spend it. Having so little myself, I'm always wondering about this when I see people driving expensive new cars or dining in the pricey restaurants that line the streets in Palo Alto. Or how they afford those houses, for that matter. According to a local realtor I'd buttonholed at a party, the tiny house Peter and I squeeze into would sell for a cool million. Of course, no one would actually buy it to *live* there. It's what they call a "scrapper" in these parts, and Peter and I dread the day our landlady tells us she's cashing out.

"I know you're on shaky ground," I tell MJ. She looks startled, so I add, "legally." She sighs deeply. "Deborah could conceivably claim this house as a part of John's estate that she's entitled to."

"I've consulted a lawyer. Deborah would have to sue me in civil court. She's assured me she won't go to the trouble," says MJ.

"Why not? $1.7 million plus whatever equity has accrued in the past five years is a lot of money," I say.

MJ shrugs. She looks unhappy. "I think she sympathizes with me. I think she knows that my life is shattered enough," MJ says. "I couldn't give this up." *This* being the garden. Of course she couldn't. But somehow I don't see Deborah as an altruistic benefactor. I wonder what her game is.

"I mean, I'd just *die* going back to a small townhouse or apartment," she says. "For the first time in my life I have a real home. This means everything to me."

So she would die for it.

Would she kill for it?

I bring out Claire's photograph. She shakes her head and waits for me to explain.

I quail a little inside, but start.

"We have reason to believe that Dr. Taylor intended to marry this young woman, and . . . separate . . . from the rest of you. Start a clean slate with a new wife. A real wife, like Deborah was."

A long pause.

MJ stares at me, her face impassive. "Well?" she asks.

"Do you understand what I've just said? Dr. Taylor intended to leave you. All of you. Supposedly he was planning to break the news on May 11, the day after he was killed. He never got the chance."

MJ surprises me. Deborah had greeted the news with her usual reserve and stateliness. Frankly, I expected histrionics from MJ. Instead, something crystalizes in her, right in front of my eyes. Is she sitting up straighter? Looking at me more directly? Tensing her jaw? Whatever it is, I honestly have no clue whether MJ had known about Claire. She isn't descending into hopelessness or panic. She isn't falling apart, as I would have expected. Rather, she appears resolute. As if she's preparing to fight a battle.

"Do you want to talk about it?" I ask her. But she's shut down, as if she's closed the door on old adversaries, of which I am one.

MJ begins pulling the flowering buds from the basil plants clumped at the base of the bench. She does so with expert hands, as if snapping off little green heads. A deft assassin, I think, and suddenly feel uncertain. The afternoon is still. No noise except for the drone of bees. The butterflies flitter silently around us. We're so far from main roads I don't even hear any traffic noise. I can't remember the last time I'd been in a place without the hum of cars. I see certain possibilities in MJ that I hadn't before. A ruthless hardening within. She snaps off another bud and I think again, *assassin.*

"Why should this change anything for me?" she finally says, not looking up. "He'd already gone and married someone else, so I was already betrayed once. Why does another betrayal matter?"

"It *is* different," I say. "With Helen, he had no plans to leave you. You still had your life together, your house, your garden. But if he'd gone through with marrying Claire Fanning, you could have been left with nothing."

"You're saying I have a motive for killing my husband," she says, and the air is so charged I actually find myself wondering whether I 'd put my gun on that morning. Then I think, *crazy.*

"Yes," I say. I see now that any warmth I felt toward MJ was just stupid me wanting to be liked. We are opponents, have been from the start.

"You have my alibi. I assume you've confirmed it," she says.

"Yes, but . . ." I hesitate, knowing that what I'm about to say might be even more unwelcome than the news about Dr. Fanning.

"But my brother has none, right?"

"How did you know?"

"He called me. What did you think, that he would keep it a secret? From me?" She laughs, and it is a harsh sound.

"Don't think about going after my brother as a suspect," she says, and it is a warning—a command, not a plea. "You won't find anything to hold against him except that damn ticket. So my brother is a pothead. You'll look like a fool in court." The unspoken phrase was, *even more than you do now.*

"I'm tired of going over and over the same stuff," she says. "You keep hounding me and asking me the same questions."

"Actually, Claire Fanning is a new topic," I say, and she turns on me fiercely.

"I told you, *I didn't know about this so-called fiancée.* And what would I have done if I'd found out? While John was still alive? Why kill him, ha-ha. Seriously, I would have been pissed. Or as we say back home, *really riled."* She exaggerates her Tennessee twang. *Reely rawled.* "And after I got over being angry? Then . . . then . . . we would have had a long talk. I know that makes me sound pathetic. But it's really no different from finding out about the other wives, about Deborah and Helen. My husband's other women. So what if there was one more?"

I catch movement at the entrance to the butterfly garden. Thomas is here. He comes forward quickly. He is frowning. I see what looks like genuine concern on his face as he sees his sister.

"What's going on here. *What have you done?"* he hisses at me as he gets closer. I stand up, and move away from the bench. He takes my place, puts an arm around MJ. She doesn't shrug it off so much as repel it with the same force that is sending me away.

I quietly make my exit. Two down, one to go.

47

Deborah

TODAY IS MY BIRTHDAY. I'M fifty-five. I must say, I don't feel it. I don't feel *middle-aged*. If I had to choose my age based on how I felt, I would say thirty-five, no older. Still alert. Still physically nimble. And certainly my desire for physical intimacy hasn't gone away with age the way I would have expected. This is something that John and I talked about, oddly enough, just a couple days before he went missing. We always chatted in the early mornings when he came home, showered, and grabbed some breakfast. I insisted we sit down together, to have coffee at least. "Don't you miss sex?" he'd asked. We never lost the ability to communicate easily about what others might consider difficult subjects. Well, of course I miss it, I told him. Of course. And then he reached out his hand and tried to touch—no, caress—mine. I was holding my coffee cup. His fingertips brushed across my knuckles. I couldn't help it, couldn't stop myself. I recoiled, so fast I spilled hot coffee on his fingers. The fact is I didn't want him anymore. Not *him*. Whatever compatibility we'd had in that way was long gone. Replaced by something other than indifference, something darker. Bitterness, perhaps.

John surprised me then. I usually can predict every move. I know that sounds grandiose, but it's true. Still, that morning I was taken aback when he pushed his chair away from the table. He then very deliberately walked to my chair and stood behind me. I tried to see what he was doing, but he had his hands anchoring my shoulders so I couldn't move; I could only turn my head, which gave me a sideways view of his rather expansive chest. My cheek scraped against the buttons on his shirt, and I felt his breath on the back of my neck. It was incredibly unnerving. Then he took his right hand and, reaching over my shoulder, placed it on my breast. I immediately slapped it away, of course. But the feel of his hand lingered. He'd managed to give my nipple a slight pinch and I felt that most of all. I was enraged, but the anger was shot through with shame, and if I could have cut off my breast in that moment, I would have. Anything to erase the feel of that unyielding palm, that burning pinch. The brute. The brute. By the time I had composed myself, he was gone, out the door and to the hospital. And good riddance, I thought.

48

Samantha

SUSAN RELUCTANTLY OKAYED ANOTHER TRIP down to LA. I insisted that I needed to talk to Helen face-to-face, confront her with the idea of Claire Fanning in person. So here I am on United Flight 42 to LAX, jammed next to a middle-aged older man who started out the flight working on an Excel spreadsheet, but is now playing Spider Solitaire. He swears loudly when he can't find a solution and has to reshuffle. I find myself thanking God for Peter, who only opens his laptop when he's ready to bang out another chapter of his dissertation. *Be grateful for small things,* I tell myself. Even if those chapters are slow to come. Peter seems to be making an effort recently. He even packed for me, and when I opened my purse to get my driver's license out for airport security, I found a bar of dark chocolate with almonds in it. I almost drove home to give Peter a kiss.

When I reach the UCLA hospital, I have to show my badge about ten times. I suppose that means the media are still trying to get through to Helen. I think of Claire. *If they only knew.* Especially if they managed to get a photograph of her. That face would sell a lot of magazine covers.

When I knock on Helen's office door, it is opened almost immediately by a woman with a blond pixie cut.

"I'm here for Dr. Richter," I say.

She laughs. "Sam," she says. "It's me." Now I recognize her, but barely. And it's not just the hair. Helen also appears younger and much less serious—like a schoolgirl, lighthearted.

"Well!" I say.

She ushers me into her office, which looks the same, the comfy chairs, the stuffed animals lying all over the floor.

"More about John?" she asks as she settles into her chair. She pulls a kind of black knitted shawl around her shoulders. It's too cool; the air conditioner is turned up high.

"I know," she says, catching me shiver. "We have no control in the offices and examining rooms, and they keep it chilly in the summer."

Summer. It's now mid-August. I can't think of another year where the summer has gone by so quickly, or which I've enjoyed less. Usually, Peter and I spend a good deal of our weekends and evenings outdoors at concerts and picnics. But this time all that has seemed to fall off the cliff. Or perhaps I simply haven't been paying attention due to the slow-moving Taylor case, and Peter hasn't been reminding me.

"What happened?" I ask, gesturing at her hair.

Helen smiles. "An experiment," she says. "One that turned out splendidly." It is only then that I see the slight bump at her waistline. After any number of social gaffes, my rule is to never ask anyone if they're pregnant unless I see an actual baby coming out. But this time I can't help myself.

"You're pregnant!" I gasp. She nods. "Is it John's?" I ask, then curse my stupidity. Of course it is.

We sit for a moment in silence. Helen doesn't seem to find the pause uncomfortable, but I am squirming in my chair.

"I thought you had a deal that there'd be no children," I say.

"We did," says Helen. "But life had other plans."

"Did John know?" I ask.

A shadow passes over Helen's face. "No," she says abruptly. "I never got the chance to tell him." She then changes the subject to signal that part of the conversation is over. "That's not why you're here. What do you need from me at this point?"

"It's about John," I say. "Or rather . . ." I hesitate. "About the situation." My mind is still reeling.

"Yes?" she asks, but doesn't really seem interested. She's looking extraordinarily healthy and happy, almost obscenely so in this room, which is likely viewed as a chamber of death by her patients' parents.

"Another woman has turned up." I say, and wait.

She laughs. Whatever reaction I'd expected, this wasn't it.

"Not another wife," she says.

"No, but someone who wanted to supersede all of you," I say. "A fiancée." Then, curious, I ask, "How would you have felt if John told you he wanted to end the relationship?"

She appears to give my question serious consideration.

"Before," and she pats her bump, "I would have been devastated. But now? I'm not particularly concerned."

We sit and look at each other. "And when did you find out you were pregnant?" I ask.

"Not until after John was dead," she says.

I consider this.

"I don't believe you," I say suddenly.

She smiles. "Well, I'm afraid you'll have to assume I'm the ultimate expert witness in this regard," she says. I'm struck by the fact that she seems to be treating this like a game.

"Your alibi is the most porous, you know," I tell her.

"Do you have any evidence against me that places me in Palo Alto? Hundreds of miles from home?" she asks.

"No," I admit.

"So I must have been particularly clever," she suggests. For the first time, I find myself actively disliking her.

"A man is dead," I say. "And one of you three almost certainly did it."

She smiles again.

"If you can guess who," she says. "You win the prize."

49

Samantha

"TALK TO ME, PETER," I say. "You've got three women, no, make that four women, all feeling extraordinarily possessive of the same man."

I've just returned from LA and we're having a lazy Sunday, of the type that used to delight us, sitting outside in our tiny patch of garden that borders the creek. It's almost sunset, and the cicadas are starting up but the mosquitos haven't come out in full force yet. The perfect time in what should be a perfect August afternoon. Yet Peter is mostly absent, playing some game on his phone. Not that I particularly *need* his attention. I'm half reading a library book, and thinking about the Taylor case. But I sense some hostility in the way he's holding his phone at arm's length—positioned precisely so it blocks my face.

Peter reluctantly puts it down when I speak. "And?" he asks. "'Possessive' is the word? I notice you didn't say 'in love with a man.'"

"You're right, I didn't."

"So what's the question?"

"You find out about these other women. You realize your existing life is basically over. Total wreckage. What do you do?"

"You're asking, does this make a woman crazy enough to kill her husband?"

"I guess," I say. "Yeah. Is it enough provocation? Forget about alibis, opportunity, whatever, for now. Just think in terms of motivation."

Peter stretches. His long 6'2" body overhangs the cheap deck chairs we got from some garage sale. He's taller than me by almost a foot and has a fairly massive amount of facial hair. I used to call him Sasquatch. We no longer have nicknames for each other, I think, sadly. Some phase of life has passed by while I wasn't paying attention.

"Give me before and after pictures of these women's lives, and I'll tell you who killed him," Peter says.

"Let start with Helen," I say. "She's the easiest, because she had the most independent marriage of the three. With John, she had the occasional companionship of a man she seemed to quite genuinely love. She sounded sincere when she described the relationship."

"And if this sexpot young doctor takes Taylor away from her?" asks Peter.

"Well, she loses that companionship. And from things she's said, I don't think she's had a lot of romantic attachments in her life. So that could be a real bummer for her."

"Not to mention the whole woman-scorned aspect of things," Peter says.

"Yeah, there's that. Female rage and jealousy." I say. "Bo-ring."

"That's the one who's pregnant, right?" Peter asks. "Making this guy a father from the grave?"

"Yes. And he wouldn't have been happy about being a father again," I say.

"She wants the baby, though? She's happy about it?"

"Absolutely," I say, thinking of the transformed woman I saw in LA.

"But her financial position doesn't change, does it? Presumably as a doctor she's raking in some pretty big bucks on her own. Enough to support a kid."

"She didn't need him financially," I say. "Not like MJ did."

"This MJ, she had the most to lose, right?"

"It depends on your values," I say. "She would certainly have suffered financially if Taylor left her to marry Snow White. She's now in a tenuous legal situation regarding the house. Legally, Deborah could make the case that the house belongs to her. Leaving MJ with nothing."

"Which brings us to my favorite wife, Deborah," Peter says.

"Why is she your favorite? She's the one that gives me hives," I say. "I kinda get MJ. And I have a healthy respect for Helen. But Deborah?" I stop talking.

"I'm just teasing," Peter says. "You stiffen up when talking about her, and your voice gets deeper. Unconscious mimicking."

"Deborah had the most to lose in the case of a divorce as far as her social standing in the community. That seemed awfully precious to her."

"What's interesting about that?" Peter asks. I see him glance back at his phone. I'm losing him. And here I am, trying to engage in a conversation, spend some time together. Anything to dispel the heavy silence that we've had between us all day.

"She also had the most to gain from the death," I say. "A ten-million-dollar life insurance policy. Hey," I say, louder, as he continues to poke at his phone, "I'd shoot you in a heartbeat if you had that kind of bounty on your head."

"I bet you would," Peter says without looking up or smiling.

I smack my hand on the end table next to my chair. My glass shatters as it hits the brick pavement.

"Goddamn it, Peter," I yell. A couple of crows that had been feeding on crumbs from our late lunch spun off into the air.

"What?" he asks. He finally looks up.

"You know *what*. You've been in such a mood. Out with it."

He doesn't speak for a moment. Then, "It's just all the cracks you've been making about marriage. The disparaging remarks."

I'm puzzled by this. My voice loses its heat. "Have I?"

"You've been pretty damn scornful of these women. You find something at fault in each of their ... marital arrangements. Well, if there's a perfect model for marriage, some ideal standard that none of these relationships meet, I'd like to know what it is."

I have to think about this.

"I don't think I've been scornful of Helen," I say. "I even admire her for carving out happiness under such extraordinary circumstances."

"Oh, great," says Peter. "You admire the woman who saw her husband once a month for two days."

"That was twice a month, for three days," I say.

"Whatever."

"And it isn't the time aspect of their marriage that interests me," I say. "It's the intensity of the emotional engagement."

"The passion thing again," Peter says.

"Yes! The *passion thing.* Which has nothing to do with sex, by the way," I say.

"So you've said."

"Peter, what do you want from me?" I bend down and start picking up the shards of glass. As I should have predicted, the sharp edge from one piece slices into my finger. Great. Bloody hands just as I need to start prepping dinner.

"Sam, the question is what do *you* want from me? I'm apparently incapable of rousing passion."

I stand there, my hands filled with broken glass. "Don't step in your bare feet until I get it," I say and go inside, discard the glass in the garbage, wrap a bandage around my hand, and return with the hand-held vacuum cleaner.

Peter is again playing with his phone. He's already over dealing with me. I stare off at the creek, at the manzanita trees that are darkening as the sun dips toward the horizon.

"Why don't we get married?" Peter asks suddenly. I see that he's sitting up straight. "Most of our friends have, and we've been together much longer than any of them. Last year, we went to so many weddings that rice got into the seams of my suit."

"It was the approach of the dreaded thirty. Everyone thought they needed to get serious."

"And don't you?"

"Not really," I say. "So much is still unknown. You have to finish your PhD. And find an academic job in a lousy hiring market. You know how that goes, Peter. You could be moving to Arkansas or Florida or Alaska. If you're lucky enough to even snag one of those."

"Are you saying you wouldn't come with me? To Arkansas or Florida or wherever?"

"Definitely not Arkansas," I say, "And Florida is plain weird." I'm trying to make a joke out of it, but I can see that makes Peter angry. "Look, Peter, I just can't commit to saying, 'Yeah, I'll follow wherever you lead.'"

"Your commitment problem. I know." His voice is deeply sarcastic.

"Hey, dude, I don't think it's unreasonable for me to not commit to being a barnacle on your ship when I don't even know if it won't sink." I surpass myself: a quadruple negative in one sentence. And as soon as I say this, I regret it. I'm well aware of Peter's anxiety over his dissertation, over the job market for PhDs—the last thing I want to do is exacerbate it.

His face tightens.

"Sam," he says, in a low voice, not looking at me. "What you don't understand is that we've got what people hope to have after the passion and initial excitement have burned out. We're best friends. It's what you want when you're fifty, sixty, and beyond. The marriages that last get *here*. After all the other stuff is finished. Where we were lucky enough to start."

"So you're saying we're already done with that ... *stuff*," I say. "Shit, Peter!" I'm speechless for a moment, which is good, because bad things are coming, terrible things. "Do you think I want to go through life missing one of the most profound human experiences there is?"

"And what's that, may I ask?" Peter says. I hate it when he gets sarcastic. It doesn't suit him, and it just about sends me to the moon in rage.

"Falling in love," I say. The cicadas have come out with the darkening sky, and now sound loudly in the silence that greets my words. I
slap at a mosquito. More blood on my hands.

"Well!" Peter says, and stops. He seems too choked up to continue,
but eventually manages to say, "That's a pretty damning statement."

I panic. "Peter, no, wait. Don't take it the wrong way."

"I don't think I possibly could," he says. "You were extraordinarily
clear."

50

Samantha

WHEN I GET TO THE station house this morning, I can tell something has happened. Grady is sitting at my desk, talking to Mollie, who seems terribly excited. Susan is standing next to her, the inevitable Diet Coke in hand. She's nodding and smiling.

"Way to go," says Grady when he catches sight of me. "Good police work."

I ask Mollie. "You got a hit?"

She is all smiles. "Yes! I was interviewing about the millionth person from that conference attendance list, and showing the photos, when this woman tells me, 'Wait a minute, I know *him*.' And pointed." Mollie grins. "Guess who?" she asks.

Susan breaks in. "No time to be coy, Mollie, just tell Sam." Mollie looks abashed for about three seconds, then says, "One of the doctors from the clinic. That Epstein guy."

"Is the witness sure?" I ask. I'm getting excited. After a sleepless night with me in the bedroom and Peter on the couch, I can use the good news.

"Absolutely. She rode the elevator with him to the second floor. She remembers him because he was a relatively short man with what she called 'wispy' facial hair. Apparently she can't stand small men with ineffectual beards. She was no lightweight herself, which is why I believed her. She probably could have eaten Epstein for breakfast."

"And he got off on the second floor?"

"Better than that. She got off, too, and happened to be staying in room 225—which is directly across the hall from John Taylor's. So they both ended up walking down the corridor in the same direction. Then, he fell behind her. She says she had the distinct impression he was dragging his feet on purpose."

"So she didn't actually see him go to John Taylor's door?" I ask, disappointed.

"No, but after she closed her door, she heard a knock, close by."

"Well, that's something," I say, and turn around to go right back out the door. I've got some questions for Dr. Epstein. "I'll keep you posted," I call to Susan.

"You do that," she says, and I know she is smiling.

51

Samantha

THIS TIME I KNOW HOW to find the entrance to the clinic. I nod to the security guard, but he still insists that I show him my badge. Must be bored. I certainly would be, doing nothing but sitting in a little booth, waiting for visitors. When I walk into reception, I'm told that Dr. Epstein is busy, so I settle down to wait in the plush waiting room. After an hour goes by, I approach Ms. Perfection at the reception desk. She lifts the phone and whispers into it. No, she tells me. Not yet. I go back to my comfy seat in the warm room.

Some time later I jerk awake. I'd been drooling while I slept, and my chin must be glistening with saliva. Embarrassed, I wipe it off with my hand and look at my watch. I was asleep for nearly twenty minutes. Enough is enough. I march up to the receptionist again.

"I must see Dr. Epstein *now*," I say, and flash my badge. "This is important business." She obeys me with such alacrity that I'm embarrassed, only this time at having meekly accepted her earlier statement that the *doctor couldn't see me yet*. She pushes a buzzer and waves me through the double doors. I know the way to Dr. Epstein's office. He's sitting in an easy chair to one side of his desk, reading a medical magazine. I curse myself again for not insisting on seeing him right away.

"Ah yes, Detective," he says, and reaches out to shake my hand. He doesn't bother getting up. I know it's petty, but I don't extend my hand in return. Instead, I let his hover awkwardly for two or three seconds.

There's a chair in front of his desk, but I remain standing.

"Dr. Epstein, why were you at the Westin in Palo Alto the evening of Friday, May 10?" I ask.

He keeps a smile on his face, and I remember what the witness had said about his beard. As a petite woman, I don't mind the fact that he is rather small himself. But coupled with facial hair that seems to be nine-tenths air and his general aura of complacency, I could see why the witness remembered him with contempt. He *is* annoying. You want to kick him just to jar the smile from those thin lips.

"You told me the first time we talked that you'd been at home that evening. Your wife backed up your statement."

"So why are you questioning it now?" he asks. He is still smiling.

"Because we have a witness placing you at the Westin, on the second floor, in the corridor of John Taylor's room, within the time frame that the death occurred," I say.

He is quiet for a moment, calculating. Then he shrugs. "Yes," he says. "I was there."

"What time precisely?"

"Around 7:40, 7:45," he says.

"And was John Taylor alive when you left?" I ask.

"No," he says.

I hadn't expected that.

"What?" I ask.

"No," he says. "John was dead. But he was dead when I arrived. I didn't kill him."

"You'd better come down to the station house," I say, "And tell us everything."

52

Excerpt from Transcript

Police interview with Dr. Mark Epstein, August 26, 2013

[preliminary introductions, explanations of police processes and procedures, notification that the session would be videotaped]

Mark Epstein: John and I had been arguing on and off for the better part of the previous month. Along with Edward—you know, Dr. Kramer. Edward and I were eager to bring on more associates so we could grow the business through increasing the volume of cosmetic procedures. John refused. But we felt very strongly that it wasn't fair to take us on as partners and then force us to leave so much money on the table.

    John hadn't shown up at the clinic for two days. It was quite unprecedented, really. Whatever the man's faults, he never shirked work. But he cleared his calendar with a call to our intake director, first Thursday morning, then again Friday morning. He wasn't answering his cell phone, returning any texts, or replying to his emails. I asked Dr. Fanning where he was.

Samantha Adams: Did you know they were involved?

Mark Epstein: Not officially. Though it didn't take half a brain to guess. They were always around each other, and although they never left the clinic together, each one always seemed to leave within five minutes of the other. But it was none of my affair. I didn't know about *all* the women, of course. Just that he was married to a woman named Deborah. And if that's the way he wanted to play it, who was I to interfere? So Claire—Dr. Fanning—told me he'd checked in to the Westin, and gave me his room number. Frankly, that surprised me. For two reasons. First, why would he check in to a hotel in his own hometown? And, secondly, why would Claire give me what was clearly privileged information? She always took John's side of things. But I took it they'd had a fight as well, and she was as frustrated with him as the rest of us.

Samantha Adams: Dr. Fanning willingly told you that Dr. Taylor was at the Westin?

Mark Epstein: Yes, that's right.

Samantha Adams: Please go on.

Mark Epstein: So I went to the Westin Friday evening after dinner.

Samantha Adams: What time was this again?

Mark Epstein: I told you, 7:40, perhaps a little later. I knocked on his door. There was no answer, but I noticed it was ajar. I walked in and found him, already dead, on the floor. It was quite a shock, I have to tell you.

Just then there was a knock at the door. I'd shut it all the way behind me, and whoever it was couldn't get in. I panicked. I thought, I can't be found here with a dead body, so I kept quiet. The knock came again, and this time a man's voice identified himself as room service. I held my breath and waited, and, after calling a couple more times, he went away. Once I was sure he was gone and the corridor empty, I left the room myself and drove home. I told my wife what had happened, and we agreed that there was no need to explain that I'd been there; it would only complicate matters. When we found out later that foul play was suspected, we felt it was too late to speak up.

Samantha Adams: You didn't struggle with John Taylor?

Mark Epstein: No! I'm telling you he was dead already!

Samantha Adams: How did you know he was dead?

Mark Epstein: I'm a doctor.

Samantha Adams: So you examined him?

Mark Epstein: Yes. I felt for his pulse. I was quite satisfied that he was dead.

Samantha Adams: You didn't inject him with potassium chloride?

Mark Epstein: *He was dead already.*

Samantha Adams: But with John Taylor dead, your way forward at the Taylor Institute was clear. You could expand the cosmetic part of the practice. You could take all that lovely money *off the table* as you put it.

Mark Epstein: Look, I know that sounded kind of flippant. Even callous. But that doesn't mean I would kill someone for a bigger paycheck!

Samantha Adams: What about the fact that your fingerprints weren't anywhere in the room?

Mark Epstein: Once I understood the situation I was careful not to touch anything. And I wiped down everything I had touched coming in, the door, the doorknob, the lock. I know, I know, that seems suspicious. But I was trying to avoid what is happening now—the police making a grave mistake.

Samantha Adams: Mistake or not, I've been instructed to book you for the murder of John Taylor.

53

Samantha

MARK EPSTEIN WAS NOT ARRAIGNED after all. We booked him, and he immediately got on the phone to his lawyer, who got on the phone with the district attorney's office. The filing deputy at the DA rejected the case as not having sufficient evidence to stand up in a jury trial, and sent it back to us with the instruction to get more proof.

This made Susan boil, as she had been the one who instructed me to arrest Epstein. Against my better judgment, I must say. I wasn't convinced it was him, and here's why: because he's so damn small. Not much bigger than I am, really. I couldn't see that he had the strength to overcome a large, heavy man like Dr. Taylor. In any event, we're back at square one, still looking for evidence. If Mark Epstein had been the killer, he'd been a clever one. If it's someone else, they're cleverer still. Either way, we don't have sufficient evidence to arraign anyone yet.

54

Samantha

I WOKE UP TODAY THINKING of Helen, about her pregnancy. *Was it intentional?* I wonder. A deliberate attempt to thwart John Taylor's edict against conceiving children? We'll never know. Would it be motive enough for murder, wanting to keep her child? That didn't make sense to me. Helen could simply have divorced John Taylor and had the child on her own. Although she possessed such an odd affect when I saw her in LA. And there is that issue of no alibi. My mind is going around in circles.

Peter and I have done this dance. Peter wanting a bunch of kids one day, me not being sure, naturally. Once we actually got pregnant, Peter and I. We took a chance one night after drinking too much, when we didn't have any protection in the house or any safe way to get to the store to buy some. We got totally busted. I missed my next period and there we were—still in school and facing early parenthood.

Nature took care of it. I was surprised to find out that 10 percent of pregnancies end in miscarriages. I got every symptom in the book: the morning sickness, the bloating, the mood swings. And then we didn't even have a chance to pick our jaws off the floor after the test revealed we were pregnant. The next day I started bleeding. End of the story. That night, in bed, Peter, trying to comfort me, placed his hand on my belly. But having those long fingers splayed out on my stomach repulsed me. As if he were probing for something. A center. My center.

Those twenty-four hours changed us. He began to truly long for grown-up status whereas I began pushing it away. I would have been up for the job of being a mother. But if I didn't have to be? I *celebrated* that mattress on the floor, and the mismatched dishes. So it brought us together briefly and established just how far apart we were. We didn't have to discuss it. Everything crystalized for us. Then we fell back into a rhythm: wake up, coffee, shower, work . . . but it was a different rhythm.

Poor Peter. Honest Peter. He's not really cut out for this tough world. He once found a wallet with five hundred dollars in it, and promptly returned it to campus lost and found. This was during our starving days, and well before I became an arm of the law. I didn't speak to him for three days.

But he's got such a big trusting heart. Really, Peter is a sweet man—I'd be hard-pressed to find a sweeter one. Yet he lacks the backbone to forge his way in this world and get what he wants. I think of John Taylor's skill as he changed lives, pulled skin away from thighs and attached them to cheekbones, made incisions, built up chins and noses, transforming dysfunction into beauty. He was truly a god, whereas Peter is all too human.

55

MJ

I HAD TROUBLE GETTING UP this morning. Even knowing the day was forecast for more glorious late summer sun couldn't rouse me. I had that bad feeling. The feeling I thought I'd vanquished with years of therapy and yoga and mindfulness.

I don't talk about that particular *thing that happened* very often. That's how my parents referred to it. But all this bustle of police officers, this being called repeatedly to the station house, this aggressive, almost bruising questioning, reminds me of it.

I kept a diary of that time. Well, of the time before. Afterwards, I didn't want to engage in any introspection. I took the diary out and read it the other day. How vapid and shallow was that girl! Nothing on her mind except boys, boys, boys. Everything in her world soaked through with budding sensuality. What a fool.

I was fourteen. I practiced walking differently, talking differently. I liked it when I was in town and men's eyes lingered on my long legs; I realized they, and my breasts, were precious assets. My parents did the usual, sent me back to my room to change when I dressed *inappropriately*. So I went underground. I'd leave the house with a bare face and *decent* clothes, and change and apply makeup in the bathroom at school. I wasn't the only one, of course. Some of the girls were able to wear their makeup openly, but many of us, especially from the more religious families, had to hide it, and strip it off at the end of the day before going home. I can't blame my mother. I'd do the same with a daughter that age.

But that *thing*. It was the end of eighth grade. May. I was walking home from school. I was alone, having left my friends at their houses along the way, mine being the farthest one out. A bunch of high school boys were huddled by the side of the road, taking turns pulling on a joint. "Hey," they called when they saw me. My makeup had been scrubbed off, and I had my *decent* clothes on, but I was wearing them differently than I would if my mother were watching. I looked young and, doubtless, eager to please. I remember their words exactly, because they thrilled me. "Hey, sexy thang, come here for some part-ay-ing." So I walked over. I recognized a couple of them, mostly the older brothers of kids in my class, although there were a couple boys my age. They offered me the joint, and I took it, tried to act casual as I inhaled with a deep breath, but predictably just choked and coughed. The boys laughed, and one said, "That first toke is a killer," in a friendly way, so I felt okay.

One boy I'd had a crush on for years. Richard. Something was wrong with his heart and he couldn't play football. This was usually the kiss of death socially for boys at my high school, but he managed to hang with the football players from sheer force of will. When we were six I'd drawn him a valentine heart with a tiny hole in it, the way my mother had described. The teacher took one look and crumpled it up. Richard never saw it. Still, I'm sure he could tell I liked him. Certainly, the other boys noticed, because they subtly pushed him forward to be by my side as they suggested a walk into the woods.

I'd thought nothing of it, the woods being my backyard. Afterward of course, everyone took my easy acquiescence as proof that I understood exactly what I was getting into. I didn't, not even when it started. We'd stopped in a clearing, and I thought they were going to light up another joint, but instead Richard got pushed forward again, and I blushed as I saw he was going to try to kiss me.

You can probably guess the rest. I don't want to go into it. It hurt, certainly it hurt, but mostly it was the shame. The awkward scrabblings at my breasts. A rock under my shoulder blades. I could glimpse the blue of the sky through the leaves of the trees above. A couple of the boys had trouble, and that hurt most of all as they tried to poke their way to success. Then, suddenly it was over and I was alone. I got dressed and went home. My mother had been frantic, had been on the phone calling the whole town. Any thoughts I had of not saying anything vanished when she saw me, my dirty clothes, my face. She had the story out of me in about five minutes, and we were on our way to the police station in ten. The whole time she was lecturing me that it was partially my fault, the way I dressed, the way I walked. "You can't tempt those boys," she told me. "At that age, they're hogs in heat." *Hawgs in heet.* I will say she fought for me, though. When my daddy arrived he was angry that my mother had gotten the police involved. Said it was a regrettable incident, but we all know what boys are. My mother for once ignored him; they nearly came to blows in the police station. Then the questioning began. Yes, I knew the boys. Yes, I went with them willingly into the woods. *What was I thinking?* I told them that I guess I wasn't. The police officer on duty reluctantly took my statement and said they'd look into it.

So began the first worst period of my life, the second being of course when I was married with two kids stuck in a small garage apartment. But that was later. I was told that the boys said I agreed to it, that they were good boys, they wouldn't lie. A couple of them were from prominent families in town with money and lawyers and in the end, after the hours of questioning and fuss, somehow the tables got turned and we were on the spot, we were going to be in trouble if we didn't drop the charges. So we did. One policeman had placed a heavy hand on my shoulder. "You don't want to end up in the Odditorium yourself, young lady."

I'd see those boys around town, sometimes with older girls, and I'd think, *I've had knowledge of you.* Some phrase I'd gotten from church. One of the reasons I married my first husband was that he was one of the few boys who was kind to me in high school after word got around. *MJ pulled a train.* That's when I started to wear the long skirts, the shapeless blouses, to hide my figure, even pants were too revealing.

John helped me with all of this more than the therapists I've paid over the decades. He took on my pain. When I told him, I saw him weep, and with each of his tears I felt lighter. It was miraculous, really. "You had a heinous crime committed against you, and they should have been punished," he had said. "But they won't be. So the least you can do is not punish yourself."

But yesterday, today, tomorrow, I feel as though the world is punishing me. Threatening to take it all away. Time hangs heavy. I feel the tick of every second of the clock, and the empty hours stretch in front of me. I honestly don't see a way out.

56

Deborah

AFTER I HANG UP THE phone, I move around the house, breaking things.

So that . . . person . . . that Helen, is pregnant. She broke the pledge.

Smash goes the blue living-room lamp, the one John and I picked out in Florence together for our first house, amazed that money was starting to come in after the years of penury. He said the blue matched my eyes. A pang at that memory. Then, smash goes silverware from the drawer. I hurl forks and knives onto the floor. A hailstorm of sharp edges, and I am sorry there is no one here to get pierced with them. I am utterly alone in this house. Not even a goldfish, hamster, lizard, the pets of the children's innocent years.

This wasn't part of the plan. The plan has gone awry. I was to live the rest of my days with dignity. Mrs. John Taylor. Not to have a trail of litter behind me, false wives, bastard children, child brides. It is disgraceful. It is undignified. I even did what certain people suggested that I do when this stink became public: I resigned my posts. My chair at the head of the South Peninsula Garden Club. Member of the board of the Palo Alto Junior League. Member of the steering committee for the Peninsula Open Space Preservation Society. I shed them all.

I can't help but blame this all on the messenger, that girl detective. She called me again after she visited LA to interview Helen, and casually dropped the bomb in passing. No doubt she enjoyed breaking the news. But I won't go down easily. An agreement is an agreement.

I book my flight to LA.

57

Helen

A BOY. I AM CARRYING a boy. This is shocking news. This is unwelcome news. Unacceptable. What can I do with a boy? There is no *boy* in my future.

I found out this morning, got the call from the laboratory. The woman on the other end of the line, the technician, was inclined to be playful. "You have a healthy child," she said, "Nothing to be alarmed about from the amnio." "That's a relief," I said. My whole body relaxed. What would I have done with a Down syndrome child or child with some other severe birth defect? It would have been aborted. That would have been my only option.

"Don't you want to know the sex?" asked the woman. I had forgotten about that, so sure was I that my child was female. "Of course," I replied, and waited. But the technician turned coy. "Want to guess?" she asked. This irritated me. I said, "Boy" just to be ornery, and heard a congratulatory, "That's right!" "A boy?" I asked, incredulously. "Yes, and it sounds as though that's what you wanted!" I hung up without saying goodbye.

What do I know of footballs and lizards and wet dreams? I was prepared to deal with the PMS and first love of a girl, but not the onslaught of testosterone. This will take some adjusting. This will take some thinking about.

It has been a rough day so far. Even the overwrought parents got to me in a way they usually don't. Often I retreat to a zone in the center of my brain that controls all the outgoing signals. The eyes, opening wide while listening and narrowing in thought at the right moments. The voice, firm yet full of compassion. The hand, reaching out to almost touch an arm, but holding back in case that's too much of an imposition. It doesn't mean I'm not capable of being kind. I just get so fatigued and cranky and unable to do my job well. For their sake, it's better that I fake it, look at the children without seeing them, pat their little heads, smile at them. Good oncologists are good actors. This doesn't make them bad people.

I would have thought so when I was younger, even post medical school. I thought sincerity was the requirement. Now I strive for *authenticity*. Quite a different thing altogether.

But today things aren't going well. My control center isn't operating properly. Earlier, I reached out and actually touched a father who jerked back angrily. To him I was the big bad cancer monster delivering the news of the impending death of his beloved son. Beloved *son*. I think of blue blankets, and tiny infant footsie suits printed with bats and balls or outer space or railroad motifs. I shudder. I am ashamed in the midst of my irritation. I slip off my shoes, prepare to change into the sneakers I wear home for comfort.

Sally, my favorite nurse, knocks, then opens the door to my office. "There's someone here who won't leave," she says, and grimaces.

"A parent?" I ask wearily.

"More of a grandparent, if anything. But I suspect it has something to do with . . . that matter." Sally has always been circumspect about my relationship with John—before we were married, when we were trying to keep it from the gossips throughout the medical center, and certainly after his death, when the media piranhas swarmed.

"She says her name is Deborah." Sally's look turns resolute when she sees my face wince. "Okay, I'll get rid of her."

"No," I say. "Show her in." I am resigned. From what I know of Deborah Taylor, she will not take no for an answer anyway, not if she knows I'm in here, which somehow I'm sure she does. I slip my shoes back on.

When Deborah enters my office, I feel the dynamics of power shift, just like that. I could be the patient on the examining table in the paper gown rather than the doctor. I stand to assert myself, but my move backfires as she graciously says, "Sit down, please." I obey her, feeling like a visitor in my own office.

She remains standing until my assistant closes the door behind her. Then the graciousness vanishes. "How dare you," she says, almost hisses. I don't even try to pretend not to know what she is talking about.

"I don't *dare* do anything," I say, with more spirit than I feel in my tired bones. "But what's done is done."

"Is it a boy?" she asks. I wonder briefly why she thinks this is important.

"I won't tell you," I say. "You have no rights here."

Deborah's mouth twists and her eyes turn ugly. "So it is," she says, then she takes a step forward so that she is pushing against my desk. "Be certain of one thing. You will not use the Taylor name."

This honestly throws me for a loop. "What?" I ask.

"Nor does this child have any claim on John's estate," she says.

I put up my hands. "There's no question of that," I say. "Of either thing."

Deborah stares at me for a full minute. Then I see the tension visibly begin to leave her body.

I gather strength as she subsides. "I don't see what any of this has to do with you," I say. I struggle a little getting to my feet; she is still standing, so close that I have to maneuver around her. "And I don't know why you intrude like this when a simple phone call or even email would have been enough."

"Because I wouldn't have trusted the answers," she says. "I had to see you myself."

I am suddenly more tired than I can ever remember being. Not just tired, sleepy. I could curl up and sleep for days. It's only Monday and I have a full week's worth of patients.

Deborah's eyes stay on me, and, as if against her will, she looks concerned.

"Are you all right?" she asks.

"Of course," I say, but as I say it my knees buckle and Deborah reaches out and catches me, gently sitting me down in an armchair.

"You're not," she says. "You're pale. When did you last eat?"

"Not today," I admit. I was too nauseated to eat breakfast, and too busy to grab lunch.

"That's ridiculous," she says. "When I was pregnant I was eating every minute of the day, and I was still hungry. Here," she's rummaging in her purse, and comes up with a power bar. "I always carry these when I fly."

I accept the bar, unwrap it, and take a bite. "Eat the whole thing," she says. "Don't try to do anything until you've had a chance to increase your blood sugar."

I manage a smile. "Who's the doctor here?" I ask.

She's serious. "You should be asking, 'Who's the foolish pregnant lady?'"

That makes me laugh. I take another bite, "Somehow I never pegged you as having a sense of humor."

"On occasion," Deborah says solemnly, "I've been known for my wit." Then she does smile.

Deborah turns to go. Funny how vulnerable she seems to me now, from behind, how fragile her shoulder blades stick out of her thin shoulders. I try to think if she was this thin at the funeral. I decide she's lost a considerable amount of weight.

"Hang on," I say. Against my better judgment and my intense tiredness I find I want to make a genuine gesture toward this woman.

She stops and looks at me questioningly.

"Are you flying back tonight?"

"No," she says. "I'm going to find a hotel, and then leave in the morning. I can't face the airport and those security lines more than once a day."

I hear my voice inviting her to stay with me. "I have a pullout couch in my home office," I say. "It wouldn't be any trouble." This is a lie, which gives me pause. I rarely tell an untruth, and when I do, it is for a good reason. But I have no reason to invite John's wife into my home. The words *common human decency* come to mind.

She appears to consider the offer. "I wouldn't impose," she says.

I'm about to argue with her. "We're nearly family," I say, and find my hand reaching out in a gesture, but somehow I miscalculate the space between us and touch her arm. This is too much. We both recoil, and I think, *Well, that's that.*

Then she accepts my invitation.

58

Helen

SEEING DEBORAH SITTING IN JOHN'S favorite chair, sipping wine out of a glass he almost certainly used at some point, is unsettling. More than unsettling—crazy-making.

She's been in my condo for about an hour. We ordered in some sushi—vegetarian for me—and while we wait for it to arrive I take a shower and put on my pajamas. She's still fully dressed—I can't imagine her any other way—and hasn't even taken off her shoes.

"Do you miss him?" she asks. She is openly looking around my living room and dining room, which is minuscule compared to her Palo Alto home, but more comfortable, in my opinion. Not as funky and full of character as John's fantasy San Francisco Victorian, of course. There's a plush taupe sofa, love seat, and matching large armchair, the one Deborah is sitting in. An antique pine coffee table, and a similar square table with four upright chairs for the dining alcove. Walls mostly bare. My wall art is in my office, which is covered with photos of children. Patients. Many of them dead, although many have survived, too. I like to be reminded of that fact. Though all this will be quite different in a few months. The office turned into a nursery, toys and blankets and diapers strewn around.

I wonder how I'll handle it. I like everything in its place. I hang up my clothes the minute I take them off. I wipe down the sink and bathtub immediately after using them, wash my dishes as soon as my meal is finished.

When John entered my life, I found myself trailing after him, picking shirts and socks off the floor, putting dirty glasses in the dishwasher, constantly tidying. I remember Deborah's pristine house. Perhaps we have more in common than I'd thought.

"Did you follow John around, cleaning up after him?" I ask Deborah. She seems surprised for a moment, then smiles. It is not a particularly nice smile. I must remind myself if I start to soften towards her—she is not a *nice* woman.

"No, I had him trained. What, did he do that to you? He knew he could get away with it, then. I made sure he understood that everything had a place."

"Right, that's my rule, too," I say, and Deborah lifts her wineglass in a mock toast. "But I could never get him to follow it." I say.

Two women, complaining about their man.

"You'll be interested to hear that in the . . . other . . . household, John was the neat one," Deborah says. She smiles again, but this smile has anger in it. "He told me that MJ was impossible as a housekeeper, impossible in the kitchen, leaving pots and pans and dirty saucepans in the sink. So he took over the housekeeping. Can you believe that? I wonder how that creature is doing without her personal maid service."

"At the reception, all she could talk about was tending to her garden," I say.

"Yes," says Deborah, but curtly. "Well, she'll get to keep her damn garden. And house too."

I don't respond. I don't know what arrangements have been made between the two of them, and I don't care to know. Deborah doesn't strike me as either a generous or merciful woman. As a judge she would have been a hanging judge and would have adjudicated to the strict letter of the law. Yet MJ, that mess of a woman, apparently got something out of her. Squeezed a drop of benevolence out of that stony heart.

Deborah breaks the silence with a strange question. "Tell me, how did you meet John?" she asks. She pauses, and then says, "He never told me. He refused. Which was unusual."

"Through the hospital," I say. I'm pleased that John refused to share this part of our lives with her. And I'm not sure I want to, either.

"You won't give me any more than that?" she asks, and I am surprised by the pleading in her voice. She has put her wineglass down, still half full, and there is a plaintive look on her face. Is this some sort of trick? But what advantage could she have tricking me into telling my love story?

"No one has ever asked," I say. This is true. To my friends, "I met a guy" had sufficed, largely because the news had so astounded them that they then pestered me with questions about John himself rather than the details of our courtship. They were overjoyed, too. My dearest friends, who had never quite accepted that I was happy on my own.

I take a deep breath. "A new patient came in, a ten-year-old boy who'd been born with a lump on his forehead. They determined it was a benign mass at birth, and the family didn't have insurance for what was considered elective surgery, so the boy just lived with it. I saw pictures. It wasn't that noticeable when he was very young. Or when he wore his hair in bangs later on. But by the time the boy was nine, other lumps—they were tumors, to be precise—began growing all over his face. They brought him to me, to ensure these tumors really were benign. In fact they were hemangiomas, benign tumors of the endothelial cells that line blood vessels. Since they were beginning to interfere with the boy's functioning—his breathing and his eyesight—the insurance would now cover removing them. He had the surgery. But the poor boy was horribly disfigured due to a careless surgeon.

"I began calling around for a plastic surgeon who might do some pro bono work for this boy. I'd heard of John's clinic, of course. It's well known in medical circles, especially among pediatric specialists. I put in a call, got the forms, and began the tedious process of filling them out and documenting the case with photos and lab reports. Then, a colleague told me that John was actually here at UCLA on an adjunct professorship teaching a seminar on facial reconstruction after burn trauma. So I emailed him directly, and surprisingly, he got right back to me. And since he was already in the hospital, agreed to come by my office that day."

"What was your first impression?" asks Deborah. "I'm curious."

"He had clearly once been handsome, but I remember thinking that he was going to seed: overweight, and with a red face. I immediately thought of hypertension, or vasculitis, or perhaps alcoholism. But the redness subsided after a few minutes and I realized he had been blushing. A man of sixty, blushing to meet me!

"I had pulled the patient's file, and we went over the photos together, and right away he said he could help this boy. No hesitation. We scheduled the surgery. The boy and his family were terribly nervous, and for some reason, so was I. There seemed to be a lot riding on the outcome of this operation. I wanted it to be successful. I *needed* it to be successful. I was invested.

"In the meantime, we exchanged a series of businesslike emails. Yet I understood it was a courtship of a kind. He called me several times to discuss the techniques he was planning to use—taking skin from the boy's thigh and grafting it onto his face over the scars, rebuilding the shape of the face with borrowed cartilage. At one point I asked him if I could observe the procedure. He warned me it would take a long time—six to eight hours—but I was welcome to stay for as much of it as I liked. I was rapt during the whole thing. I positioned myself in the observation room above the operating theatre in such a way that I could see John's hands.

"Whatever slovenly habits he had in civilian life, none of this passed the threshold to the OR. He was gentle and delicate. I stayed for seven and a half hours. I hadn't realized how tense I'd been until John completed the last suture, and turned to his team members and gave a triumphant thumbs-up. Then he looked up at the observation room, where I was getting ready to leave, and pointed to himself, then to me, then made a drinking motion. I nodded.

"In the waiting room I still felt tense. I was feeling . . . how can I describe it? Like I was about to see my beloved after a long absence. I remember a quotation my father recited when he saw my mother enter the room, a kind of inside joke between them. 'Who is this that cometh out of the wilderness like pillars of smoke, perfumed with myrrh and frankincense, with all powders of the merchant?' *My beloved*, he'd exclaim.

"Those are the words that came to mind when he finally approached me, his hair still slick from his shower. I saw his face was crimson again. Another blush, deeper than the first. He said, and it amazed me how close our thoughts had been. 'I had to succeed on this one. 'I had to win the hand of the princess in her tower.' No other explanation. We didn't go for a drink. We went straight to my place with very little more discussion."

Deborah doesn't say anything. I hadn't looked at her while I was speaking, and turning to her now, I'm surprised to see that her eyes are closed. She is leaning against the back of the chair, her hands clutching the ends of the armrests, and that's what tells me that she isn't asleep—the tendons showing white from stress on the backs of her hands.

59

MJ

I'M FEELING BAD, THAT BAD feeling again. The very bad one. I just can't shake it.

I haven't felt like this in more than twenty-eight years. When I'd just given birth for the second time, and was breastfeeding and changing diapers in the middle of the night while caring for a hyperactive toddler during the day. My husband was off at the Odditorium, and doing extra shifts on construction sites whenever he could get the work. We needed the money. The suffocation of the soul. That shortness of breath. That heavy feeling, as though some beast was sitting on my chest. The urge to disappear, to get on the road and *go* was ultimately strong enough to make me move across the country.

Of course some of it was sleep deprivation. And part of it was utter, brutal boredom. Most of my friends were in similar situations, so we'd get together with our babies at the playground, or for coffee at someone's house, and that eased the feeling somewhat. I understood back then why certain women turn on their children. The urge to smack the little whining behind, to direct a blow to the head, anything to stop the noise and the demands.

I made the mistake of telling some of this to my husband. It was after one of the night feedings, I was exhausted and murderous and could have killed them all while they slept, my small family; I had a fantasy of turning on the gas and leaving the apartment. That scared me enough to wake up my husband. What I said was, "I'm having some trouble with the kids."

He was tired himself, spent because of his job, but he tried to listen, and heard enough to be alarmed, because in the morning he talked me into phoning one of Gatlinburg's five therapists. The therapist's advice—or rather, lecture—was that everyone went through this when their children were young, and how I needed to basically put up and shut up and be thankful I had healthy kids.

I nodded, but my heart was growing murderous again. I left the office and drove to the nearest gas station, bought a map of the country, and began plotting my escape. That map saved me in the months it took to steel my nerves and gather resources for the trip. I put aside a little out of the paychecks every week, in a special account in my name only. I got myself a credit card. I used a magic marker to chart my way on the map from Tennessee to LA. I envisioned freedom.

Without that map to inspire me, I'd likely be in some female penitentiary. God help me, I was so close. I was a madwoman. But once on the road, the kids strapped into car seats and the windows open and road clear before me, I became the doting mom that everyone thought I should be.

But the heavy feeling, the shortness of breath, has returned. I can't shake it this time. And there's no map, no guide to my future. My children are grown and largely self-sufficient, my husband gone. There's Thomas, of course. In fact, he was the only person I told of my plans to leave Tennessee, and I'll always remember his white face when he realized I was really going without him. But he can't save me this time. No one can.

60

MJ's Note to Her Brother

Dearest Thomas,

So this is it. This is how life has narrowed to one path and only one path for me to follow. The heaviness has returned and it has proven too great a weight for me to bear after all.

I know you will take this hard, after all we've been through, both apart and together, but mostly together. You've been my life's true companion, and for this I am eternally grateful. I have no regrets. You mustn't either. Life is what it is, that unit of existence we are allotted, and I shaped mine the best way I knew how. But I only had so much to give it. I found myself praying to St. Jude the other night. Just like Mom would in times of stress. Patron saint of lost causes. Will you implore him to intercede for me? That's all I ask. And that my ashes are buried in my garden, which is now yours. Everything I always had was always yours. You knew that. Take care of the garden. Please.

Tell the boys I'm sorry. And I *am* sorry—sorrier than I ever could have imagined. It is wrong to take a life, no matter how much one is owed.

Love,

MJ

61

Samantha

PETER PICKED UP THE PHONE when it started ringing at 3 AM, then handed it wordlessly to me. The Los Gatos police had been on the scene since midnight, when MJ Taylor's brother, Thomas, had called them. Unable to reach his sister for two days, he finally drove down from the city. He readily admitted he was drunk when he found MJ, and delayed calling the police until the alcohol wore off.

When I arrive, it's almost over except the taking away of the body. MJ lies on her bed dressed in a kind of blue sparkling sari that dips over the edge of the bed like a brilliant blue waterfall. She has makeup on, too. And jewelry. She went out dressed as a bride.

"Was there a note?" I ask the officer in charge. He nods and hands it to me, encased in a clear plastic evidence ziplock. I read it, then approach Thomas, who is sitting in the corner of the living room, his face in his hands. When I get near him, he raises his head, and—honest to God—I've never seen such utter despair on a human face.

"Without her, I'd be dead, or close to it," he says before I have a chance to open the conversation. "I would have ended up a meth addict or worse."

"I'm sorry to have to ask you questions right now," I say, as gently as possible. When he just looked at me, I added, "Did you read the note your sister left?"

He nods his head in the affirmative, then buries his face in his hands again.

"What does it say to you?" I ask. I consider putting a hand on his shoulder, I suppose that's the natural instinct when you see a wounded animal—to comfort. When he didn't answer, I said, "Much of it seems awfully abstract. Do you know what was troubling her?"

Thomas just shakes his head.

"Thomas, did she kill John Taylor? I'm asking you a direct question."

He doesn't reply.

"Thomas?"

He finally speaks, slowly. "I guess it doesn't matter anymore. Nothing matters anymore."

"What are you saying?"

He gets to his feet. "I'm not talking to you without a lawyer," he says.

62

Deborah

SO THAT MJ CREATURE IS dead. And that brother of hers has practically admitted that she killed my John. For once I feel pity for that woman. She suffered. And I'm surprised to find that I'm actually glad she had six years with John. Six apparently happy years. She filled a hole in his life that I never knew existed. The thought of John as her housekeeper and chief gardener will amuse me for a long while to come.

May God have mercy on her soul.

63

Samantha

THOMAS GIVES HIS STATEMENT THE day after MJ's body is discovered. And it's a doozy.

According to him, MJ had somehow found out that her husband was not in LA as he had told her. She somehow found out that he was at the Westin. How she discovered these facts Thomas couldn't say. But she'd called Thomas Friday evening, May 10, very agitated. The time was approximately 7 PM. As per his previous statement, he was already at MJ's house, waiting for her to return. She told him that she needed his help. She instructed him to go into her closet and get the long blond wig that resembled, at a distance, MJ's own long graying locks, bought for a Halloween party in which Thomas and MJ had dressed up as each other. MJ gave Thomas explicit instructions that he was to put on her clothes, and—complete with the wig, one of the more conspicuous hats from her wardrobe, and sunglasses—immediately make the rounds of the grocery store and drugstore. And to get himself noticed. He dutifully knocked over the cereal display at Trader Joe's, bought some toiletries at Walgreens, and then returned to Walgreens via the drive-through window for MJ's prescription. All as instructed. Then they met back at MJ's house at 7:45, where Thomas put his own clothes back on and she insisted they dine at a local restaurant. "We must be seen there," she had said.

Thomas swears that he didn't know what it was about at the time. MJ had merely ordered a vodka and tonic from the waiter—a very unusual move on her part—and refused to say anything else. It wasn't until Sunday that Thomas heard about John Taylor's death.

"It would have been perfect. No one would have known," Thomas says during his statement. He begins to cry. "MJ didn't have to kill herself."

"Her conscience decided," I say, not unsympathetically. "But why would you agree to do this, if John Taylor was going to be your golden goose? Weren't you expecting money from him?"

"I didn't agree!" he says, sitting up straight. "I knew nothing!"

"You didn't ask why you had to dress as your sister? I have a hard time believing that."

"Of course I did!" he says. "She simply said she needed to be in two places at the same time. And I trusted MJ. Unconditionally." Here he began to cry again.

"Do you know why she did it?" I ask. "Why she would want to kill John Taylor?"

Thomas gives a sort of defeated half shrug. "She must have found out about the other wives," he says. "That's the sort of thing that would set MJ off."

"No idea how?"

"No idea."

And that is pretty much it. MJ Taylor, RIP.

But I'm not satisfied. They take Thomas away. And I return to my desk and begin filling in the paperwork for a new subpoena to examine MJ's phone and email records for the week before her death.

64

Samantha

SUSAN CALLS ME INTO HER office.

"What is this?" she asks, waving my request for the subpoena.

I steel myself. "I'm not convinced that MJ was the murderer," I say. I'm not completely comfortable saying this.

"But Sam," Susan says. "You were right. You've been saying all along that we had to keep putting the pressure on MJ, that she wasn't telling us everything. You weren't fooled by Mark Epstein, either. You called this one. Now's the time to close the case and move on."

I shake my head.

"No," I say. "This doesn't feel right."

There's a knock on the door. It's Grady. "Congratulations," he says to me. "You kept on it, and followed your instincts. Good work."

I look from Susan to him. "I'm not done," I say. "This isn't closed yet."

I see a glance pass between them.

"What is it, Sam?" asks Susan. She is trying to be patient, I can tell.

"For starters, how would MJ know about a potassium overdose? And where would she even get it."

Grady shakes his head. "Sam, as you said yourself, it's common knowledge that an overdose of potassium can be fatal. I mean, for chrissakes, that's what a lethal injection is in death row cases."

I feel stubborn. "Well, where did she get it from, then?"

Grady laughs. He motions to Susan's computer. "May I?" he asks. She nods. He pulls the keyboard toward him and types in l-i-q-u-i-d p-o-t-a-s-s-i-u-m and hits enter. I can see the list of sites from where I'm standing. "Sam, it's a common health supplement for both people and pets. Hell, for all we know, Dr. Taylor prescribed it for himself or MJ."

I shake my head. "We checked their pharmacies. No prescription for potassium chloride had ever been filled."

"So she called a Canadian pharmacy," says Grady.

I turn to Susan. "Does this mean you won't allow my request to see MJ's phone and email records?" I ask.

She sighs. "Sam . . ."

"I don't feel we can let this one slide," I say. "We've put too much into the investigation. Just do me this favor, and then I'm done. I promise. I'll accept that MJ was the perp."

Susan hesitates, then pulls out a pen and signs the forms. "Okay," she says. "Go ahead and submit these. But after this, it's back to the burglary beat, Sam."

"You mean the barking dog beat," I say under my breath, but I suspect Susan hears me because she turns her head sharply.

"And one more thing," I say, meekly.

"What's that?" Susan asks, visibly annoyed now.

"I'd like permission to interview Deborah Taylor one more time."

Susan shakes her head. "Absolutely not. City Hall is roasting my butt on that. According to Deborah, you've been harassing her. For no good reason. Asking the same questions over and over again. She's well connected in this town, Sam. I can't let this continue."

"Just one more interview," I say. "To tie up some loose ends."

65

Excerpt from Transcript

Police interview with Deborah Taylor, September 5, 2013

[Preliminary introductions, explanations of police processes and procedures, notification that the session would be videotaped]

Samantha Adams: I take it you've heard the news.

Deborah Taylor: Yes. Yes, I have. It was MJ all along. I wouldn't have thought she could engineer such an elaborate plot. And I wonder how she found out. Or what she found out. Was it just that John had other wives? Or did she find out about Claire, too? That her little idyll was coming to an end?

Samantha Adams: We'll never know.

Deborah Taylor: Why have you asked me here yet again? I understand that the case in closed. Certainly you must have everything you need. I don't know what I can add, except that I'm glad you have settled this very unsettling situation.

Samantha Adams: We feel there are some holes.

Deborah Taylor: Such as?

Samantha Adams: Such as MJ assuring her brother in the note that he would get the garden, get the money, get "everything." What did she mean by that?

Deborah Taylor: I assume she meant that I agreed not to claim any equity in the house in Los Gatos.

Samantha Adams: Isn't the equity worth more than two million dollars by now?

Deborah Taylor: Yes, but as I told you, I have enough to be comfortable. John had the insurance policy, and with our savings I could afford to be generous. It was the least I could do, given the . . . unusual . . . household arrangement I had set up. With Helen, there were no issues, she wanted nothing and asked for nothing. But MJ was anxious about this until we settled it.

Samantha Adams: When did you have a discussion with MJ about money?

Deborah Taylor: Oh, not until a month or so after John's death. I told her she could keep the house, that as John's sole beneficiary I would sign the deed over to her. She could also keep what was in their joint bank account, a considerable sum. She would have been taken care of financially. And if she decided to pass that along to her brother, I have no reason to object.

Samantha Adams: And you really believe MJ had it in her?

Deborah Taylor: Absolutely. She wasn't the simple hippy child she liked to portray. Clever, really, to have her brother act as her surrogate. They had an interesting relationship, those two. Something I've never had, a close sibling. Or, I suppose a close anything once John and I lost our connection. My children have yet to forgive me for this whole thing. Even Charles, my eldest, who I could generally count on to support me, has disappeared. Refuses to return my calls. So MJ was an object of envy to me in that regard, she had a genuine relationship to call her own. You might laugh at me for such an unambitious desire. Most people, I can only assume, have these types of connections. Yet they've never come easy to me. John was it. Too bad I didn't realize it in time.

Samantha Adams: Realize what?

Deborah Taylor: How much I still loved him.

66

Helen

MJ. POOR THING. YOU COULD almost see her gasping for breath, how foreign the air of this world was to her. I can't grudge that she found a safe harbor, however temporary, with John. At least she apparently had six years of happiness. John gave her that. Not the greatest deal, but not the worst either. I daily see families torn apart, families that will never recover from loss, people who are scarred for life.

My situation is so different from MJ's that I should feel some sort of survivor's guilt. But I don't. I am merely elated. I know at least part of this high is due to the second trimester hormones beginning to kick in; I feel as though I can conquer the world. I'm showing now, and people are cautiously commenting on it, tactfully trying to determine if I'm happy about the baby or not. My face alone should show how I feel about it. I had envisioned the second half of my life to be a solitary one. Then came John. And now a child.

I'm adjusting to the fact that it's a boy. Enough not to let it affect my moods. I'm careful to eat all the nutrients I need, I'm careful to take my vitamins, and my OB says that things are looking very well after the last ultrasound.

I had a strange encounter the other day. I ran into an acquaintance, a friend of a friend who I had met at a party, and looking at my belly, she congratulated me openly, without any sense that this pregnancy had dubious origins. "And how is that delightful husband of yours?" she asked. "Is he over the moon?" "John is dead," I said, and I realized that was the first time I had voiced it out loud. I'd always interacted with people who already knew the facts. The woman had turned pale and took a step back. I only half listened to her fumbled words of condolence, hit once again with the reality that John is dead, and of the weight of my great loss. The world had been a better place because he was in it. But this child wouldn't have existed if John had been alive. I know that much about myself. I was not in control of my destiny or my body. When I realized I was pregnant I took a sick day from work—unprecedented—and went to the beach at the Pacific Palisades and walked for hours. John or the child? John or the child? I knew that telling John about the pregnancy would seal the child's fate, that soon it would cease to be a child and become a mass of bloody cells in a medical biohazard waste container. It was the biggest decision I'd ever had to make, and I couldn't make it, could not for the life of me make it. John's death decided it absolutely. I didn't have to choose. My way was clear.

At this stage, a little over four months, the child has fingers and toes, and is covered with downy hair. He floats in the amniotic fluid, and I'm careful to protect him from loud voices, cigarette smoke, angry people, even unpleasant images. I turn my eyes from anything that displeases me. I wish to remain a calm vessel for this child, to let no ugliness penetrate the lining of my womb. My patients' parents look at my left hand, naked of any ring, and can't decide whether to congratulate me or not. Some of them are openly envious; as I help usher their children out of this world I am bringing a new life into it. In the midst of terrible suffering, there is joy.

Yesterday I saw a patient, a terminal case, and her heartbroken parents wanted another round of chemo—more suffering and for naught. So I vetoed it. I sent the child to the waiting room in the care of her nanny and was blunt. "If you love your daughter, you will not do this," I said. "You will allow me to prescribe palliative measures so that the rest of her life is easier." They were silent at first, the man weeping, the wife more stoic. Then the wife burst out, "Easy for you to say," looking at my belly. "I remember when I was like you," she said. "We were so happy to be pregnant. We didn't know our baby already had this seed in her, that she was broken from the beginning. She seemed so perfect."

I put my hand on my belly and shuddered to think of what I might have done to this child if John had lived. Then, I place my hand over the woman's, and said, "I'm so very sorry. But you must think of the child first."

I suppose the case of John's murder is now closed. Well, thank God for that.

You seem like a sweet girl, Samantha Adams, but I am happy to see the back of you.

67

Deborah

RELIEF. THAT'S WHAT I WAS feeling as I got up this morning, showered, ate my breakfast fruit. MJ gone is a problem solved. The last big one, really.

It's a misty day outside, so thick a mist that you actually get wet stepping outdoors as I do at 10 AM to do my grocery shopping. I take my cloth shopping bags and walk over to Whole Foods, two blocks away, ignore the large homeless man who always positions himself at the entrance, holding up what he considers are clever signs. *Only $100,000 gets me a meal and a Mercedes,* and *I take my cappuccino dry,* and *Please no filet mignon, I'm a vegetarian.* I've never seen anyone give him anything, but it must be a productive post or he wouldn't be stationed there at all hours.

I walk through the aisles, picking out one avocado, three tomatoes, a can of soup. I tend to shop for only one or at most two days at a time. The structure of my life is gone without John around, and I've almost stopped expecting him to come home every morning. But I find myself still purchasing his favorite fruit, raspberries, and other treats that I'd pack for him to take to work in case he didn't have time for lunch. These chores punctuated my life, gave it shape. Now there's an amorphous stretch of time, bookended by sunrise in the morning—I still wake early—and sunset in the evening. I rarely stay up after ten. I look at my watch a lot.

Not all my friends have deserted me. Not all were appalled at the lies I had told them over the years. So I have lunch two or three times a week with these loyal women. I'm looking for something new, to fill the hours. Knitting won't do it. Perhaps animal rescue or another satisfying charitable activity that involves working with your hands and body, not just organizing ladies for meetings and dinners and luncheons.

I go to the computer, surf the latest news. It's only 1 PM. The day stretches out in front of me, but now the hours aren't full of anxious dread, rather they hold promise. I am resourceful. I will find my way, again. Thank goodness money isn't a problem.

I've just started scanning the headlines when the doorbell rings. I'm not expecting anyone, and when I peek through the curtains I see with horror that it's the young police detective again. I arrange my face in an appropriate smile for greeting her and open the door. She is not smiling.

"May I come in?" she asks.

I am not happy, but I don't let it show. I usher her into the living room, gesture to one of the chairs, and sit myself down on the adjoining sofa. She starts talking without preamble.

"So I was going through the telephone records of MJ Taylor's cell phone for the week leading up to her death." She pauses and looks at me, as if waiting for a comment.

I merely incline my head and say, "Go on."

"The day of her death, she first phoned Helen Richter, then yourself." She pauses again, but I don't give anything away. "The call to Helen was short, less than a minute. But the call to you stretched for twenty minutes. That was at approximately 5:15 in the evening. We estimate she died shortly after that, as early as 6:30 PM, or at the very latest, 9 PM."

I say nothing.

"What did you talk about?" the detective asks. "Helen Richter says that MJ just wanted to chat, but that she, Helen, didn't want to be embroiled in any of MJ's messy emotional stuff, so she politely but promptly got off the phone. Then MJ tried you. What did she want?"

"To blather on," I finally say. "About John, about how sorry she was, about how much she missed him."

"Did she actually confess to you?"

"Not in so many words. But amidst all the *I'm sorries* and *how can I live with myselfs* I gathered that she was trying to," I say.

"And you didn't contact me?" The color is high in the detective's cheeks. She has stopped taking notes. "You seem to be taking it all very lightly."

"I didn't have anything definite of use," I say. "As Helen correctly predicted, it was quite messy. I listened for a while . . ."

"Twenty minutes," she interrupts.

"Yes, twenty minutes. Then I said goodbye and hung up."

"Did you get the sense that she was in a desperate state?"

I pause while calculating what to say.

"Deborah, did she tell you she was going to commit suicide?" Her voice is louder.

"Yes," I say finally. "She mentioned she was thinking about that. In fact."

"And what did you tell her?"

"I'm not a suicide hotline. I haven't been trained or coached in what to do in such situations. I didn't offer her any false comfort, if that's what you're asking. I told her, yes, John is dead and he isn't coming back. I told her that if she had anything to do with his death it made sense that she was experiencing despair."

"Cutting words," the detective says. She isn't looking at me, but is fiddling with her hands the way I've seen her do before. A nervous habit.

"I wasn't patient or encouraging, that's true," I say. "But I wasn't sure she meant it. I thought it was just her hysteria."

"People do rash things when they're emotionally out of control."

"I truly thought she was bluffing. A way to get sympathy."

"And so you presented a hard front." Her voice is cold.

"I told her to go ahead and do it if she felt that way," I finally erupt.

The silence in the room is absolute.

"I think that's all for now," the detective says, still not looking at me. She gets up to leave.

"Wait a minute," I say. She stops.

"Why are you continuing to hassle me about this case?" I ask. "I understand from my friends in Palo Alto City Hall that the precinct is satisfied with the outcome."

The girl appears to be calculating something. She decides, clearly, to not play straight with me. You can always tell when people with these open, honest faces are trying to lie.

"Yes," she says. "We're completely satisfied." And she leaves. I don't believe her for one minute.

68

Samantha

I'M STANDING IN FRONT OF Susan in her office at the station house. Her face is stern. "We"—she doesn't say who is included in that *we*—"have gotten complaints again from Mrs. Deborah Taylor that you continue to harass her. Samantha, what game are you playing? My ass is fried from the heat I'm getting from the mayor's office. I gave you permission for one more interview. Yet I understand you went back to her again after that. For a surprise home visit, no less."

"I'm not satisfied that we fully understand what happened," I say with bravado, but I suspect Susan sees right through my loud voice, my upright posture.

"*You're* not satisfied?" The sarcasm is palpable.

"No," I say, more loudly. "It doesn't make sense."

"And it won't make sense. It's a frigging mystery what those people were up to. I'd be surprised if you *could* understand it," Susan says. "That doesn't mean you keep wasting time and resources on trying to work out the kinks in human nature, Sam. Sometimes you just accept that things are the way they are."

"It's not that I don't understand the situation," I say. "If anything, I understand it too well. Hell, if I'd known Dr. Taylor I probably would have been the fifth wife." Susan looks at me strangely, but I continue. "It's the circumstances of the death that don't add up. How could MJ both overpower John Taylor enough to manage to inject him with the potassium? Even if she had been able to get hold of the potassium herself?"

Susan's voice is calmer now. "Sam, those might have been good questions before we got the statement from MJ's brother. But the fact is, he *did* give us a statement making it obvious that MJ had both motive and opportunity."

"No, he never directly asked MJ if she killed John Taylor, and she never directly admitted as much to him," I say.

"But asking her brother to dress up! Isn't that damning enough for you? Why would anyone bother to establish an alibi like that unless they were guilty?"

Something nags at me. "What did you just say?" I ask. "About establishing an alibi?"

"Sam. Enough. I want this to stop. For the next three days, you're on administrative leave. I can't have my detectives running amok on me."

As I walk out of her office, my phone goes off. A text from Peter. Odd—he rarely texts me, preferring what he calls *old-fashioned conversations*. And I find the text makes no sense. *Tell Peter to call James.* Why would Peter text me such a thing? It's not like he asks me to remind him to do things, the way some couples remind each other not to forget birthdays or parents' anniversaries. So I give him a call on his cell.

"Hey," I say, when he answers with an uncharacteristically abrupt *yeah?* "What's up with the text?"

"Hi, Sam, it's James," says the voice, which I now recognize as belonging to Peter's best friend. I just wanted Peter to know he left his cell phone at my house last night."

"I didn't know Peter was at your place yesterday," I say. As usual, I'd stayed late at the station, and didn't ask Peter about his day when I got home after 8:30 PM. We haven't been communicating all that well.

"Yeah, he stopped by for a few beers. But he forgot his phone. Just let him know in case he's freaking out about it."

After assuring James I would tell Peter, I hang up. Then, after thinking for a moment, I get in my car and head straight for Deborah Taylor's home.

69

Samantha

"I'D LIKE TO CONGRATULATE YOU on a job well done," I say. I'm sitting on the edge of a plush chair in Deborah Taylor's living room, trying not to give in to its comfort. Deborah Taylor is standing in front of me. She does not look pleased. I interrupted her arranging a huge bunch of flowers for her dining-room table. Cut flowers—I am reminded of MJ and feel a pang of sadness. A muffled roar from a vacuum cleaner upstairs. The maids' day. I'm actually shocked Deborah let me in to the house. But her manners are too good. She automatically stood aside as I pushed my way in.

"What job, exactly?" asks Deborah. She remains standing.

"The murder of your husband John Taylor," I say. I wait. What will I get? Shock? Outrage? Cool denial? My bets are on the latter. Deborah is always cool.

But Deborah surprises me. She's cool, yes. But no denial.

"You'll never prove it," she says. She is dressed as impeccably as always, a tailored red blazer over a white blouse and a long thin black skirt. The clothes show off the slimness of her figure.

She walks over to the stairs, looks up, and listens to the sound of the vacuum roaring in an upstairs room. "We don't need this conversation to be overheard," she says, coming back into the living room, but still not sitting down. "Especially since I gather you're not exactly in step with the rest of your precinct. Have gone rogue, in fact?"

"Let me tell you how you did it," I say. "And you correct me if I'm wrong."

"No tape recorder," Deborah says. "No notes. This conversation is not happening. And after this, no more visits to my house."

"I just have to know," I say. "I *must* know." And, then, reluctantly, I add, "You were too good. This murder was almost too perfect. But you slipped up. Twice."

"And how was that?" asks Deborah.

"First, when you took the room key with you when you left the Westin. And second, by involving MJ. She was too emotional—too unpredictable. You would have been better off with a simpler plan. Or using Helen as your dupe rather than MJ."

"Helen would hardly have sufficed, given that she lives four hundred miles away," Deborah says. She sits down, but slowly, without haste. If she is worried by what I'm saying she doesn't show it.

"Go on," says Deborah, after she's smoothed her skirt. "Say your piece. But try to speed it up. I'm giving a dinner party this evening and need to prepare for my guests."

"You were the brains, and MJ was the stooge," I begin, and cross my fingers. "You got her in over her head. And she didn't know what to do."

"*If* I were to indulge you in your little fantasy," says Deborah, "I would have to say that you're making a mistake about MJ. Poor creature. To be thought a murderer! Or, perhaps worse, to have believed it about herself."

"But surely MJ was there—either with you or because of you."

Deborah interrupts me. "You're coming at this all wrong," she says. "Think logically for once. First tell me: why would MJ want to kill John?"

I am quiet. This is what makes no sense to me. Would MJ want John dead out of anger? Did she find out, somehow, about Claire and about John's divorce plans? But MJ wasn't the murderous kind. She would get upset, yes. Perhaps even get physical. But cold-bloodedly plan a murder? No. And then I remember Peter's text and suddenly I have it.

"Here's what I think happened," I say, slowly. "MJ stumbled upon John Taylor's secret. Perhaps she learned only about one of his other wives. Perhaps she discovered Claire Fanning—who knows? Somehow she realized she wasn't the only woman in his life. She was devastated. She confronted John Taylor Thursday morning at their home. He admitted it—he was a polygamist, but he wasn't a very good liar. She kicked him out of the house, told him he wasn't welcome there any longer. So after his usual shower and breakfast at Deborah's, he went to Claire and told her he needed a place to stay until he calculated the best way to proceed. Only they fought, too, about when John would make their relationship public. John Taylor was certainly caught between a rock and a hard place. Or should we say four rocks and a hard place? He was vacillating from one moment to the next. On Friday afternoon he checked in to the Westin to get some thinking space. MJ was summoned there via a text sent at 6:45 and immediately went to meet him."

I pause. "That's when you come into the picture," I say. "You murdered John Taylor. And set it up so MJ would provide you with an alibi, and perhaps even take the rap."

"And how do you figure that?" Deborah asks. She seems amused.

"You yourself went to the Westin sometime before 6:30. Let me do the math and work backwards. You were in Menlo Park at your Women's Auxiliary meeting by 6:25, and since you needed fifteen minutes to drive there, let's say you showed up at the Westin at around 6 PM."

"And why would I have gone to the Westin?"

"You found out about Claire Fanning—about the fact that John was about to divorce you. My guess is that John slipped up somehow— you're pretty sharp, it was frankly astonishing that Claire and John were able to fly under your radar for as long as they did. Once the cat was out of the bag, John didn't really have a chance. You started pressuring him to change his mind, causing him to waver in his commitment to Claire. But I think that John was afraid to admit that—he didn't want to appear weak in front of Claire. So all Claire knew was that he was becoming less . . . let's say enthusiastic . . . about their plans. She began hassling him, too." I stop for a minute to catch my breath and organize my thoughts. "I really feel sorry for the guy," I say.

Then I continue. "When John disappeared from your radar Thursday afternoon you suspected he was swinging back toward Claire. That was unacceptable. So when he didn't show up as usual on Friday morning, you called him—and called him. God knows why he picked up your call in the afternoon when he was refusing all other calls—out of force of habit, I assume. And you managed to get him to admit where he was. That would have been easy for you. You knew him so well.

"You went there to meet him—I imagine you told him you simply wanted to 'talk.' You were there long enough to stick a hypodermic needle filled with potassium chloride into his back. He might have felt the prick, or might not, but in any case the deed was done. And then you left, knowing that MJ would arrive soon—only to find him dead of cardiac arrest."

"And how did I know that MJ would show up?" Deborah asks.

"Because you called, then texted her, from John's cell phone. That was your alibi. While at the Westin, you stole John's phone. You were safely at your meeting by 6:25. Then you excused yourself on some pretense—probably to go to the bathroom—and made a quick call to MJ's phone, hanging up when she answered. You then texted her that urgent message. John would then be on record as being alive at 6:47, and you'd have an ironclad alibi. MJ would arrive at the hotel, find John dead of an apparent heart attack, and no one would be the wiser. That was the plan, anyway."

Deborah appears attentive, nothing more.

"Although the text and the phone call were essential for establishing your alibi, they also opened up possibilities for complications," I say. "And complications did occur."

"John didn't die right away," Deborah said, nodding. "I must have miscalculated the dosage. Of course, he was a large man. That probably had something to do with it."

"So when MJ arrived, John was still alive. He let her in to the room, and they immediately begin fighting again. My guess is that MJ got worked up enough to grab John, perhaps even strike out at him, which caused the bruising on his arms. Already not feeling well, John lost his balance and fell, striking his head in the process. But that didn't kill him. The heart attack that shortly followed did."

"MJ is partly culpable," Deborah says. "She's not the innocent you'd like to make her."

"No doubt MJ was horrified to see John dead in front of her, and assumed of course that it was her fault. Again, my guess. If she'd stayed calm, called 911, who knows what would have happened. But she panicked and fled."

"Although not so panicked that she made a call from her cell phone," Deborah says.

"Yes, she was surprisingly clearheaded about that," I say. "It's a little after seven o'clock by then, and that's when she called Thomas from the house phone in the lobby, so it couldn't be easily traced. Ironically, he must have just arrived at her house from his ill-advised meeting—and parking ticket—in Palo Alto. She told him to immediately do his dress-up routine, placing her firmly in Los Gatos close enough to the time of death to keep her safe."

"I wouldn't have believed that creature would have thought quite as fast on her feet," Deborah says.

"Not only that, she had the presence of mind not to call Thomas from her cell phone, but to find a pay phone somewhere so there'd be no record of the call. Then, she started calling John and the Westin once she got home, to back up her story that she'd forgotten her cell phone when she went out to run errands," I say. I'm still puzzled by a few points. "But here's something I don't get. If you took John's cell phone with you, how did he have it on him when he was discovered on Saturday?" I ask.

Deborah smiled. "*If* I were to have planned it the way you're describing, I would have had to have taken the room key as well. To return and put the phone back in John's pocket."

"But what if MJ had simply found John dead, and called 911?" I ask. "You wouldn't have been able to put the phone back during all the fuss and bother."

"Again, *if* I were in charge of such an operation, I would have contingency plan upon contingency plan," says Deborah. "I would have bought an iPhone the same model as John's phone, and left that with him at the Westin. If I were prevented from getting back into his room to put back his real phone later because emergency responders were there, the police would find the substitute phone and assume it was his."

"That was risky, though."

"Yes, as it would have a different phone number assigned to it. But if John had simply died and MJ had found him dead, it would have been ruled a heart attack, no questions asked. There would have been no need to examine the phone or search phone records."

"So you drove by the Westin on your way home at 9 PM. Seeing that all was quiet, you slipped into John's room and swapped out the phones."

"That sounds plausible."

"Only you forgot to leave the key," I say.

"The perpetrator of this scheme certainly forgot to leave the key," Deborah agrees calmly. She uncrosses her legs. I almost expect her to yawn, she appears so disengaged. "You haven't told me my motive yet," she says.

"You had two motives," I say. "First, you didn't want to lose your status as Mrs. John Taylor. You'd have had to suffer through what would be the ultimate shame—for you, anyway—a public divorce."

"Interesting," says Deborah. "And my second motive?"

"Simple, unadulterated greed," I say. "You didn't want the money to dry up. You knew that Claire Fanning and John wanted to start a purely pro bono clinic. That John wouldn't be able to pay the type of alimony that would keep you in your current lifestyle. And then you thought of that tempting ten-million-dollar life insurance policy."

"You'll never prove this," says Deborah. "Never. It seems to be, as you said, nearly the perfect crime. And if John had died right away, before MJ arrived, it would have been perfect, since without the trauma marks the police wouldn't have suspected a wrongful death. MJ would simply have found John dead of a heart attack. End of story."

"But I don't think that's necessarily the important part," I say.

"How do you figure that?" Deborah asks.

"You're not exactly walking away from this with a sweet deal," I say. "You've lost your husband. From what you say, you've lost your family as well. And your social standing in the community will never be the same. In fact, you've lost all round. And one of the things that really gets to me is that you took the life of a good man. A flawed man, yes, but a good one nevertheless."

Deborah makes an ugly noise, so ugly I can't be sure it came from her.

"But what really hurts about this case is poor MJ," I say. "She suffered the most. She had a conscience. She wouldn't have gotten any enjoyment from her house or garden after John's death. She was doomed from the minute she walked into that hotel room. You let her think she killed another human being, and for that, if nothing else, you deserve to be punished."

"She took my husband from me," says Deborah. "It all started with her."

"The polygamy thing was your idea," I say. "MJ was an innocent bystander."

Deborah shrugs. "I have no pity for her."

I am done. No more to say. I get up and leave Deborah sitting silently.

Once outside the house I pull my phone out of my pocket and click the *record audio* button to off. Even if it's not admissible in court, Susan and Grady will be most interested.

70

Samantha

LATE AGAIN. I LET MYSELF softly into the house, tiptoe around as I get a glass of water from the kitchen, and head for the bedroom. But here I stop. The bedroom door is open—Peter always closes it when he goes to sleep, he claims it reduces road noise although I've never noticed a difference. The bed is still made, is empty. Where could Peter be? He's never out past 10 PM on a weekday—at least, not without me.

I have no doubt it's a signal, a message, that Peter can't deliver any other way. I feel momentarily chilled because I've told him jokingly that I would probably find out he no longer wanted to be with me by coming home to find his possessions gone, and I'd never hear from him again. A vanishing. I try not to rush, but still stumble in my haste to get to the closet. His clothes are gone. I go back to the living room and finally see the tactical omissions, the gaps in the bookshelves, the holes in the stacks of CDs and DVDs, his favorite blue blanket gone from the sofa that we would huddle under on cold winter evenings. Peter has flown.

I sit down, unsure of my emotions. Am I relieved or distressed? This has been coming for a long time. What does this leave me with?

Fantasies of a dead doctor. Hopes of someday finding with one person what John Taylor needed four women to satisfy.

I open my laptop and begin writing a report of my conversation this afternoon with Deborah. I stop, thinking of the three wives. Two, now, since MJ's passing. Each of them, each of *us*—for now I consider myself one of the sisterhood—left alone, ultimately. But despite my sorrow for MJ, it is Helen I think of as I sit here. It's a surprisingly cool night for September, so I go searching for a sweater, then return to my laptop. Yes, it's Helen who haunts me now. Devoting her life to sick kids, building an independent life, then being *surprised by joy*. That phrase again.

And what is left to me?

The shell of an amicable but less-than-nourishing relationship— and the fear that it was as good as I can expect to get.

I drift off to sleep and begin to dream almost immediately, a lucid dream in which I know I'm dreaming but am powerless to wake up.

I am one of John Taylor's cases, lying on the operating table, the anesthesia rendering me helpless. "When you ain't got nothing you got nothing to lose," John Taylor says to me, and I vaguely recognize the quotation from another master of the double negative. I am immobile, but conscious. Dr. Taylor is going to make an example of me; I am starting out with a normal face and he is going to sculpt me into something else. Something better. My life is in his hands. He is now by my side of the operating table, his face as benevolent as in his teaching videos. "This is what you deserve," he says, and begins cutting.

Acknowledgments

Heartfelt thanks to all the people who read and commented on early drafts of this book. That includes David Renton, Mary Lang, Marilyn Lewis, Talila Baron, Frank LaPlante, Marie LaPlante, Teresa Heger, Gayle Shanks, Rich Seidner, and Mitch Rotman. My bottomless gratitude to the amazing editorial work of Corinna Barsan and Elisabeth Schmitz at Grove Atlantic and for the extraordinary sharp-eyed copyediting of Briony Everroad. And, of course, special thanks to my beloved agent at Levine-Greenberg Literary Agency, Victoria Skurnick, for her help, support, and friendship.